HODAK

WITHDRAWN
UTSA LIBRARIES

Books by Tom Pendleton

THE IRON ORCHARD

HODAK

HODAK

TOM PENDLETON

McGRAW-HILL BOOK COMPANY

New York Toronto London Sydney

HODAK

Copyright © 1969 by McGraw-Hill, Inc.
All Rights Reserved. Printed in the United States of America.
No part of this publication may be reproduced,
stored in a retrieval system, or transmitted,
in any form or by any means, electronic, mechanical,
photocopying, recording, or otherwise, without
the prior written permission of the publisher.

Library of Congress Catalog Card Number: 68-55423
First Edition   49257

LIBRARY
University of Texas
At San Antonio

For
Los Tres

HODAK

1

As he shaved, Mike Hodak regarded himself in the mirror with the flat gaze of a man long accustomed to the knowledge that he was ugly. A homely face was one of the things in life he could do nothing about, and he did not hold with brooding over what he could not help. Each scrape of the razor exposed more of the solid, lumpy jaw. But it was not a mean face, for the deep lines across the forehead had been etched by concern for men other than himself. The squinted eyes looking straight under fist-scarred brows had heated the cheeks of many a boot in years gone by, yet they were eyes that had caused lonesome Marines to share their sorrows with him in foxholes and bars from Bougainville to Da-Nang. The nose, broken beyond repair before he learned to take care of it in the ring, added a touch of pathos to the otherwise formidable visage. His short-cropped hair was the color of gray mud.

When he had washed the scraps of lather from his face he went out into the bedroom, a towel around his waist. He was a powerfully built man but he noted his girth in the mirror with displeasure. He was eighteen years older and thirty pounds heavier than the honed young tiger who had been light-heavyweight champion of the Pacific Fleet, but that was still the physical standard by which he measured himself. He slapped the slab of his middle with contempt.

I

Scrubbing a brush through his stubble of hair he considered irritably the problem of what to do with the rest of the evening. Sensible thing would have been go to bed. He had just come in from one of those interminable midday banquets so dear to the hearts of Latin American military men. *Commandante* Somebody had been promoted to *Coronel*. Patriotic orations flamed by numberless toasts in pisco had proliferated far into the afternoon. Attendance at such dreary functions was a part of Embassy duty. He was tired, mainly from boredom, and he remembered that tomorrow was another heavy day. Yet he felt a deep restlessness with an edge of vague, unfocused anger.

The real unadmitted cause of his distemper was that coming home from the *almuerzo* he had seen Sadie Flippo riding horseback in the park with Lupo Machia. Lupo, *El Lobo*, the wolf—fit name for a scurvy sonofabitch. She had been tearing through the late-dappled shadows of the bridle path along the *avenida*, hair streaming across her child's face as she yelled raucous, unladylike taunts at the big man who galloped heavily after her. Sadie Flippo was another of those hard facts of life, like ugliness, he could not change. But this one he brooded about.

Tossing the brush onto the chest with a clatter, he moved to the door and shouted an order down the hallway. Moments later a slight *mestizo* youth in an oversized white jacket glided in with a martini on a tray. As Mike Hodak lifted the drink the boy cocked his head attentively to see if the potion pleased him.

"The *Capitán* is going out tonight, of course?" the youth murmured.

Mike stopped the drink halfway to his mouth. "What makes you think so, Nestor?"

2

"It is a good night, *Capitán*."

"Good?" Mike grunted. "For what?"

"For many things, *Capitán*." The youth gave a slight swagger of his head. "For banging the *chicas*, eh?"

"You been associating with too many Marines, *hijo*."

Nestor laughed shrilly. "But every night is good for *poosey, Capitán!*"

Mike Hodak grimaced at the boy, aware that despite his impertinence he was prescribing for him, like a doctor. An evening of bedroom athletics would have a therapeutic effect upon the Captain's chronic mental malaise.

"You're a real swinger, you are," Hodak said. "You wouldn't know a *poosey* if one whistled at you."

His words were harsh, but there was fondness under the gravel. Mike had developed a genuine, almost paternal affection for Nestor. The boy was loyal and intelligent, and his household pilfering was restrained and within reason. His *café con leche* complexion and thick black hair branded him Indian, but the fineness of his features bespoke a lusty Spaniard somewhere back along his bloodline.

Of this Castilian stamp Nestor was very proud. When he applied for his present position he had related gravely, by way of character reference, that his maternal grandmother had been a servant girl at the *estancia* of one Don Alfonso Monsalve in the early years of the century, and further that she had been effectively seduced by one of Don Alfonso's lusty teen-age sons, with the result that Nestor's mother had been born.

The Monsalves never admitted any such thing, of course. Everyone knew they were descended from the same family as the great Simón Bolívar, and it was unthinkable that Monsalve seed could be sown in such common ground. The girl had merely fallen victim to the malady of fiesta time when the

3

young town bucks, waiting in ambush, would up-end any young female foolish enough to come down the mountain unchaperoned. Babies originated in this fashion were referred to as Juan or Juana Fiesta, depending on sex. Nestor considered this a gross calumny on his grandmother. Though only fifteen, she knew with certainty the father of her child, and that certain knowledge had been passed with pride down to Nestor.

Awareness that the same strain of blood which had pulsed through the great Simón Bolívar also flowed in his veins instilled in Nestor a fierce proprietary interest in the political affairs of his country. And the present state of things in Maragua filled him with disgust. One day, not far distant, he would assure you, the good people of Maragua would rise up and drive El Lobo and his rotten People's Revolutionary Party into the river and watch them drown like rats!

Mike drained the glass and tossed it to the boy, who nipped it neatly out of the air.

"All right, *hijo*," the big man said mildly. "It could be a little close-order drill with the *chicas* is what I need."

Uncinching the towel, Mike Hodak started to dress. Fifteen minutes later, with Nestor standing at attention, he canted his Panama at a sharp, military angle and went out the door into the night.

The air was soft and fragrant with cape jasmine that spilled over the walks. As he went toward the *avenida*, he mulled without enthusiasm over the possibilities: a couple of corn-fed belles at the Embassy who were always ready to wrestle, an airline pilot's wife who liked to "party" when the pilot was a-flying, a wealthy but fading nymphomaniac; others. The prospects ranged from titty-pat in the parlor to orgy. All seemed dismal, even painful, this night. The one possibility that beguiled him he would not even round out in his mind, for

4

whatever else he was, Mike Hodak was a practical man, and he knew that Sadie Flippo was not anywhere in his deck of cards.

Still, a man had to do something with himself and with his time. . . .

When he reached the *avenida* he flagged the first taxicab that came along, an ancient rattletrap with dim, flickering headlights. He climbed into the back seat, grimly determined to go out on the town and raise a little hell and have himself a time. Like the Mike Hodak of old. The one who took his jollies on the run and never let love get its hooks in him.

The cab driver looked around expectantly.

"Let us go down to Doña Maria's," Mike Hodak said in Spanish, "and see what the tender young whores are doing."

2

Michael Hodak, Captain, United States Marine Corps (Retired), was a Mustang: one of that thorny breed of professional noncoms who as a matter of battlefield necessity had become officers, but who by no stretch of a national emergency could ever become, also, gentlemen. At least not in the view of the high gods who rule the destinies of fighting men and to whom the word *fraternize* is abhorrent. An enlisted man, so the saying is, never changes his stripes. He is expected to be a rollicking fellow with nothing more profound on his mind, off duty, than booze and broads, yet disciplined in bar-

5

racks, competent and tough in the field under fire, and in all circumstances absolutely dependable in knowing his place, or lack of it, in the military social order.

Thus it was that while young officers of the Corps who bore the official stamp of "gentlemen" were polishing their manners in the genteel halls of Richmond and Alexandria, Mike Hodak received his schooling in the social graces in the whorehouses and saloons of San Diego and Norfolk.

At thirty-six Mike Hodak had long outgrown whoring and saloon brawling, but when he set out to find relief from the heaviness of heart that weighted him this night it was perhaps understandable that he should make for the red-light district. There at least he would feel at home, and with luck could breathe again for an evening the carefree air of his youth.

"Ah, Señor," Doña Maria gurgled with laughter that shook all of her three hundred pounds like a balloon full of jello. "You come to see the *chicas,* no? You been here before, no? Long time ago, yes? Where you been, you rascal?"

"Here and there," Mike said, pushing past her into the dim blue light of the big room.

"Ah-ha-ha," Doña Maria gurgled on, nudging and guiding him to a table. "Everybody come to see the *chicas,* soon or late. Doña Maria got mighty fine ones, fresh ones since you was here. *Mira!*" She swept her enormous arm grandly toward the half-dozen young women seated in chairs along the far wall. They wore cheap satin evening gowns of atrocious hues and were variously reading magazines, filing nails or gazing with boredom into space. As Mike sat down at the table the only emotions that kindled in him were a kind of wry nostalgia and a sadness tinged with pity. He was sorry he had come.

Doña Maria clapped her hands sharply and the young

6

whores stood up and began to parade, in file, across the room toward Mike, trying to walk sexy on their unaccustomed high heels, as the good Madam had taught them.

"*Por favor!*" Mike protested, holding up his hands. "Later. In good time. I haven't had a drink. First things first, Señora."

"*Quítase!*" the fat woman bawled at the girls and waved them back to their seats along the wall. Then she cackled, "Ha-ha, goddam, you *gringos* all the same. Got the cold blood, no? Has to work you up slow, like a woman, no? How about nice filthy picture show, to start? No? Then, how 'bout —how you say—*circo?*"

"Circus."

"*Sí*, cir–cus. I make good live circus for you. One man, two womans. Thirty-three different position. Okay?"

"Later, *corazón*, later." Mike sighed heavily, loosening his tie. "First the drink."

In a moment the bartender came from the dingy bar with a bottle of pisco and two glasses. The native brandy of Maragua was cheap, more or less pure, and *fuerte*. When the bartender had pulled the cork and poured an inch into the glasses, Mike lifted his and said, "Your health, Señora, and to the good times."

"You goddam right," said Doña Maria, raising her glass. "Now you talking!"

Mike took the drink down and shook with the jolt. Then he picked up the bottle and, through watering eyes, read the label. He felt grim satisfaction in the thought of reducing the entire bottle to emptiness, single-handed. Mike Hodak was not a boozehead. He drank only for pleasure, or as a cathartic for a sluggish spirit. And in the latter case, he didn't fool around with inadequate doses.

After the second glass, the harshness faded from the brandy

7

and a pensive languor began to spread through the barrel of his chest. There was lacking only the solace of music. It was solace, not sex, that he needed tonight, and perhaps this was too much to hope for in a supermarket-type whorehouse.

"*Hay música?*" he said tentatively.

"*Sí, cómo no?*" said the Madam. "Doña Maria got everything." She arose and waddled away into a dim, recessed doorway at the end of the room. Moments later she returned, leading a slight, dark-haired girl by the arm. Mike saw at once that the girl was blind. She had a sweet, trusting smile on her face that made Mike, unaccountably, want to cry. She also wore an ill-fitting satin evening gown that revealed the fragile bones in her shoulders and upper breast. In one arm she carried a zither and in the other a cigar box with a slot in the top for coins. Guided by the Madam, she placed these on the table and seated herself opposite Mike. Then she smiled sightlessly in his general direction.

"My daughter," said Doña Maria, shrugging, which could have meant anything. "Play for the Señor, Antonia."

"Señor, what is your pleasure?" said the girl in a small sweet voice. With one thin hand she smoothed the dark tresses that fell to her shoulders.

"Please yourself, *hija,*" Mike said solemnly. "I expect it will please me."

The girl drew a breath, closed her blind eyes and drew the plectrum across the strings. Then suddenly the music began. Deep throbbing chords filled the room, threaded with a delicately picked air in a minor key that spoke of lofty mountains and eternal sadness. With a slow expulsion of breath Mike capitulated to the mood. The old built-in defenses went down and his thoughts drifted irresistibly toward forbidden country —the fair young land of Sadie Flippo.

8

3

He had never thought of himself as being in love with Sadie Flippo. The polar difference in economic and social status made the possibility that he should be in love with her absurd. To say nothing of the difference in model and mileage.

Still, a background consciousness of pain had been with him since the first day he saw her. It was his only experience with this preposterous malady. That he had been spared until the late summer of his life, then afflicted with a case so virulent, once reminded Archie Pringle of an old Mohican proverb (no doubt composed by Archie for the occasion): "Those so ugly that a painful expression would improve their looks will surely be blessed with pain."

Mike met Sadie soon after he arrived in San Felipe. He had stayed at the country club for a few days while he was looking for quarters. The natives called the place "El Coontry." Late one afternoon he had jogged out across the lawn to the swimming pool, having in mind some hard exercise to tighten up his belt line. Ignoring the little groups of *gente decente* around the blue-and-white umbrella tables, he hit the water and set about the business of laps in a workmanlike manner. After a dozen or so he pulled up to poolside, blowing heavily. A cheery voice right beside him spoke his name. He remembered the sound later—it sparkled like sunlight in crystal. Turning, he looked straight into a small wet face, framed in a white bathing cap, not a foot away.

"Hello," she said.

"Hello yourself," he replied.

"You're the Ambassador's bodyguard."

Mike wiped water from his face.

"Aide-de-camp sounds nicer."

"I'm Sadie Flippo. We met at the reception for the Ambassador. With all the new people you wouldn't remember me."

Mike smiled at her. "You're the only one I do remember. You're Mrs. Clinton's sister." Alden Clinton was First Secretary at the Embassy, but that wasn't why Mike remembered. It was a physical memory—the way certain females are put together that reaches down inside a man and grabs him to attention.

"Do you like this place?" she asked.

"Better than some others."

She fixed him with a bright smile, tiny pearls of water clinging to her clear amber skin. "Are you training for the Olympics?" She arched her brows and nodded toward the still-swirling waters.

Mike grinned and shook his head. "Just a little weight problem."

"Care for a *copita?*"

"Why not?"

Sadie puffed out her cheeks and sank beneath the water, then she pushed up from the bottom, broke the surface like an arrow and with a flash of motion was standing on the pool rim above him, slim and dripping. She looked back at him as she unfastened her bathing cap and shook loose her short dark hair, then she pulled down her suit which had ridden up, revealing the firm white of her buttocks. Mike started out of the pool, then stopped, transfixed, gazing up at her. She was not a big girl, but her limbs were slim and wonderfully shaped, and there was a disturbing fullness to her figure in the right places. Looking down at the block of a man poised half out of the water, she laughed and extended her hand down to him.

"You need help?"

Ignoring the hand, Mike hoisted himself out of the pool and followed her to a table on the lawn, shaking water from himself as he went.

"Well, Captain," she asked, smiling, when they had sat down. "What'll it be? Tea or booze?"

"I can drink anything you can," he said, toweling his face. "You name it."

For a long time as the late sun slanted across them and lighted the darting white figures on the tennis courts beyond, they sat sipping *Cuba libres* and talking, chatting easily about nothing in particular. Mike thought he had never met anyone so easy to talk to as this girl. A naturally close-mouthed man, he found himself sounding off more than he had in a long time. Sadie Flippo seemed interested in everything he had to say, and she broke up with laughter when he said anything that was close to funny. Flattered by this and numbed by her physical desirability, his native caution slipped out of his hands and flew away like a bird. He decided that this girl was somebody very special in the way of a human being. She was intelligent, obviously a thoroughbred. Her talk was fresh, to the point, without a trace of banality. Yet he noted in her responses a wry twist of cynicism that made him wonder.

While they talked she drew a comb through her short, damp hair, revealing the taut swelling of her breasts along the edges of her bathing bra, and the molded clean-shaven hollows beneath her beautiful arms. Her hair was the color of mahogany with sunlight on it. Her eyes were a deep and lovely amethyst that sparkled with almost elfin gaiety one moment, then speared him with the most disarming frankness, the next. Once or twice Mike saw an unreadable sea change come into her eyes, as if something he had said touched a tender, unhealed wound. Seconds later, when the bad moment had passed, the sparkle returned.

This one has a loose bolt somewhere, he thought. Too much money. No discipline, ever, probably. Spoiled-brat-that-never-grew-up type. Still, the quicksilver changes captivated him. In fact, everything about her did. The tiny beveled planes at the tip of her small nose. The dark, thick eyebrows. The petulant mouth that was like a pale, tempting fruit. The oval perfection of her chin.

It was almost dark now. They had talked through several drinks. Sadie became suddenly silent, as though she had tired of a game. Mike assumed that the pleasant interlude was at an end, and he was sorry. The girl sat quite still, studying his face, as if trying to memorize its rugged topography. Then, impulsively, she said, "I like your looks, Mike Hodak."

In an old boxer's gesture, involuntarily, Mike brushed his thumb across the battered shape of his nose. Narrowing his eyes at her, unsure whether she was kidding him or not, he said, "Now you mention it, I like your looks, too. What can I do for you?"

She studied him intently for a moment, pulling at her short forelock. "Not fishing for such extravagant compliments, Captain. You have doubtless guessed this meeting wasn't accidental. The first time I saw you I knew you were A-OK. Semper Fi, ta-ta-ta-taa, and all that. I need a friend. I haven't got any. Not a damn one, here or anyplace else."

Mike frowned. This was truly the remark of a sophisticated child. It caused him to wonder if she was one of those sad characters who were put together wrong when they were made. He had known a few. They always seemed to lose touch with reality after a few drinks. This one had suspicious earmarks. At the same time she seemed completely self-possessed.

He said, "Friendship isn't something you jump up like a picnic, sugar. Good ones take a while to build."

She looked at him. "That's a pretty fat thing to say. And from a bloody Marine! When I see something I like, I grab it!" She frowned about this a moment and shrugged. "Maybe that's my problem." Then she flashed him a dazzling smile and gave a petulant laugh. "Oh balls! You're either going to be friends with me, or you're not. So why worry about it?" She stood up slim and beautiful before him and put out her small brown hand, white palm upward. *"Amigos?"*

Slightly shocked, Mike got to his feet and found himself closing his big hand around her fingers. As he did, he experienced, for the first time, the electrifying sensation of touching her.

He said, "Honey, if you want to be my friend, that's it."

In this moment Mike Hodak felt something he had not known in a long time, perhaps not ever. It was exhilarating, and it was near happiness.

Later, when he thought back over this ridiculous first meeting, he had the good sense to realize that the alliance this beautiful, strange and desirable girl was seeking was a far different thing from the feeling that had already begun to disturb the deep centers of his being. Obviously she was seeking an ally, for reasons yet unknown to him. Maybe she was only a rich and lonely waif looking for a big-brother type to cushion her from the rude shocks of an alien world. Or perhaps she had a specific problem and merely wanted somebody killed.

In any case it was clear that her motives were far different from his.

4

From that first meeting by the pool it was as if they had been lifelong friends and confidants. They made a strange pair, the slender, beautiful girl and the big Marine with the fist-scarred face. So strange, in fact, that not even the most ardent gossip-mongers in the foreign colony connected them romantically. Gradually and hopelessly, however, and despite his refusal to admit what was happening, Mike Hodak fell in love with Sadie Flippo. In the process he discovered beauty in a world which, all of his life, had been rough as a cob and ugly as sin. When he was with her it was as if she stirred in him a remembrance of lovely things he had never experienced—as though he were momentarily afforded a glimpse into some earlier and happier incarnation.

The week after they met, Mike rented a small house with a patio on a side street near the Embassy. Sadie immediately made herself at home there. She would stroll in any time of day or night, barefoot and in shorts, likely as not. If Mike wasn't at home, she'd make a drink, visit with Nestor or have a romp with Nestor's cat. If a few people, including her sister, thought this camaraderie with an unpolished ex-sea-soldier was hardly proper, Sadie could not have cared less. She felt good at Mike's.

Archie Pringle said she reminded him of a small, expensive

Swiss watch that someone had wound too tight and nobody knew how to fix. Being with Mike seemed to give her a kind of relief from the torment of this tension.

Two or three times during those first months she called him on the telephone after midnight, almost in tears, unable to sleep, and minutes later was nervously tapping the claxon of her car in the street below. Those times they drove down through dark orchards and fields to the ocean and sat on the beach, talking and watching the surf roll in until it began to get light. It was then that she told him about her childhood—about all the bad things that had happened to her, and all the good things that hadn't.

Sadie was a Wharton of Tulsa and points east, the grand-daughter of Joseph T. Wharton, known with facetious envy in the petroleum world as "Dry Hole Joe" because of his phenomenal success in finding oil. Starting as a near-illiterate tool dresser, he saved his money, bought a secondhand drilling rig and hit a sweet spot on his first well. An incredible string of wildcat discoveries followed. When he died, years later, he was one of the richest men in America. Sadie's mother was the former Brenda Tennison, the much-photographed beauty of New York and Palm Beach. She spent most of her time being the much-photographed socialite beauty, and almost none being a mother. Sadie, a pale, delicate child, was reared by a series of governesses. She saw her mother as infrequently as she did her father, who divided his time between shooting elephants in Africa and recuperating from these taxing labors at Nice and Cannes.

At sixteen, when the first inkling of what she was missing in life began to dawn, Sadie, in a fit of depression and rebellion, ran away from her fashionable boarding school in Switzerland, flew to Paris and married Charles Flippo, III. Charlie was a nice boy of good family, one of the few "men" in her life to that point, she having met him the previous summer at Newport, where they had had a brief but passionate romance, consisting of a little timid nuzzling and the exchange of some deathless vows.

Sadie's mother, by now married to a penurious Italian count and traveling the international society circuit in an advanced state of alcoholism, cabled congratulations and five thousand francs' worth of gardenias. Her father cabled from Africa that he was going to thrash the fortune-hunting young whippersnapper and have the marriage annulled as soon as he finished his current safari.

"Charlie Flippo really was a nice boy," Sadie said, wistfully flicking at her bangs and gazing out over the whispering surf. "Earnest and nice, though I sometimes wonder if I married him just because I was fascinated by his name. I kept waiting for him to do something extravagant, maybe even acrobatic. He never did. Pappa was breaking in a new mistress when he got back from his hunt, and forgot all about thrashing him."

Charlie, who was a few years older than Sadie, had been drafted into the Army and was stationed in France. Two months after they were married, during training exercises, he held onto a live grenade too long after pulling the pin and blew himself up.

This left Sadie a very immature, very rich and exceptionally beautiful young widow. Dry Hole Joe Wharton, who detested his son, had left a substantial part of his fortune in a testamentary trust for Sadie. This all added up to a very unhealthy situation. No strong family ties, no firm lines moored Sadie to anything. She went to London and played aimless games with the rich mod set for a time and got herself mixed up with some bad types. She became briefly pregnant and underwent the indignity and shock of an abortion. She brooded and cried over this, though she hated the young man who had put her to the trouble.

When she came, inevitably, face to face with the utter pointlessness of her existence she experienced an emotional flyapart and ended up in the misty, unsatisfying refuge of tranquilizers and endless talk, provided by an expensive psychiatrist. After a time Sadie concluded that the psychiatrist was worse off than she was, and fled from him. She began to travel, constantly, without plan or purpose, taking up with any sort of people, with other bad experiences resulting, including three days in jail in Los Angeles on a marijuana charge. All of this reinforced her growing conviction that life was basically no damned good. Whenever she stopped moving, restless anxiety was always sitting there staring her in the face, grinning at her like an obscene dwarf, setting her off again. This is how she came down to San Felipe, to visit the Clintons. Arlene Clinton was her older half-sister by one of her mother's previous marriages, and though the two sisters were virtual strangers, there was at least an excuse for coming here. It was some place to go.

By the time Mike Hodak crossed her wandering track she was completely without direction or compass. As a kind of substitute for purpose, she constantly and deliberately flirted with disaster. Her affair with Lupo Machia was typical. It was almost as if she were exposing herself to destruction in hope that in the danger zone, someone or something, perhaps the very danger itself, would fan flames from the dark embers that smoldered inside her. Then perhaps the meaning of the grotesque little playlet of her life would in some way be illuminated. If a meaning existed.

17

These things and more went through Mike Hodak's head this night, floated on brandy fumes and the strains of the sad zither strummed by the thin blind girl. The bottle of pisco was nearly empty and he was adequately poisoned. He looked forward with grim satisfaction to the punishment of a hangover of magnificent proportions. Outside a hint of gray was coming into the street.

Sometime during the night Doña Maria had summoned a comely young whore and planted her in a chair very close to Mike. The fat Madam sat close behind them and extolled the girl's whorely virtues in low, breathy whispers into Mike's ear.

"Observe. Is she not a lovely creature, Señor? Beautiful in face and form, expert in movement. I give you my personal guarantee. Warm and tender-hearted she is, holding back nothing. Generous to a fault, completely dedicated to her career. At times she has even extended credit to young gentlemen temporarily embarrassed for funds. In this way she has risen to the very top of her profession, esteemed by all!"

Mike shrugged. He did not mind the girl being there. It was even rather pleasant to feel the young, plump flesh. She was a pretty little thing despite the heavy paint and the flat Indian features and cheap perfume. She reminded him of a magnolia blossom already spotted with decay.

Sensing the big man's impending departure the young whore, goaded by Doña Maria's sharp thumb in her ribs, began to whine at him, promising delights he had never experienced if only he would come to her *cuarto*.

Mike drew himself together, shook off the brandy fog that swirled in his brain and arose stiffly. He set the Panama squarely on his head. Then he tucked a small bill into the girl's hand, a kind of consolation prize.

"You do not like me," the girl cried, tears of frustration cruising down her painted cheeks.

Mike chucked her under the chin. In English, which she did not understand, he said, "I like you all right, sugar. I just can't stand penicillin."

Then he took a fifty-peso note from his pocket, folded it and slipped it into the slot of the cigar box of the blind zither player.

"*Gracias, amorcita,*" he said, touching the blind girl's cheek with his knuckles. Then he stalked out into the early morning mist.

5

Five o'clock the next afternoon Mike was having tea at the Hotel Bolívar when Robert Sanders came in. The first look at the man made Mike wince and aggravated the dull pain behind his eyes. His business for twenty years had been men, and this one had trouble marked all over him. How much trouble he could not then have guessed, but he muttered "poisoned pup" and hoped the fellow was just stopping over between planes.

The man obviously was no ordinary business traveler. Nor did he look like one of those self-styled soldiers of fortune who turned up regularly in San Felipe, looking for Romance and an easy peso. Something about him was different. Something about his eyes, a fatal look, as though he had a broken-off knifeblade in his liver.

La Rotunda at the Bolívar was an elegant watering place. Set in the center of the spacious lobby, it was surrounded by tall columns of dove-colored marble twined with lush tropical

19

vines. Exotic little birds sang from their cages in the interstices. The girls at the American Embassy called La Rotunda "The Snake-pit" because it was the clearinghouse for all the fashionable gossip in San Felipe. It was also a place where a presentable and unattached female could parlay a dull cup of tea into a martini and, sometimes, other more exciting sports.

As a part of his service to the Ambassador, Mike made it his business to know as much as possible about everybody important in Maragua. La Rotunda at five o'clock was a regular checkpoint. Being an old military man, the Ambassador had a salty thirst to know what was going on in his theater of operations. Thanks largely to Mike, he was probably as well informed as anyone in the capital outside of Lupo Machia himself.

Mike was seated at a table treating his grinding hangover with tea and Beefeaters, straight, when he saw Robert Sanders come through the revolving doors at the front of the lobby. The man carried a worn Army Valpak and had a trench coat slung over his shoulder. He stopped, put down the bag and took in the place with a sweeping gaze. Then a bellboy skated over, grabbed up his bag and led him to the desk.

He was a man who turned passing glances into stares—what the Maraguans called *un hombre formidable*. Yet he wasn't much above average size—Mike pegged him at five eleven, one eighty—but compactly built and perfectly balanced, like a boxer. Mike could tell this from the way the fellow handled the fat señora who barged head-on into him as he crossed the lobby. She was wearing an absurd hat that billowed from her head like whipped cream and was waving madly at someone in La Rotunda. Robert Sanders caught and held her, deftly, firmly, but very politely, until she regained her balance, then with the slightest bow sent her giggling on her way.

He was plainly American. His suit was wrinkled. Mike guessed he had come on the afternoon plane from Balboa. His dark knit tie was loose at the throat, his collar unbuttoned, and he wore no hat.

Other eyes besides Mike's followed him as he moved through the lobby. Any new arrival was welcome grist for the gossip mills of San Felipe, and this one plainly was no *turista*. When he had registered at the desk and disappeared upward through the ceiling with porter and luggage in the little wire-cage elevator, Mike excused himself from the table and went to the men's room. After he had finished there he strolled across the lobby to the *administración*.

A young clerk with small mustache smiled as though he had been expecting him. He was a regular contact of Mike's and had a taste for tax-free American cigarettes, which Mike could supply at Embassy cost. In a friendly exchange during which Mike inquired about the health of the clerk's wife and his children and his father and mother and his two grandmothers, the clerk casually turned the register around so that Mike could read. The open-handed scrawl said *Robert Sanders, Corpus Christi, Texas*. Mike glanced at the man, who with the slightest shrug murmured, "Routine airline reservation," indicating that he knew no more.

Nodding, Mike turned and recrossed the lobby to the public telephones. He dialed the number of the airport and asked for the customs office. In a moment the absurd voice of Inspector Alvaro Rodriguez came on the wire.

Mike said, *"Hola, cholito. Habla* Mike Hodak. *Qué te pasa?"*

"Mike, *amigo mío!* How you are?"

Alvaro was a clown who claimed he could butcher five languages with fluency. He never missed an opportunity to practice. "It makes *mucho* time I have not seen you," he cackled, pleased with himself. "What passes? I say well the Englis, no?"

"You speak English like an educated chicken, Alvaro. Try Spanish. A gringo calling himself Robert Sanders just checked in at the Bolívar. I think he was on the four-thirty. What about him?"

As Inspector of Customs at the San Felipe airport Alvaro Rodriguez was afforded an intimate look at everyone arriving in Maragua by air. He, too, had a highly developed taste for American cigarettes.

"*Momento,* Mikecito." Alvaro left the phone. Half a minute later he was back, mumbling names from a passenger list.

"Martinez . . . Obregon . . . ah, *aquí está!* Sanders, Roberto! Corpus Christi, Texas."

"That's the man. What do you know about him?"

Alvaro's voice took on an offended tone. "I believe he's mother is a dog."

"Oh, come on."

"Truly, he growl, like a—how you say—sonebitch."

"Oh, knock it off, Al."

"Truly, *amigo.* I am very extremely nice man. I tell him mos' politely 'Open please you valise.' So? So, he growl at me. R-rr-*off!* I am only conform to the duty of my post. I inspect the content with greatest delicacy. He growl once more. *Rr-off!* I smile. I make leel' joke about the onderwear. So then? Eh? He snap like he gonna bite me. *Qué sinverguenza!*" Alvaro Rodriguez finished with a rattle of uncomplimentary phrases.

"Okay, Al. What else?"

The Inspector of Customs sniffed as if overtaken by sudden ennui. "Personal stoff. Two honder dollar U.S., more or less. *Nada más.*"

"I don't think you're trying, Alvaro," Mike said, a trifle wearily. "What else? Think, please."

The Inspector of Customs was a clever fellow, but lazy. When he put his mind to it he could divulge many things about a man from what he had observed in rummaging through his suitcase.

"What kind of clothes? Tuxedo? Golf shoes?"

Alvaro made a sound of disdain. "Nothing like that. A *peón*. Maybe he got another suit. Old pair of slippers. Shirts, socks—but wait, aha!" His voice brightened. He gurgled, pleased with himself. "One thing more I remember. In a leather whatchucallim with teethbrush and razor he has medal. Two medal, eh? In a leel' black box. Also picture of baby with curly hair. Ho-ho, he act very nasty about the picture. Like my hands is dorty, eh?"

"What kind of medals, Al? How did they look?"

Alvaro sounded a trifle crestfallen. "Goddam if I know. So many question, Mike. One like a star, maybe? On a ribbon, eh? The other—oh, hell, Mike, *carajo!* I know nothing of *condecoraciones!"*

"You're okay, Al. Thanks." Mike said in a placating tone. "How're you fixed for smokes?"

His friend groaned. *"Carajo!* These local trosh! I have not have a decent poff in a week."

"I'll send you some tomorrow."

"You would be so kind." He lowered his voice. "But to my house, eh, *amigo?* You know how goddam stupid peoples talk."

"Sure, *chico,* to your house."

Back in La Rotunda Mike took a small table by himself, aware that he hadn't learned much. Rusty Cobb, a strapping Texas girl with sandy red hair, leaned over his shoulder and buzzed in his ear. "Well, who is he, Mister Moto?" Rusty worked in the Embassy typing pool and was a snake-pit regular.

Annoyed that his sleuthing had been so obvious, Mike looked around and said, "Who is who, Rusty?"

"Let's not kid one another, honeybug. The dyspeptic all-American who just went up in the birdcage," the girl said.

"I surely must not have seen him," Mike replied, turning back to his drink. Rusty gave him a sweet smile with acid in it. "That's all right, acorn-pie. You call me up next time you need some after-work typing. I'll tell you to go bite yourself."

Mike returned to his drink, wishing that he did have some information to withhold from the girl. This fellow bothered him. Call it what you would, he had a tainted look. However, at this moment, something else took charge of Mike's thoughts. With the casual but methodical thoroughness of a trained observer, he let his gaze sweep slowly across the now crowded room, from left to right and back again. He was looking, of course, for Sadie.

He had no business looking for Sadie then or ever, and he knew it. But he always did. And he guessed that he always would, as long as he lived. It was the one completely pointless activity in which he knowingly engaged. A slight depression settled on him when he did not see her. But it was early yet and he made the hopeful prediction that she would breeze through the revolving doors any minute now. She would glide over to his table, cool and sparkly as a small summer cloud. Then she would sit with him and they would talk for a little while. The world would take on an excitement and a glamor it had not had before, and he would feel young and almost handsome—or at least not so battered up—and life for a moment would be good and beautiful and have *shape*. The prospect was as enticing and illusory as a frosty highball in the eye of a parched alcoholic.

It was then the firing started.

The sound was faint at first. When he heard the opening burst over the tinkle and babble of La Rotunda he doubted what his ears told him. But one who has learned over a long span of years that respect for a particular sound can mean the difference between staying alive or not does not mistake it for anything else. The sound came again and he was sure—the hard, repeated slam of an automatic weapon and the sharp, contrapuntal pop of rifle fire not far away. It was impossible to tell the direction.

No one else in the room had noticed, yet. Mike was annoyed, almost angry with himself. Because he could not assign any cause for this shooting. There wasn't the smell of a revolution in the air. El Lobo and his secret police held the country firmly by the throat. The Army was still respectfully obedient to the old Marshal, General Ugarte, dotty as he was. The remnants of the liberal Populista party were scattered and disorganized. All of the Populista leaders who hadn't been lucky enough to escape into exile had gone to the wall, except Rafael Benavides, and he was safely neutralized in the Colombian Embassy in diplomatic asylum. It didn't add up. But those were serious weapons firing. No doubt about it now.

Suddenly the sophisticated tea-sippers in La Rotunda seemed to hear it too, or sense it. All at once they became silent, alert, like sheep when the smell of wolf comes on the wind.

The next moment a man burst into the lobby from the street, yelling *"Revolución! Revolución!"*

Then all hell broke loose in La Rotunda. In the past when the revolutions came, one of the first places hit by looters was

25

the Hotel Bolívar. In the minds of the sandalfoots the hotel was the symbol of their oppression. The tearoom crowd jumped up and stampeded in all directions.

Rusty Cobb grabbed onto Mike as he arose, almost knocking him over, for she was a big girl.

"Mike!" she cried indignantly, frightened. "It's a goddam revolution! What do we do? It's not in the book!"

Righting himself, Mike smacked her sharply on her ample rump. "Knock it off!" he snapped. "It is not a revolution. I don't know what it is. Get under the table before these animals run over you. And stay there till I say come out!"

Clamping his fingers onto her neck, he shoved her down under the table and kicked her legs in under the draping cloth. Then he stepped quickly out into the lobby and crossed to the front windows of the hotel. Hugging the wall, he peered around the window's edge and had a clear look across the plaza. The gunfire was popping steadily now, like firecrackers. It came from beyond the cathedral, but there was nothing in sight except two or three scared people scattering across the plaza for cover. He was extremely irritated. The General would be raising hell for an explanation as soon as he heard the shooting, and Mike didn't have the remotest idea what it was about.

He had just assured himself that his job did not include rushing out into a fire-fight to ask silly questions when Robert Sanders came pushing his way through the crowd now spilling out of La Rotunda into the lobby. Sanders shouldered through the mob like an angry fullback and hit the revolving door at full speed.

After twenty years in the Marine Corps, a sizable number of them in combat, Mike Hodak had no intention of winding up his career with a stray bullet in his gizzard. But this stupid

26

Robert Sanders, who had arrived in San Felipe an hour ago, appeared to have an urgent interest in what was going on out there in the streets. Which created a whole new situation. The idiot was American, and, rightly or wrongly, the General considered himself personally responsible for all American citizens in this country. The old man had always been that way about his troops. Mike saw the thing taking on the ugly shape of duty. Buttoning his jacket over the hard barrel of his middle, he shoved his way through the revolving door and took off after Robert Sanders, cursing him at every step.

6

San Felipe's central plaza is very old and very lovely, and is named for Simón Bolívar, the Liberator. Fat pigeons rubberneck around on the walks and fly up and whiten the bronze shoulders of the Great Man, equestrian in the sunlight.

Hotel Bolívar, a large graceless pile of weathered limestone, occupies the entire block on the west side of the plaza. Avenida Sucre, the principal artery leading from the residential district of Miraflores, runs along the far side of the square. Across the plaza, opposite the hotel, the spires of the cathedral rise above the streets like the doom-telling fingers of an ancient prophet.

As Mike came out of the hotel the firing stopped, then started again angrily. It seemed to center somewhere south of the plaza, not far away. The rattling sound had swept the streets clear of people. There was no one in sight except

Robert Sanders angling across the square at a dead run. Giving his hat brim a yank, Mike charged down the steps and ran after him.

A ripple of fire which sent sparks skating up Avenida Sucre froze Sanders to a palm tree on the edge of the plaza. Then Mike saw him break and run across the street and through a gate in the walled grounds of the old seminary which adjoined the cathedral. Keeping low, Mike followed. He sprinted across the street and through the open gate after the man, wondering what kind of fool's mission he had in mind.

Inside the grounds Mike pulled up, scanning his surroundings quickly. He was in a large, poorly tended garden and no one was in sight. For a moment he thought his man had escaped. Then his eye caught something—nothing more than a flicker of movement through the thick growth of ferns at the top of stone stairs leading to the second story of the old seminary building.

Seconds later, breathing hard, he was at the top of these steps. Straight ahead he looked down a covered veranda overhung with vines. After ten paces the veranda elled abruptly at the corner of the building. He ran to the corner and looked around cautiously, but saw no one. The firing was very close now. The rear loggia of the building overlooked a side street which came into Avenida Sucre from the suburbs toward the ocean. A haze of acrid blue smoke filtered upward through the leafy branches above the street.

Puzzled and highly annoyed, Mike ran back down the porch to the top of the stairs. He hesitated, then he turned through a tall doorway into the cool, dark interior of the building. In the dimness of the long hallway he saw no one. The air had the smell of a school—stale lunches and chalk. At a recessed doorway on his right he stopped again, then pushed

28

through the door and entered, cautiously, into the shadowy room. He found himself in a classroom whose dirty windows opened onto the rear loggia. The room appeared to be empty. He was turning to leave when a brilliant light flared behind his eyes, like a flashbulb exploding in his head. Streamers of liquid multicolored light trickled down inside him and died in blackness.

He came to, lying on the floor. A knee pressed painfully against his backbone, cramming his face against the cold tiles. Something hard and sharp gouged into his neck just above his collar. This, he assumed correctly, was a knife.

Immobilized, he cut his swimming eyes upward and made out parts of a man kneeling on top of him.

For seconds he concentrated on regaining his breath and shattered vision. "Nice chop," he said. "You musta took Karate by mail."

"Who are you?" Robert Sanders said. "What do you want?"

"That's just what I was gonna ask you," Mike said in a heavy strain. "Take it easy with that shiv. I'm strictly non-belligerent. I'm not mad at anybody."

"Who are you?" The knife point punctured the leathery skin of his neck, demanding an immediate, no-nonsense answer.

Mike got the message. "My name is Hodak," he said in the most pleasant tones he could summon. "I work at the U.S. Embassy. I figured you were American and headed in the wrong direction."

At this instant the dirty window on the loggia came in with a crash, taken out completely by a burst of automatic weapon fire from somewhere down the street. Plaster, dust and flying glass filled the air. Instinctively Robert Sanders and Mike Hodak rolled headlong across the floor and ended up in a tangled heap against the wall by the blown-out window.

When his wits returned, Mike said querulously, "Put *up* that goddam knife, will you, Mac?" He pushed the blade away from his face.

Robert Sanders snapped the blade closed with one hand and began to disentangle himself.

"What's going on?" he said, closely, angrily. "Who's doing that shooting?"

"It beats the hell out of me," Mike said, truthfully. "But if you'll get off we might go and find out."

Shoving apart, the two men crawled cautiously to the window, Hodak in the lead. Gingerly they picked their way over the shards of glass left in the frame, then rolled quickly across to the heavy stone baluster of the loggia. Rising slowly to hands and knees, they peered over the worn limestone slabs.

From this point of vantage they could see for nearly a block down Avenida Sucre, a wide tunnel of shade overhung with eucalyptus trees. Directly below them Avenida Diez de Mayo angled into Sucre, merging with it at the corner of the seminary grounds. The cause of the shooting lay in the intersection of these streets.

Directly opposite, across Sucre, loomed the Colombian Embassy, a pretentious pile of Victorian sandstone. Parked in front of the Embassy stood a panel truck. There were ladders on racks on its roof, and its rear doors stood open. The sign on the side of the truck said *Hnos. Ortega—Pintores—Reparaciones.* Smoke poured from the hood of the truck and the front tires were flat. The door on the driver's side was open. A man hung limply, face down, over the wheel, his arms dangling.

Bullets slammed into the truck from all directions with the

sound of hail beating on a tin roof. Mike spotted muzzle flashes in clumps of hibiscus and in the thick foliage of trees down the block. The street was full of thin blue smoke, and there seemed to be dead and dying painters in white overalls all over the place—four or five of them sprawled like rag dolls on the pavement and sidewalk around the truck.

It was a weird, unreal spectacle in the late-afternoon light. In a flash of comprehension Mike knew what it was: an attempt by the outlawed Populistas to rescue Rafael Benavides from his diplomatic prison house. Their plan was suddenly, pathetically clear. The crew of pseudo-painters would work briskly for a while spreading paint over the trim of the old house, then when they left, Rafael Benavides, in a smuggled suit of white overalls, would leave with them. Some Judas had leaked this inept scheme to Lupo Machia, and the would-be rescuers had been ambushed by a picked platoon of Lupo's *soldados*.

Presently an arm with a hand holding a large paint brush was thrust out of the rear doors of the panel truck. The hand, raised aloft, waved the brush frantically, like a surrender flag. For a moment Mike thought the party was over. The man inside the truck clambered out of the rear doors. He was a tall, bony man, dressed like the others in painter's white overalls and cap. He shouted frantic protests and held up his arms, the brush in one hand, a bucket of paint in the other, as if this proved beyond a doubt that he was only an innocent house painter.

The firing had stopped abruptly when the man appeared. He now circled round and round in the center of the street, arms upraised, like a Greek dancer. Then a rifle cracked, then another. The bucket, twice perforated, began to spurt streams of paint onto the pavement and over the man. It was as if the

31

hidden gunners were playing with him. Two or three other bullets nicked playfully at his feet. The man began to jump up and down like a jumping-jack.

"No, señores, no!" he screamed. *"Por Dios! Soy pobre pintor! Nada más!"*

The precision firing at the bucket and his feet continued. Then his mind must have snapped. He broke and started running straight down the street, yelling in terror. He did not know much about running. His long, thin legs moved as if he were running in slow motion, as if trying to escape something in a nightmare.

The gunners quit playing then and zeroed in on him. First one, then four, then all of them, mounting to a solid, angry roar. As the slugs hit, they spun him this way and that, and he sloshed paint in a wide arc, but amazingly he didn't fall right away. In a crazy, limber-legged walk he somehow kept his feet, kept reeling down the street, bucket in hand, his shoes slapping against the pavement as if he were doing a spastic tap dance.

Something made Mike turn away. It could have been disgust, or it could have been the sound of a car's horn down the street. Or perhaps it was something stronger, something unheard, extrasensory. As his shocked gaze came into focus, his scalp tightened. Two blocks away on Avenida Diez de Mayo a powder blue Cadillac convertible, one of a kind in San Felipe, was coming on fast. A brilliant scarf streamed from the unmistakable head of Sadie Flippo. In another fifteen seconds she would reach the intersection and drive right into the meat grinder. Andean *soldados* with hot rifles will shoot at anything that moves.

It was strictly a reflex situation when the genes and chromosomes take over the thinking. Mike punched Robert San-

32

ders and jerked his thumb at the oncoming car. He said, "Climb down my back, then catch me. We've got to stop her."

Robert Sanders' chromosomes reacted admirably. As Mike Hodak slithered over the balustrade, then caught and clung to one of its balusters, legs dangling eight feet above the street below, the younger man vaulted quickly over the limestone slab and slid down the big man's frame, then dropped lightly to the ground. With a quick glance at the approaching car, he did not wait to break Hodak's fall. There was not time. He picked himself up and dashed down the middle of the street toward the car, waving his arms like a wild man.

The girl hit her brakes, but she couldn't stop. Hanging by his fingers in midair Mike heard a solid thump and, turning his head, saw Robert Sanders spreadeagled across the Cadillac's hood. Tires screaming, the heavy car swerved sideways, carrying Sanders like a bull with a matador on its horns. The front wheels jumped the curb and the car bounced to a stop in a flower bed twenty feet short of the intersection.

There was nothing for Mike to do now but drop. The ground eight feet below his dangling legs was concrete. Mike tried to remember his paratrooper training and let go. The impact jarred fresh stars loose in his head. A shoot of pain in his left ankle made him wonder if it was broken, but he couldn't worry about that now.

Picking himself up, Mike charged across the street to the stalled car. He jerked open the door.

"Get over!" he snapped.

Sadie sat looking at him, her eyes wide with shock. Shoving her roughly across the seat, Mike slid under the wheel.

"You've gone mad!" Sadie cried in an oscillating voice. "I just hit a man! You hear me? There he is!"

At that moment the firing broke off again. A whistle shrilled and a jeep came roaring up the *avenida*. It skidded to a halt beside the thin man now crumpled in a smear of paint and blood in the middle of the street. He had too much lead in him to be alive. The jeep driver wearing the mud-brown uniform and white Sam Browne belt of the elite troops of the Army, on a nod from the man beside him, gunned the little car toward the smoking truck. Mike knew the other man riding in the jeep. So did Sadie.

"Lupo Machia!"

One of the "painters" by the truck was still alive. As they watched, he raised to his elbows and struggled to his knees. Blood blubbered from his nose and mouth. He staggered to his feet and fell back against the trunk of a tree. A spreading stain crimsoned the bib of his white overalls. With painful slowness he raised his hands above his ears. The jeep driver gunned up close to the curb beside him. Mike's intestines grabbed when he saw what was coming. Machia looked at the dying man, his face expressionless. Without removing his gaze from the man Machia held out his hand to the driver, who placed his large service revolver in it. The man propped up against the tree began to shake his head in protest. Spinning the cylinder, then cocking the hammer almost casually, Machia raised the pistol and fired three measured shots into the man's heart.

With a convulsive, voiceless cry Sadie lurched against Mike, clawing his chest with her fingernails. The *coup de grâce* had not been necessary, but it cost only a few bullets and it served to show that the junta was not to be trifled with.

Lupo Machia returned the pistol to the driver, then he took out a cigarette. The driver whipped out a Zippo lighter and lighted it for him. Machia then nodded to the driver, who blew three quick blasts on his whistle. Whistles answered all up and

down the street. Squat *soldados* came climbing out of shrubbery and dropping down from garden walls.

Almost immediately a few frightened faces began to appear
in doorways and windows up and down the street. Mike knew
that Avenida Sucre would be jammed with people in a matter
of minutes. In San Felipe they swarmed like hungry flies when
blood had been spilled and the danger was past. Sadie shud-
dered hysterically in his arms. He hugged her against his chest,
fighting off the lethargy of his own shock.

Robert Sanders had picked himself off the hood and was
limping around the side of the car, holding his knee, grimacing
with pain.

"Pile your ass in the back and let's get the hell out of here,"
Mike said, "unless you want to be picked up as a witness."

Throwing a leg over the door, Sanders sprawled into the
rear of the car as Mike shoved it in reverse. Backing in a tight
arc, he spun the wheel and headed back down Avenida Diez
de Mayo, the way Sadie had come. The big engine responded
as Mike pressed his foot to the floor, hoping some enthusiastic
soldado wouldn't snap off a reflex shot at them.

7

Six blocks later Mike let up on the foot-feed, and the unbearable cramp of tension eased out of his shoulders. Sadie lay
against his chest moaning, still covering her face with her
hands.

"Why did he do it, Mike? He shot him. He was already dying."

Suddenly she lurched forward, spread her knees and vomited wildly on the floor. Mike reached out with a hand and gripped her hair in his fingers, supporting her head until the paroxysm of sickness had passed. Then he shoved a clean handkerchief at her and pulled her, shuddering and weeping back against his chest.

"Think about something else. Breathe deep and don't think about it. We'll get a drink." He cranked out the ventilator to let the windrush blow against her face. At Calle Panama he turned south and headed for El Gallo de Oro.

El Gallo was the number-one nightclub of San Felipe. It was a barny place in a wooded park in the district known as Miraflores. This was where the important families lived, in the southern arc of the sprawling city, the play-and-living-ground of proud *gente decente,* who maintained the purity of bloodline in their acknowledged children, as in their registered cattle, with stern discipline. Some of the homes here covered entire blocks. The car sped past iron-grill gates with curving, palm-fringed drives beyond leading to great houses with swimming pools and tennis courts and stables. These were the homes of the Fuentes, the Corderos, the Villanuevas, and a dozen lesser families, the silent rulers of the country for two centuries.

These families didn't care for publicity and so one didn't read much about them except, occasionally, in the society columns, for they owned the principal newspapers. The Economic Attaché at the Embassy estimated that, one way or another, they controlled two-thirds of the wealth of the country. They ran the country as well, subtly, without seeming to, but effectively, floating on top of political upheavals undisturbed. Cynics said they secretly financed all serious contend-ers in the periodic political wars, hence always backed a win-ner. A proud, inbred colonial gentry, their deep affinities were for Mother Europe. They sent their young back to Spain, France or Italy to be educated, and they felt no more kinship with the broad-faced Indios, who made up eight-tenths of the population, than Pizarro felt for Atahualpa the Inca when he hacked him in quarters.

It was early for El Gallo, but Mike knew Miguel Llona, the *gerente,* and he wanted a quiet place for Sadie to collect her-self. Turning the Cadillac through the gates, he rolled swiftly under the porte-cochère.

An attendant in shirtsleeves came out. Mike gave him a bill and pointed at the floorboard. "Clean up the lady's lunch, will you, *amigo?*"

Then they all piled out and went up the steps. Mike rang the bell. In a moment Miguel Llona came to the door in his shirtsleeves. With a smile of recognition he bowed them in and they went up more stairs and along the end of the darkened ballroom and out onto a balcony that looked over a little lake in the small forest of eucalyptus trees. Sadie turned off to the ladies' room for a face wash and a hair comb, for she looked a wreck. Mike pointed out a table to Sanders.

"I'm going to make a phone call. Order a couple of straight Scotches and whatever you want."

In the phone booth Mike called the Embassy and asked for the Ambassador.

"General, this is Mike—"

"Well, well, Captain Hodak, is it?" The General's big voice purred with sarcasm on the other end of the wire. "I thought maybe you'd gone over the hill." The sarcasm changed quickly to official anger. "All hell has broken loose and I'm

37

sitting out here in utter purblind ignorance! What am I supposed to do, Captain, buy a newspaper?" The old man considered it dereliction of duty amounting almost to mutiny for a subordinate to know anything he didn't know. Less than ten minutes had elapsed since the shooting had stopped and the verbal hiding raised blood to Mike's face. This showed in his tone.

"Sir," he said stiffly, "I have been down on Avenida Sucre watching some people get shot. I came to the closest place I could telephone."

The General had a sense of humor like a bullwhip. He took delight in stinging his favored subordinates with it. His laughter raised static on the telephone wire. "All right, Captain. I guess you're doing the best you can, such as that is. What's it all about?"

In slightly hackled tones Mike told him what he had seen. When he recounted the ambushing and unnecessary killing of the Populista "painters," the amusement died out of the older man's voice. "It sounds as if Colonel Machia was in excellent form."

"It was a typical Machia operation, General."

General Gatch was not given to strong language, but the three things he could not tolerate were cowardice, the unnecessary taking of life, and treachery. When he came in contact with these deformities of the human spirit, something in his big Scottish soul revolted.

"The skunk-eating son-of-a-bitch!" He expelled the words as if they were filth in his mouth.

Mike could not stay peeved at such a man. "Well, that wraps it up, General," he said, warming to the old man's anger. "The Populistas are finished. Wiped out—except for Rafael Benavides. Looks like he's gonna be a permanent

38

boarder at the Colombian Embassy now. If I get anything else, I'll call you."

When he returned to the balcony Sadie was coming out of the ladies' room. She was pale but composed now. And, Mike thought, more incredibly, tenderly beautiful than ever. They converged on Sanders at the table. A *mozo* brought two whiskeys and a plain Coca-Cola, setting the soft drink in front of the young American.

Sadie took her drink down neat. Then, with fingers still trembling, she lit a cigarette and inhaled deeply. Blowing out the smoke she said, "Sorry I came unstrung, gents. Those were the first murders I've seen all day."

The residue of shock that still clouded her eyes pained Mike to see. In spite of the tough road she had traveled in her short life, she was still an amateur in an ugly professional world. He tried to smooth the ugliness into a happier thought.

"Your rabbit's foot was working real good, sugar. If this gent hadn't showed up, you would have frammed into real trouble."

Staring, Sadie seemed to see Robert Sanders for the first time, as though the horror she had witnessed had dashed the memory of him from her mind. Instinctively she reached across the table and touched his hand.

"Thank you."

Mike said, "This is Robert Sanders, Sadie. From Corpus Christi, Texas—he says."

"I guessed you saved my life, Mister Sanders," Sadie said, her dark eyes still liquid. "Not worth the risk, but I'm grateful."

Making a derisive sound, as though her gratitude annoyed him, Sanders moved his hand from under hers.

"There was no risk involved. The shooting was out in the

other street." The way he said it sounded as though he was disappointed that the danger hadn't been greater. In the fading light Mike had his first close look at him.

In sizing a man up, those who have been in the ring pay attention to the hands, for that is what you get hit with. A glance at Sanders' hands told Mike that he was dealing with a strong man. The fingers had a good shape, but they were stout and tough. One of the nails was split and blackened. Whatever Sanders' business was, it had recently involved working with his hands. The wrists were thickly sinewed.

Mike guessed him to be twenty-seven or -eight. Then he wasn't sure. He could have been younger or older. He had an almost boyish look about him, except for his eyes. There were lines and shadows of hard dissipation around the eyes.

He had a short but well-made nose—a part of the anatomy about which Mike was particularly sensitive. His mouth made a straight, noncommittal line. His ears were set rather close to his head, and his reddish-brown hair grew upward from a widow's peak in the center of his forehead, which was creased as if from much squinting in the sun. One could almost say he was good-looking, in a rough-cut sort of way. Yet there was something wrong about him.

It was surely the eyes. They were the eyes of a man years older than twenty-eight, who had seen things that it does not benefit a man to see. Deep-set under dark brows, they gave the first hint of the trouble in him. When Mike looked squarely at him, Sanders returned the look for a second, as a man should, then his gaze flickered away. It was as though he feared the other would see through his eyes and read what lay behind them.

Mike said, "In five more seconds this lady would have been in the intersection. Those idiots would have shot the Virgin Mary if she had showed up just then."

"Forget it. There was no danger to me," Robert Sanders said emphatically.

Mike gave a short laugh. "It was a good move just the same."

"Captain Hodak is the den-mother of all weak and helpless *gringos* in San Felipe, but he's getting a little slow," Sadie said, trying to force a timbre of gaiety into her voice. "He's really jealous because you saved me." She was still trembling slightly and trying to get herself under control. Looking curiously at Robert Sanders, she said, "If you're wondering who you saved, I'm Sadie Flippo."

"Mrs. Flippo is the sister-in-law of the First Secretary at the Embassy," Mike interposed. He didn't trust this fellow and he wanted him to know with whom he was dealing.

Unimpressed, Robert Sanders glanced sharply at Mike and demanded again, "What was that killing about?"

Mike looked back at him cynically. "You wouldn't try to kid a feller, would you? A man don't generally go jackin' around in a fire-fight unless he knows what it's about." Neither Mike's words nor his smirking expression fazed Sanders, who said coldly, "Who were those men? Why were they killed?"

Mike studied him. He was either serious and stupid or a damned good actor. He *seemed* to be very much in earnest. In either case Mike decided to go along with him, for the moment at least. And so he told him about Rafael Benavides. He explained that Benavides had been the duly elected president of Maragua—maybe the only president honestly elected by a majority of the qualified voters that the country had ever had. He had held office for about eighteen months. Then, almost two years ago a military junta, nominally headed by General Ugarte, a senile Army general of great prestige, had seized power. The mastermind and moving force of the junta was *Coronel* Lupo Machia.

41

With the support of a handful of ambitious young officers and the People's Revolutionary Party—a Castro-oriented group of extreme left-wingers—Machia had staged a bloody *coup d'état* and taken over the government. He disbanded the Congress and shot most of the top Populistas, the political party that backed Benavides for the presidency. A few lucky Populistas had got out of the country. Benavides hadn't been so fortunate. He hadn't been sent to the wall only because he had been taking a drive at the time of the *coup*. His chauffeur, a wily old Indian, hearing sounds of shooting, had driven him straight to the Colombian Embassy on Avenida Sucre instead of back to the Palacio. The Colombian Ambassador, though of different political hue, had given him diplomatic asylum as a political refugee. And there in the Embassy of another country Rafael Benavides had remained, virtually a prisoner in the heart of his own capital city, ever since.

Diplomatic asylum, Mike explained, was an old South American custom founded on the principle that the embassy of a foreign country is a small plot of sovereign foreign soil, hence immune from invasion by the local authorities. It was a kind of political Kings-X generally respected by the locals, not only because a breach would set off international repercussions but also because those riding the uneasy seat of power never knew when they might need to invoke the privilege for themselves.

Rafael Benavides had been an embarrassment and a threat to the junta since he had taken refuge in the Colombian Embassy. Not because he commanded any battalions or tanks, but simply because he was idolized by the poor people of Maragua. He had been a university economics professor who advocated social reforms the ruling families considered intolerable, and which, at the same time, were not drastic enough to satisfy the Castro-Communist element in this land of very rich and very poor. He had been elected to office, almost by default, during an indecisive time when the far right and extreme left in the country were sparring with one another, trying to decide which had the strength to grab and hold the reins of power.

After the *coup,* the Colombian Ambassador had requested safe conduct out of the country for ex-President Benavides, but the junta refused. Machia didn't want him loose, even in exile, where he could speak with his disarming logic and influence hemisphere opinion against the junta, and perhaps even rally the scattered exiles into some kind of counterrevolutionary action. At the same time the old man's presence in San Felipe was extremely aggravating to Machia. Every afternoon after five o'clock a long procession of working people would walk slowly past the Colombian Embassy in a kind of mute tribute to their captive champion. And nearly every day they could catch a glimpse of Rafael Benavides walking, exercising on the loggia of the Embassy, his long hands clasped loosely behind his back, his leonine head bent as if in deep, sad thought.

Lupo Machia kept a close guard on this deceptively dangerous prisoner. Hard-eyed agents of the secret police—called *números* because of the numbers on their hidden badges, and because they were held in contempt—drifted up and down the walks around the Embassy. Armed *soldados* were stationed at each corner of the block, day and night. They were tacitly ignored by the Colombians, but their presence did nothing to promote good relations between the two countries.

The junta denounced Rafael Benavides as an ordinary criminal and demanded that he be surrendered to stand trial. There was little doubt that if released he would be executed. The matter had been kicked around the International Court of Justice at the Hague for nearly a year. A lot of toothless international law had been written on the case, but ex-President Benavides was still the houseguest of the Colombian Ambassador, and that worthy gentleman had no intention of turning him out.

There had been much brave talk in the *barrios* of San Felipe about rescuing Benavides. A tunnel would be dug into the Embassy from an adjoining house. A helicopter brought secretly from the States would pluck him off his balcony and whirl him away to freedom, and so on and on. Mike never took any of this talk seriously. It was inconceivable that the handful of impractical old dreamers and smooth-cheeked students who were the survivors of the Populista party could carry through any such fantastic scheme.

But the streams of patriotism run deep in the South American *paisano*. Prudence and practicability had finally been overbalanced. The result was the bloody debacle these three had witnessed in the afternoon shadows.

"Some cheap, sell-out son-of-a-bitch took the escape plan to Machia," Mike said grimly. "With that it was no problem to arrange the ambush. You saw the rest."

He drew and expelled a deep breath and held up his hands in a gesture of finality. Robert Sanders threw him a penetrating look. Ridges stood out in his jaw. His voice was low and angry. "There was no need to kill those last two. They were trying to surrender."

Before he fully considered the effect of his words, Mike gave a bitter laugh and said, "You don't know this lady's boy friend, Colonel Machia." As soon as he said it he was sorry. It didn't help matters to grind Sadie about her friendship with Lupo Machia.

"It's all right, Mike," Sadie said in an almost inaudible voice. "I deserve that."

44

In the twilight she looked miserable. A tremor went through her shoulders and down her slim brown arms. Her dark eyes were full of revulsion and loathing, and Mike knew that most of this was directed inward, toward herself. He covered her small clenched fists with a big hand and tried to smile her out of the depths of her depression.

"Don't take it so hard, sugar. That's the way this life is. Next one got to be better."

Through the trees the surface of the small lake shone like a dark mirror in the twilight. Street lights were coming on in the *calles* beyond the park. Mike sensed there was nothing to be gained by staying here any longer, and said so. With a visible effort Sadie pulled herself together. She looked at Robert Sanders.

"We'll drop you at the hotel." With grim, forced gaiety she added, "We'll take the scenic route—by the Colombian Embassy. They should have things tidied up by now. It's really a lovely city."

"A pretty good liberty town, too, if you have a serviceable prophylactic kit," Mike said, cutting his eyes at the man. "You're here on pleasure, I take it."

With an angry, sarcastic laugh Robert Sanders gazed back at Mike and said, "You presume, Captain? You know my name. You know where I come from. Don't tell me you don't also know why I'm here."

Mike rubbed his jaw, somewhat abashed, and explained that he wasn't a gumshoe. Just kind of an unofficial greeter for the American Embassy. It was his business to find out about new people from the States and extend them any assistance that he could.

"I see," Robert Sanders said in a tone of disbelief. "Then for your information I'm here on business, not pleasure."

"Good enough," Mike said. "What line? Machinery? Cotton?"

"I represent a cost-plus import chain in the States," Robert Sanders replied without hesitation. "I'm looking for native handicraft. Pottery, silver jewelry, rugs—anything we can sell."

"That surely ought to be an interesting business," Mike nodded, trying to sound convinced and friendly, though he didn't feel either. "Drop by the Chancery in the morning. I'll introduce you to the Economic Attaché. He knows the local market. Give you some good leads."

"I may do that," Robert Sanders nodded, a little more pleasantly. "There's a wholesale dealer here I want to contact. In fact, I'd like to look him up tonight if at all possible. Maybe you know him. A man named Felix Góngora."

"Felix Góngora?" Mike looked at him carefully. It was nearly dark now and he couldn't see his face well. Frowning, he twisted his glass in his fingers and puddled it lightly in the wet ring on the tabletop.

"You remember the painter in Avenida Sucre—the tall, skinny one that took all the lead, trying to get away?" He paused for several seconds to let it soak in. "That was Felix Góngora."

8

After Bougainville and Iwo Jima, Mike Hodak, a hard-tailed, bullet-headed Marine corporal who had made them both, was rewarded for two Purple Hearts and a Bronze

Star with a tour of duty in the Embassy Guard at San Jose, Costa Rica.

In San Jose there was opportunity to gratify the sex drive, rarely available to Mike since he had been old enough to appreciate it. An enterprising native woman named Rosa developed a thriving business doing the laundry of the enlisted Marines of the Embassy Guard. She had a daughter, Maria, a precocious girl of fifteen sun-ripened summers, who pulled the little red wagon in which Rosa collected and delivered the weekly wash. Before the end of Mike's tour Maria turned up pregnant and Mike, remembering with anguish some carefree encounters on laundry day, was forced to conclude that he was the responsible party. Shortly after this unwelcome phenomenon manifested itself, his tour was up and he received orders back to the States. His first reaction was relief at being thus extricated from an untenable situation.

In the months that followed at his new station, however, an embryonic conscience grew in Mike Hodak just as the fetus grew in Maria. He tried to put the whole matter out of his mind as just one of those *c'est l'guerre* things, but he could not shrug off the fact that the girl was hardly more than a child, a first-timer, and that she had trusted him. Duty became an ugly little demon, riding him like a hump on his back. As soon as his enlistment was up, he caught the first plane back to San Jose to make an honest woman of the girl he had seduced.

Upon arrival he found that Maria, now married to a prosperous grocer, not only did not welcome him, but angrily denied ever having seen him before, despite the striking resemblance he bore to the snotty-nosed, bullet-headed baby rolling on the floor. That night Mike celebrated with a drunk of such magnificent proportions that it is remembered in the district in San Jose to this day.

Before he left, Mike had a serious talk with Rosa, the girl's

47

mother. Then he caught the next plane to the Canal Zone and re-enlisted.

In the years that followed, an allotment from every paycheck Mike Hodak drew went to Rosa for her grandson. It was only just before he came down to Maragua on this present assignment that he received from Rosa a photograph of the new graduating class at the Technical Institute in San Jose. An arrow drawn in ink pointed to a serious, American-looking youth in the back row. The old woman's message scrawled on the back of the picture said simply "Send no more. Go with God." Thus was a duty completed.

Strangely, this fulfillment of a self-imposed obligation, which should have given him a new sense of freedom, left him instead with a feeling of purposelessness. He had no obligation to anyone now, except to himself. He knew that his son, a graduate pharmacist, was now gainfully employed as a junior-grade pill-roller in San Jose. He also had a conviction that the best thing he could do henceforth for him would be to go down to his grave with his secret. He made a vow never to yield to the temptation to stop off in San Jose for a box of aspirin and just one look at what he had wrought.

Mike Hodak had always worn pride like starch in his khakis, as a good Marine should, but during and after his last tour in Viet Nam things began to change in him. The starch of pride no longer was enough. "You put in your time at what was set before you, and that's good" is the way he phrased it to Sadie, "then you begin to think about what you'll be doing a hundred and fifty years from now. Then, somehow, the old ways don't feed you any more. You figure there's got to be something more to it than this."

He had experienced the immense phenomenon of a war, a "police action" in Korea, where he was commissioned, and a "non-war" in Viet Nam, had seen the entire process, from boot camp to the dead gook in front of his bunker. All that he could make of it for sure was that winning was better than losing, and that killing was better than being killed, and in some dark hours he hadn't even been sure of that. Nothing he had seen was going to solve anything, or make men any wiser or kinder. A journeyman warmaker like himself was engaged in a holding operation, a buying of time at best against chaos and old night. But when the periodic killing cycles were over, the mindless crowd rushed back to the same old mindless routines at which they had been occupied when the shooting started. Nothing had been learned.

A deepening discontent with the life he was living settled upon him. He was moved by the same vague unrest that compels an Indian merchant, at the zenith of a successful career, to trade his worldly accumulations for the saffron robe and brass bowl of the beggar-monk in order to seek reality in the inner life of contemplation. Except that Mike had no such tradition to follow. He was merely discontented and confused.

The advent of Sadie Flippo added a ridiculous and distracting complication to the problem confronting him: what to do with the rest of his life?

Once at the beach, when the hour was late and his guard was down, he had talked to Sadie about his future. He had never had a home. He thought he would like to settle down someplace, where the ding-dong business of getting ahead in the world wasn't so important, if there was any place like that left in the world. Some small town in New Mexico or Arizona, where he could use what skills he had acquired, and make himself useful to what went on there. A place where, in time, he could feel that he belonged, like the rocks and the grass.

Then, when he was gone, perhaps a few people would be sorry. If they were, that would be sufficient.

And though he didn't tell this to Sadie, in this dreaming of his future there had always been a woman—somebody to love.

Hugging her knees, looking out at the moon-tipped waves, Sadie said it all sounded like a bunch of crud. The people in that hick town would turn out to be bastards, like everybody else. But she would be willing to try it. She might go with him.

Mike gave a jeering laugh. "I can see you now, wearing coveralls under a ten-thousand-dollar mink coat!"

9

The morning after the shooting Mike stood in front of the Embassy a few minutes before ten waiting for the Ambassador to come out. There was to be a dedication of the newly completed Instituto Militar, Maragua's West Point, in a manner of speaking. The morning was bright and pleasant. The sun warmed the pink walls of the Embassy, the bleached trunks of palms along the curving drive and the back of the old gardener, called Zapo, who was weeding in the brilliant beds of geraniums.

Mike still burned with anger at the needless killing he had witnessed the afternoon before. Robert Sanders was on his mind also. When they had dropped him at the hotel, Sadie had held her hand out to him.

"I don't know anything else about you," she said, looking straight at the man, "but there's surely nothing wrong with your guts."

As Robert Sanders stood beside the car under the dingy light of the marquee, Mike also looked for a second into his eyes. What he saw was anger and helpless pain. From that moment his dislike for the younger man was complicated by a feeling of pity. The fellow was clearly maimed. How or why, Mike didn't then know, but there was no doubt that his trouble was serious, maybe terminal.

The Ambassador's big Buick came breathing up the drive and stopped at the door. Enrique, the *chofer,* hopped out, looking like a spider monkey in his oversized uniform. He gave Mike a smart salute, whipped out a cloth and began to polish the already dazzling hood of the limousine.

At precisely ten the front doors opened and the Ambassador stepped out into the sunlight. The sight sent a surge of pride through Mike Hodak as he snapped to attention. General Rolla Z. Gatch, USMC (Ret.), in his dress blues, his gold-crusted cap canted at just the right angle, the sun sparkling off the wide colored patch of ribbons on his breast, was the finest-looking man Mike had ever seen.

The General stood well over six feet, and despite sixty-five hard-lived years he carried every inch like a model for a recruiting poster. His long, narrow legs were as secure under him as ever. His thick chest and his large, slightly inclined head, with its big features and light blue eyes under white-sandy brows, made as admirable a superstructure, in Mike's opinion, as a man ever came equipped with.

The older man acknowledged Mike's salute with two fingers lightly touched to his cap bill. The old familiar twinkle in his eyes, half hard, half bantering, was filmed with anger this morning. Still, he managed an amiable greeting for his aide.

"Captain Hodak, is it?"

"The same, sir," Mike responded.

It was an old joke between them. The General termed it the grossest miscarriage of justice in military history that Mike ever became an officer.

In accordance with naval custom, Mike ducked into the car ahead of his superior. Then as they settled themselves in the seat, the car lurched out into the midmorning traffic.

The General obviously was in dark spirits over the shameful events of the previous day. Every few seconds he made the choleric little clucking noises in his throat, which Mike recognized from long association as the sign of controlled but smoldering anger. The General was not personally in sympathy with the Populistas. In his opinion they were a bunch of bird-brain socialistic dreamers. But the killing of Felix Góngora and the others filled him with burning rage. It was completely unnecessary—killing for sport. He despised Lupo Machia as a lion despises a jackal.

A few blocks beyond the plaza they entered the slums of San Felipe. Passing through these dreary streets invariably depressed Mike, perhaps because they reminded him of his childhood. Filthy children played in the gutters. Naked, pot-bellied babies tumbled out of doorways in the stained walls. Old women haggled over beans and peppers and fly-stung meat in dingy *bodegas* along the way. The smell of onions cooking in rancid oil, of urine, of mold, all the odors that make up the fragrance of poverty, came through the car windows in a penetrating vapor.

The music of Maragua is *muy triste,* very sad, and the traveler needs only to drive through the *barrios* of San Felipe to understand why.

When they debouched from the depressing city into the open countryside the General said, "I'll wager you a bottle of McCollum's that Colonel Machia awards himself the Condor Cross for yesterday's little engagement, Captain."

"No bet, sir," Mike said with a grunt.

General Gatch did not take his own military decorations overseriously. He knew that he had received most of them merely for doing a workmanlike job of what he was paid to do, and the rest because he had a bunch of ironhead Marines under his command who didn't have better sense than to attack when they were outflanked, outnumbered and should have run like hell. Ugarte had decorated him with the Condor Cross upon his arrival in Maragua in recognition of a long career of fighting the free world's thankless battles. Though the General classed this as one of his "banquet bangles," he still felt it would tarnish the memory of a lot of dead Marines if Lupo Machia received the same hunk of metal for bushwhacking a truckload of clumsy Populistas.

Rolla Gatch was military to the core. Good order and discipline stood right alongside cleanliness and godliness in his book. A little of the old blood-and-thunder had mellowed out of him at sixty-five. He viewed life with a more philosophic eye, and was more tolerant of man's shortcomings than when Mike first knew him. But he could still rise to heights of scalding rage when he came upon one of Lupo Machia's breed.

They drove down through the dark greenness of irrigated cotton fields toward the front rank of the Andes which loomed in hazy purplish grandeur fifty miles away. Mike felt some uneasiness about how the General would react when he came face to face with Machia this morning, for the old man had been Marine for forty-four years and a diplomat for less than one.

53

Presently the Military Institute came in sight, a line of sparkling white buildings with red-tile roofs stretching nearly a mile across the plain against the backdrop of mountains. Pride was a chronic disease in Maragua. One of its symptoms was a compulsion to build everything on a grandiose scale unrelated to need.

The car slid to a stop before a building marked *Administración*. A mahogany-colored non-com snapped open the door and the General stepped out, followed by Mike. Then they entered the building and proceeded across the polished floor toward the receiving line, headed by General de Division Francisco Ugarte y Piñeda, the titular leader of the junta. Next to Ugarte, inevitably, stood Machia. An impressive contingent of high-ranking staff officers, resplendent in *uniformes de gala,* hovered in the background.

With a cordial smile, the American Ambassador saluted Ugarte and the two fell into an *abrazo,* the crablike embrace-cum-back-pounding which Maraguan males inflict upon one another when they are very friendly, or wish to appear so.

In his crimson trousers and powder-blue tunic girdled with the green sash of the Marshal of Maragua, Ugarte was a gaudy and pathetic figure. Mike judged him to be over eighty. His soft, putty-colored face was lined with a thousand wrinkles. The benign, faraway smile in his eyes told that the old warrior was living in a past and happier world of senility. His usefulness to Machia was prestige only. There was a saying current in the streets that if one looked closely one could see Machia's hand up the old man's back, working the controls.

As Mike shook hands with the Marshal, he cut his eyes to see how Rolla Gatch would greet Colonel Machia. The two big men were regarding one another with frank hostility, but the Marine General performed his distasteful duty with diplomatic propriety. After a formal handshake he said in perfect

54

Spanish, "An impressive establishment, Colonel. My congratulations."

With thinly veiled insolence Lupo Machia smiled. "You are excessively kind, my General. In our humble way we backward nations do our best, though we cannot hope to compete with the magnificent academies of the great Estados Unidos."

Machia was a powerful man, tall for a Maraguan. The darkish cast of his complexion was attributed to a strong flavoring of Zambo blood, a mixture of Negro and Indian said to distill the worst traits of both races. The pits in his flat cheeks, the square forehead sloping back to crinkly pompadoured hair, and the glint of calculating mockery in his eyes contributed to an aspect that was both fascinating and evil. But in his tailored uniform of green gabardine with golden shoulder boards he impressed even Mike Hodak. After shaking hands with him one's hand smelled for hours of the intense scent he used. There was street talk that his sexual powers were prodigious, and young women of San Felipe had been known to swoon with hysteria at the sight of him.

No one knew much about his early history except that he had emerged upward out of the ranks of the Army by force of burning ambition, undoubted ability and ruthlessness. As long ago as the late fifties he had been evaluated by the political section of the American Embassy, as a comer, intelligent, completely amoral, an opportunist of the first water, and no friend of the U.S.A. He was known to have close ties with the Castro-Communists, and it was believed that the only reason he had not gone all-out in a complete Castro-type takeover of the country was because he wasn't yet sure he could get away with it. The landed *gente decente* was very powerful, and, since Cuba, much wilier. He was too clever to risk defeat until he was sure of his ground, and so he covered himself with the prestige of General Ugarte and bided his time.

55

Mike trailed General Gatch into a large glass-walled room where a hundred guests were moving about in a slow diplomatic ballet, exchanging polite greetings and sipping pisco punch.

Presently a bugle sounded. Led by Ugarte, Machia and their aides, the distinguished assemblage filed out onto the parade, and the inspection began.

Mike strolled along near the tail of the procession glumly wishing he was somewhere else when Benito Monclova came up and linked arms with him.

"Enjoying yourself?" Monclova said with a wink.

"It's better than cleaning latrines," Mike replied.

Monclova was a short, square-faced lieutenant colonel in the Maraguan Army. He had the thick black hair and dark eyes of the pure Andean Indian and the calm, assured dignity of the highborn of his race. He had attended the Command and Staff School in the States, and he possessed the ability, uncommon in Maragua, to think with his brain instead of his emotions. Mike considered him a good man, the best of the lot in the Maraguan armed forces.

Monclova was not happy about the junta. Mike sensed that he was filled with a deep shame over yesterday's dirty little massacre in Avenida Sucre. But he was a good soldier, and for the moment at least he did not consider it proper to question the actions of his military and political superiors.

"Quite a lash-up you got here, *mi coronel,*" Mike said, trying to be nice, for he liked Monclova.

Looking off across the spacious grounds and buildings, the squat officer answered softly, thoughtfully, in English. "We got room enough here to train officers for the whole focking Russian Army. What we need was agriculture school."

During the next four hours they inspected classrooms, boiler rooms, dormitories, heads, armories, kitchens, repair shops without machinery, and barracks without furniture, all smelling of wet plaster and paint. They ate a meal that would have poisoned a hyena, listened to speeches of marathon duration, and stood in a reviewing stand while the cadet corps wheeled and turned in endless evolutions on the parade ground. It took more out of a man, Mike was sure, than a hard day in the field with troops.

All the way back to San Felipe General Gatch cursed the vanity or sense of duty or whatever it was that had caused him, when his fighting days were over, to accept this diplomatic appointment, instead of retiring to the pleasant environs of La Jolla, California, as an old worn-out Marine should. His face sagged with fatigue and disgust. As they drove into the outskirts of the city he snappishly ordered Mike to check further on that screwball Robert whatever-the-hell-his-name-was and find out what he was up to. He had no intention of allowing any halfbaked Rover Boy from the U.S. to run afoul of Machia and upset the delicately balanced relations between the two countries, which it was his assigned duty to preserve.

At Plaza Bolívar the big car paused and Mike stepped out, saluted, then watched the car disappear in the late traffic. As he crossed toward the hotel, the plaza was teeming with sundown strollers who had come out for the vermouth hour. He was bushed. He felt ineffectual and frustrated and was thinking that he should have stayed on in the Corps. He would probably be commanding the guard company at some naval ammunition depot now. That would be good, for he would never have heard of this fouled-up country—or of Sadie Flippo.

The lights of Ciné Metropol were blazing garishly against the plum-colored sky of early evening. Under the arcades around the square men sat in clusters at little tables drinking vermouth and pisco and smoking and talking with importance. Everything in this strange little land seemed foolish and unnecessary tonight, including himself. Mike wondered what Sadie was doing.

At the far side of the plaza he stepped from the curb and started across the street to the hotel. Then he stopped. Sadie was sitting in her car in front of the entrance, her bare arm resting across the back of the seat. As Mike watched, Robert Sanders came down the steps and stood beside the door talking to her. Laughing, Sadie held out her hand. Robert Sanders hesitated, then he took her hand, and for the first time Mike saw him smile. Then he got in the car beside Sadie and they drove away.

Sadie hadn't seen her mother for several years when she came to San Felipe, and she had no desire to see her, ever again. Her father had finally enjoyed as much of himself as he could stand and had retreated to the basement of the old family mansion in Tulsa with a hundred cases of Scotch, which he announced he would drink all by himself before he came out. Several earnest friends in AA tried to lure him to the surface. When he finally came, it was feet first in an undertaker's basket.

After her father's death, Sadie's sense of futility and personal worthlessness became chronic. Perhaps that is one reason she developed such an intense concern for the oppressed and downtrodden, or at least for those who in her youthful tender-hearted ardor she imagined to be oppressed and downtrodden. This is how she met Lupo Machia.

When she came to San Felipe she had been deeply touched and depressed by the number of ragged, undernourished children roaming the streets, begging, scavenging, shining shoes, hawking dirty lottery tickets. Many had ugly sores on their arms and legs.

With characteristic impulsiveness and without consulting anyone at the Embassy or elsewhere she employed two local doctors and four nurses and opened what she grandly named the Charles Flippo III Memorial Vitamin and Penicillin Institute of Maragua. The Institute set up a clinic in the heart of San Felipe's slums and offered vitamins and antibiotics, free, to any child in need of them. With candy bars and balloons she lured the youngsters into the clinic for shots, and from the first the Institute did a thriving business.

For a short while Sadie glowed with enthusiasm for her new project. Within days she imagined she could see the running sores disappearing from the streets and began to feel that there was some need for her in this world after all. Then, without warning, the Ministerio de Sanidad descended upon her benevolent little enterprise, closed the clinic, posted armed guards at the doors and enjoined all further operations of the Institute on pain of imprisonment. Ridiculous charges were made that the clinic was using old, impure drugs imported from the United States.

Infuriated, Sadie reacted with some of the resourcefulness she had inherited from Dry Hole Joe Wharton. By now she had learned that Lupo Machia was the real power in the junta. At first opportunity, a garden party at the Indian Embassy, she went out in her wispiest, most revealing minifrock, topped by a ridiculous picture hat that flopped over one eye, and stalked Machia like a youthful huntress.

Two days later the Charles Flippo III Memorial Vitamin and Penicillin Institute was permitted to reopen its doors, and Sadie Flippo was seen with Colonel Machia frequently thereafter—up the hill at the ski run, in the official box at the race track, at the roulette table in the exclusive Club Nacional.

When Mike upbraided her about the low class of people she was associating with, Sadie smiled and patted his hand. "Lupo

Machia is a rat fink. I know that. Every time I've been with him I've wanted to go home and barf. Then I think of all those little kids and I feel like Gertrude Nightingale—or whoever it was. You know, the big nurse."

"You remind me of Gertrude Sap!" Mike said.

"So it keeps the clinic open!" Sadie flared, flipping a strand of hair out of her eyes. "That's more than your stuffed shirts at the Embassy could do for me!"

Mike felt sure there was more to Sadie's interest in Machia than the privilege of shooting a bunch of scruffy kids in the ass with penicillin. He divined, correctly, that she was also fascinated by the atmosphere of danger and power that the man moved in. Mike wasn't sure how far Sadie went with him, but he knew that Machia wasn't one to give something for nothing.

In a numb fury Mike Hodak reminded himself it was none of his business what Sadie Flippo did, with Lupo Machia or anybody else, and he repeated this to himself, like a catechism, several times a day, hoping that sometime he would come to believe it.

That was how matters stood when Robert Sanders arrived in San Felipe.

10

The morning after the dedication at the Instituto Mike sat in his office in the Chancery going over a checklist for the Ambassador's reception to be held the following night. The incumbent Military Attaché of the Embassy had finished his tour of duty and, in accordance with custom, the Ambassador was giving a cocktail party for his incoming replacement, Lt. Col. Thomas Clapsaddle, U.S.A., a Viet Nam veteran who was due to arrive tomorrow, shortly after noon.

When Mike had ticked off his list and everything seemed in order, he walked down the hall to the Ambassador's office. The old man, wearing an English tweed jacket and a sporty knit tie, a little halfmoon pince-nez perched on his large nose, was intently studying a paper on the top of his desk. An impressed visitor from home would doubtless have taken this for an important document of state rather than a tout sheet for the day's *cinco y seis* at the local race track.

Mike told the old man that everything was squared away for the party and reminded him of the *despedida* at "El Coontry" tonight, for the departing attaché, given by the Attachés Association. The old man made a face.

"Jesus Christ! I was going to work on my coins." The General had collected Filipino coins for years. He had several sacks full and was always going to "work" on them, but never seemed to get around to it.

"The General *will* go to the *despedida?*" Mike observed. It was more a statement than a question. Diplomatic propriety required that the Ambassador attend the farewell cocktail party for his own departing attaché. With a put-upon sigh of resignation General Gatch said, "Ye-s, the General will go."

As Mike reached the door on his way out, General Gatch cleared his throat in a manner that would have stopped a truck.

"Sir?"

"Gunner. What have you got to report on your friend from Stateside. That Robert—"

"Sanders."

"Yes. Has Conners heard anything on him?" Conners was the CIA man attached to the Embassy.

"Not a thing," Mike said. "He radioed Washington. They don't know him. They're running a check on him."

"Sounds like a loner."

"His activities last night were strictly social, sir. He left the hotel at six-ten with your First Secretary's sister-in-law, Mrs. Sadie Flippo. They returned at one A.M. That's not all. That idiot female has arranged to get him invited to the *despedida* tonight. It's a gut cinch Machia will be there. How stupid can American women be, General?" Mike was visibly irritated.

The General sighed and shook his head. "Oh, that Sadie. I wish I was twenty years younger."

"I wish you were, too, General. Then Sadie would be three years old!"

As he went down the corridor Mike passed Alden Clinton's office and saw the First Secretary of Embassy at his desk, studiously dictating. Alden Clinton kept the Embassy running, administratively. His neat, ash-blond head was always inclined intently at something connected with his work, which he discharged with earnest and unimaginative zeal. His wife's beautiful younger sister, Sadie Flippo, had caused him untold anxiety and considerable embarrassment. In Clinton's book of rules, conformity to the norms of social behavior, especially when diplomatic decorum was involved, became quite as fundamental as observance of the Decalogue.

Before he reached his own office Mike's eye fell upon the generous shape of a girl bending over the drinking fountain. Since it was a familiar shape, he gave it, in passing, a friendly pat. Jumping, Rusty Cobb straightened, half-strangled, and made small eyes at him.

"What's the matter, Rusty?"

"Oh, there you are," she said, wiping her mouth with the back of her hand. "My hero! I stayed under that damn table at the Bolívar for two hours!"

Mike laughed. He hadn't seen Rusty since the shoot-up in Avenida Sucre. "Rus," he said, "I can't lie to you. I flat forgot you. But I'll make it up. You going to Horsley's *despedida* tonight?"

Rusty Cobb brightened. "You know me, kid. The unattached attaché's dream."

"Well, I'll tell you what. If you're real sweet, I'll save a dance for you."

"Che-sus! How lucky can I be! I haven't danced with a gorilla in a long time!"

When he got back to his office the phone was ringing. The receptionist on the front desk said there was a *Teniente* Luís Calderón waiting to see him. Mike scowled. Calderón was one of Machia's *ayudantes*. He told the girl to send him in. Moments later the officer appeared in his doorway. The young man was a junior-grade replica of his *jefe*, tailored uniform, supercilious expression, air of supreme confidence and all. Cap under arm, he clicked his heels smartly and advanced to Mike's desk.

"Accept, Señor, the renewed assurances of my *Comandante*'s high esteem," he said in stiff, memorized English.

Mike nodded. "The same to him. What can I do for you, Lieutenant?"

"*Coronel* Machia wishes to be delivered to you, eh—thees!" With a flourish he handed a white envelope across the desk.

"Eet request the answer," the *Teniente* said aloofly.

63

Slitting the envelope, Mike drew out Machia's large engraved card. On the reverse side in the man's own handwriting he read: *"Estimada Capitán*—I would be pleased to discuss a matter of importance. *Machia."*

Concealing his surprise, Mike glanced up at the man and nodded. "I'm at the Colonel's service, *Teniente,* of course."

Clicking his heels again, the young officer gave a curt half-bow. *"Coronel* Machia will be at the *Comandancia* thees morning at more or less eleven o'clock."

"Tell him I'll be there at eleven. *Hora inglesa."*

When the aide had departed Mike sat back in his chair frowning at the card as he turned it in his fingers. His first impulse was to report the matter to the Ambassador at once. Then he thought better of it. No point in starting the old man's hydrochloric acid to flowing before lunch. He would be belching and goddamming all afternoon. Mike was protective of his General this way. First he would find out what Machia wanted, then he would tell the old man, after he had had his midday toddy, lunch and short nap. He glanced at his watch. It was ten forty-five. Flipping the card onto the desk, he got up and left the office, informing the receptionist he would be back at two.

As he went toward the Plaza Mayor, where the government offices lay, threading his way through the narrow crowded streets of shops and old houses with latticed balconies, relics of colonial days, he tried to puzzle out an explanation for this summons by Machia. But when he reached the plaza he was still in the dark.

Machia's Mark X Jaguar with red headlights and sirens on the fenders stood before the ominous gray-stone *Comandancia.* The two-motorcycle escort who always preceded the car in its howling passage through the city sat idly on their machines and followed Mike with their eyes as he went up the steps. A pair of guards with submachine guns cradled in their arms lounged in the dark shadows of the entrance.

A chill of depression rippled Mike's calm as he thought of the foul operations said to take place in the subterranean apartments beneath his feet, where men and even women disappeared without trace. On still nights faint cries of anguish and despair were sometimes heard by late passers-by, as if coming, muffled, through the sidewalks. It was in these catacombs that Machia employed the infamous device called The Sweetheart, a contrivance with both male and female attachments which imparted a devastating but sublethal electrical shock when applied to or into the sex organs. Two or three applications, at most, were sufficient to make the stoutest suspect confess eagerly and in minute detail to any political crime he had committed, and as readily to any crime of which he was merely accused and had no knowledge whatever.

Inside the entrance Mike underwent the cold scrutiny of an officer of the guard. The man examined his diplomatic identification card closely, then thumbed him up the marble stairway to the second floor.

At the top of the stairs Mike walked down the wide, shadowy corridor until he came to a railing behind which another officer sat at a desk, eyeing him sullenly. This one hauled himself from his chair, flipped the latch on the gate, and before Mike could protest was running his hands expertly under his arms, between his legs and slapping his buttocks, checking for the lump of a pistol. With a jerk of his head the officer passed Mike down the hall.

In another moment, raging inwardly, he was admitted through tall doors into Colonel Machia's suite. Looking around, he saw Machia at the far end of the room sitting

65

behind a massive desk on a raised dais. Clad in a shirt of beige silk, Machia surveyed him from this elevation with an air of regal indifference. Light from windows onto the plaza illuminated dark oil paintings of forgotten dictators and generals that lined the long wall. The floor was of ancient polished marble.

As the Marine officer approached, Machia arose languidly and descended from his dais.

"It was kind of you to come, Captain Hodak," he said, extending his hand. "I trust I did not inconvenience you." Mike could not help remembering that this was the same hand that had triggered the unnecessary bullets into the dying Populista, but he shook it anyway.

"No inconvenience, Colonel," he said coldly.

Smiling, Machia took a silver box from the desk and offered a cigarette. Mike declined.

"May I offer you a pisco?"

"No thanks."

The big man studied the American for a moment; then, with a short laugh, he dropped his pseudo-cordial manner. Mashing out his cigarette he strolled to the window, turned and faced Mike, thumbs hooked in his belt, a look of mockery on his face.

"Captain Hodak, only my profound esteem for your Ambassador and—shall I say—my sincere desire to prevent an embarrassing situation arising between our governments cause me to invite you here." His manner changed now to frank hostility. "An individual who calls himself Robert Sanders has arrived in San Felipe. I presume you are aware of this."

"I met the man yesterday for the first time," Mike said. "I meet most Americans who come to San Felipe. It's part of my job."

66

"The word is *estadounidense,* not *Americano,* Captain," Machia said, with sudden anger, emphasizing the strange Spanish term for "United Statesian." "You do not have the exclusive franchise to be called American. In any case I presume you know something about this man."

"Not a thing, Colonel, except that he comes from Texas."

"Then I will tell you. He is a hired killer, imported by the Populista rebels to aid in the escape of the criminal Rafael Benavides from the Colombian Embassy, where he has been given unlawful refuge from justice. When this Sanders did not arrive on schedule, the desperate leaders of the plot proceeded without him. The results you know. It is regrettable that Sanders did not get here on time. Perhaps he would have added some polish to that otherwise laughable attempt in Avenida Sucre. He is said to be quite resourceful—an expert in explosives, I believe. We are disappointed that we did not have opportunity to observe his skill."

He watched Mike with amusement for several seconds. "We are not taking official notice of him, for the moment. We will charitably consider him a misguided fool and dupe who is unaware of the criminality of the Populista conspiracy. However, his presence in Maragua will not be tolerated. This is why I have called you here. If the man should decide to leave Maragua immediately, no one would detain him. I am sure you will know how to arrange this, Captain."

He turned and strolled back to his desk, as if to give the American a moment to organize his reply. Mike followed him with his eyes, pawing his brain for an answer. Machia's supercilious manner galled the hell out of him. At the same time he realized that the junta could hardly allow Sanders to remain in the country without picking him up. Mike wasn't fooled by Machia's professed esteem for General Gatch. He knew the man would take pleasure in showing Sanders the same mercy he had shown Góngora and the others, if there were not an important reason for restraint. Fortunately for Robert Sanders, even the slightest jarring of relations with the United States would be very bad for the junta's plans just now. The country's economy was in hard straits and an infusion of U.S. dollars was desperately needed. A pending AID grant from the American government was in the final stages of negotiation in Washington. This, Mike knew at once, was the only reason Robert Sanders was at large and still alive.

He made a rather feeble protest, sparring for time. "Colonel, *we* don't have anything on this man. Ambassador Gatch can't tell people to haul freight just because he don't like their looks. You haven't charged him with anything yet."

Machia said sharply, "What I have just told you is all the charge you require, Captain. I am sure a way will be found to arrange his departure. Your Ambassador is quite a crafty old fox, I am informed."

Sudden anger flared in Mike's face. He knew he had better get out of here quick before he lost control of himself. He said, "Your informant is a lousy judge of his betters, Colonel. But I will call the matter to General Gatch's attention."

Machia strode over and clapped a hand on Mike's shoulder in an exaggerated show of friendliness. "Splendid, Captain, splendid! No doubt you will be at the *despedida* for your outgoing attaché tonight."

"I plan to be there, Colonel."

"Then possibly we will have a drink together."

"That is a possibility, Colonel."

11

Mike Hodak's background and experience better equipped him for social intercourse with longshoremen and merchant seamen than for mingling with the gentry of the diplomatic world. His mother died when he was three. His father was a cook who worked in second-rate cafés in Philadelphia, where Mike was born. This parent, a violent thwarted man, nightly inflamed his frustrations with alcohol. The only attention Mike received from him was swift and stinging punishment for the misdemeanors he wasn't clever enough to hide.

Such upbringing as he had was from a sister eight years older than he. He remembered her as a miserable, slatternly girl who cried a great deal and whipped him with a belt when he was naughty. She left home when he was ten and he never saw her again. Though he had been glad to be rid of the whippings, she was the nearest thing he had known to a mother and he missed her sorely. After he had grown to manhood he once spent a furlough trying to locate her, and finally learned that she had died in childbirth years before.

When he was fifteen Mike lied about his age and enlisted in the Marine Corps, and that became his life thenceforward.

With its iron discipline and rock-hard men the Corps became his parents, his education, his security. Later on it even took the place of wife and family, for he had no other. By the time he was seventeen he fancied himself a formidable fighting man. He had been drilled, pounded, driven and sweated until he performed instinctively and without question the hard, simple things a private must do in all circumstances in order to wear the globe and fouled anchors of a U.S. Marine.

Having the shoulders and awkward quickness of a young bull, he won the light-heavyweight boxing championship of the Fleet when he was eighteen. The next year he took a piece of Jap shrapnel in his back and spent three months in the Naval Hospital at Aiea Heights outside Honolulu.

During this dreary time one of the significant events of his life occurred: he learned to read. Of course he already had a rudimentary knowledge of reading and writing. In the hospital he was introduced to the astonishing world of books.

While thus confined he found himself at the mercy of a Gray Lady by the name of Mrs. Boggs. This angel of mercy was a heavy woman with gray hair that swirled off in all directions like smoke, and she was by nature a missionary. She spent most of her waking hours visiting patients at the hospital, preaching with missionary fervor the gospel of literature. Later Mike knew he should be grateful to Mrs. Boggs, but to the end of his days he would remember her with a feeling of dread.

With maddening regularity she came to visit him, bringing little sacks of cookies and armloads of books. With a true missionary's zeal she read aloud to him in her husky, rasping voice for twenty minutes or more on each visit. She read Shakespeare, Milton, Wordsworth, Keats and Shelley. She even read Chaucer. It came near to driving Mike crazy. He dreaded her visits worse than the doctor's with his scissors and probe to work on his wound. He tried to figure out how to stop his ears without showing it and hurting her feelings, for her

70

reading caused him actual pain, just as the music of Beethoven and Mozart can pain people who are not brought up to it.

Mrs. Boggs always left several books for him to read between visits. When she came again she would quiz him relentlessly on what he was supposed to have read since her last visit. Finally in self-defense he picked up one of the books, *Moby Dick,* and plowed in. He found it very heavy going for a while. Then, as he laboriously spelled out the words, he found himself becoming involved in the voyage of the *Pequod* and concerned with the fate of Ishmael and Queequeg and the others, as though they were shipmates. Thus a door he never knew existed opened to him.

His appetite for books since then had been voracious and undiscriminating. This accounted for his broad if somewhat superficial knowledgeableness on many subjects, an unusual credential in one of his station. General Gatch referred to him as his "highly uneducated aide-de-camp." Mike didn't mind. He knew what the old man wanted, and he performed when better-educated careerists gave well-reasoned explanations of why they did not. This was partly why the old man picked Mike for his aide over others of higher caste. Other reasons were twenty-four-hour availability, no family encumbrances, a sense of humor, and a passable skill at acey-deucey. But mainly the General picked him because he liked him.

As he rode through the early dusk toward the *despedida* to the departing Military Attaché, Mike worried back over his morning visit with Machia. After lunch he had briefed the General fully on the meeting, for the serious turn of events made it imperative that the Ambassador be informed. General Gatch had grunted, had called Machia several varieties of sonofabitch, then had taken cognizance, grimly, of the necessity of getting Robert Sanders out of Maragua.

It was certain that Machia would attend the *despedida* tonight. He made them all. The mass, if synthetic, adulation he received at these big affairs fed his ravenous ego. He would certainly see Robert Sanders, if *he* came. If they both were there, matters would be complicated. Mike passed his hand across his forehead, trying to rub away the beginning of a headache.

When his taxi arrived at "El Coontry," the clubhouse was aglow with lights. The deep thrumming sound of guitars and many voices came through the open windows of the old, rambling building. Inside he found the grand salon filled with a humid, teeming crowd of fashionable humanity. A well-bred din laced with laughter confused his ears as he worked his way into the room. *Mozos* in white jackets served the guests from dangerously balanced trays of drinks and *bocaditos*.

Across the room the General's white sandy hair was visible above the sea of people like a beacon. Making his way toward this Mike saw another, darker giant of a man standing out above the moving sea of heads—Lupo Machia, surrounded by his usual squadron of aides and bodyguards.

Mike didn't see Sadie Flippo or Robert Sanders and felt a momentary hope that the latter had not come.

General Gatch was surrounded by his own admiring claque: his wife Molly and a squad of chattering Embassy girls, all of whom adored him. Molly was a small, wiry woman with crisp gray hair and a not pretty but good Irish face. She perpetually crackled with nervous energy. She had followed her big man around the world for thirty-five years, sticking as close to him as duty would allow. She fussed over him like a little hen over a giant chick.

With the slightest lifting of brows the General acknowledged Mike's greeting. "Good evening, Mister Hodak. Has
our young compatriot arrived?"

Mike made a frog mouth. "He was invited, General. I
haven't seen him. I'll look around."

After working his way through the crowd for ten minutes in
a circular search pattern, Mike stopped in an eddy of open
space near the terrace doors and scanned back across the
room.

He had just concluded with relief that Robert Sanders had
decided not to come when he saw the man standing against the
wall not five feet away.

Sanders was alone. He held a cup of nonalcoholic fruit
punch and he wore the same gray suit he had on the afternoon
Mike first saw him. Surveying his relaxed, compact physique,
Mike thought again: *un hombre formidable*. The man's nar-
rowed eyes took in the crowd. Without joy Mike moved over
to him.

"Hello, Sanders," he said. "How's your business going?"

Nodding recognition, Robert Sanders said, pleasantly
enough, "All right, Captain. Been to any more murders since I
saw you?"

Mike felt like saying, "No, old buddy, but you're liable to be
the star of one if I can't figure how to get you out of here in a
hurry." Instead, he said, "Nope. Things have been kind of
dull." For a while neither added to this exchange, then Mike
said, "Having a nice time?"

Robert Sanders said, "No complaints."

"Have you met our Ambassador?"

"No."

"I'd like to introduce you. He likes to meet visitors from
home."

Robert Sanders was silent for a moment. He seemed to be considering this. Then he shrugged, "It's up to you."

Irritated, Mike steered him through the crowd toward the corner where the General had established his command post for the evening. En route he gave the Machia party as wide a berth as possible, but he knew there was slight chance the big man would not see them. Very little escaped Machia's sharp, roving eye.

Molly and the Embassy girls had gone, as the General put it, "to pump ship." Puffing at his holdered cigarette, the old man stood talking with the British air attaché. After Mike introduced Robert Sanders, the Britisher remained a polite moment, then excused himself.

"Mr. Sanders, I'm told you arrived in San Felipe just in time for the nasty little show on Avenida Sucre." The General dug into the man immediately, probing, sizing him up.

Without expression Robert Sanders said, "Yes sir. That's right."

"Sorry business." The General pursed his lips and looked at the young man. "But none of ours, of course. We Americans have to be careful not to let our sympathies lead us into meddling. It's a difficult thing, but we have to remember that nobody appointed us caretakers of the world." Then he smiled cordially. "I understand you're here buying native handicraft for export."

Above the dark brows a frown creased Robert Sanders' forehead. With a restless gesture he ran his hand over his short hair. Mike received the quick impression that the man had no wish to be impolite or disrespectful, but at the same time had no intention of submitting to cross-examination. The General sensed this also. Without waiting for an answer, he came quickly to the point. "I'd be pleased if you'd stop by the Chancery for a visit in the morning, Mister Sanders. In fact I

74

think it would be advisable. We might be of some help to you."

Robert Sanders gazed at him as if he didn't know what to say. He shot Mike a glance of exasperation. This awkward silence was broken by a voice that came like sparkling light into their midst, turning them all toward its source.

"*Mi general!* There you are! I've been looking for you!" Sadie said coming toward him, almost floating it seemed, in her short green chiffon gown. She held out her hand.

"Sadie, *ma cherie,*" the General said with exaggerated gallantry, taking and lightly kissing her fingertips. In a way the old man was under Sadie's spell just as Mike was. He enjoyed having beautiful women around him, though being a practical man and aware of his age, he recognized that the greatest sin he would ever commit with Sadie would be lust of the eyes.

"You look ravishing, my dear!" he said. "Ravishing!" Mike agreed. Her filmy skirt swirling from her narrow waist when she turned revealed a length of slim brown legs that made him mutter as if with pain. The pencil straps of her gown accentuated the tanned smoothness of her shoulders and the youthful perfection of her arms and bosom. Mike watched Robert Sanders closely, but the younger man hardly glanced at the girl, and there was no more expression on his face than on a clock.

"Well, now," Sadie cried, clapping her hands together. "I see you've met my—my——. General, did you *know* that Mister Sanders saved my life?"

"Yes, I do know," the General said, inclining his head cordially toward Sanders. "And we are most grateful, for many reasons."

Robert Sanders inhaled with quiet exasperation.

"The whole affair has been exaggerated," he said. "I was in no danger whatever."

75

The *despedida* ran its normal course. By eight-thirty the old guard began to tire and drift out. The flat bellies, as the General called the younger crowd, had only just got up to tempo. The night would lead them on to other excitements and adventures.

A little earlier Molly Gatch had taken Robert Sanders in tow like a reluctant captive, to introduce him to some special friends. Mike stood near the entrance of the salon talking uncomfortably to Sadie and Cyril Corkright. Corkright was the resident managing director of Compañia Cobre, S.A., which operated copper mines and a larger smelter near Barranco in the Andean *altiplano* east of San Felipe. The man was explaining to Mike the interlocking corporate arrangement whereby the trust which Driller Joe had created for Sadie owned the controlling interest in a holding company, which, in turn, held fifty-seven per cent of the shares of Compañia Cobre.

"Sounds a trifle complicated, I daresay," Corkright said with a rather superior smile. He was a pleasant enough Englishman with a cropped blond mustache. "The short of it is that this young woman owns, beneficially, fifty-seven per cent of Compañia Cobre, an operation with over two thousand employees, producing countless tons of copper ingot per annum. And she has never been near the place. It's almost enough to turn one into a Communist."

Sadie made a sweet-acid mouth at him. "Someday I'll come, Corkright, and you'll be sorry. I'll take away your chains and lashes and raise the miners' pay."

The General and Molly strolled by on the way out. The puckish expression and rosy glow on the old man's face told Mike that he had had his quota of bourbon and branch water.

76

The General kissed Sadie's hand again and offered the men a playful, two-fingered handshake.

"Be good children," he said. "Don't fight."

Molly pecked a kiss on Sadie's cheek, then Mike followed them out of the entrance and down the stairway to the drive where Enrique was standing by with the car.

When Mike had helped them into the car and closed the door, the General leaned up to the window and motioned to him. All playfulness was gone from his voice now.

"Don't let our boy friend walk into any traps tonight, Gunner. We'll talk to him in the morning and get him on a plane out of here tomorrow afternoon. Meantime, see that he stays out of trouble."

"Aye, aye, sir."

The General sat back in the seat and the car pulled away. Making a wry face, Mike watched it until it turned out of the drive into the *avenida*.

When he returned to the party the crowd had thinned. A few couples had started dancing. Mike circled the room looking for Sadie and Robert Sanders, but saw neither.

Near the entrance he saw Alden Clinton and his wife saying good night to the Haitian Chargé d'Affaires, but Sadie was not with them. Both she and Robert Sanders had disappeared. Mike went out onto the terrace that overlooked the club pool and grounds, but neither was there. He was about to re-enter the club when he heard a sound that drew him back across the terrace to the balustrade. Peering out into the darkness he listened and heard the sound again, a coarse, raucous voice, laughing. It was Machia's.

A floodlight by the swimming pool cast pale illumination across the lawn. In a moment Mike's eyes adjusted to the semi-darkness and he could make out the figures of two people on the far side of the pool, a girl and a large man. The laughter was loud and vulgar. The man was obviously drunk, and obviously Lupo Machia.

In a second Mike realized that the girl was Sadie. Apparently she had been strolling beside the pool with Machia, who had taken a sudden notion to stop and embrace her. She now struggled to extricate herself from this unwelcome development. Her voice came to Mike shrill and angry. These facts had scarcely registered when Mike became aware of another actor entering the scene—Robert Sanders. The young American walked from the portico directly beneath the terrace on which Mike stood and headed rapidly toward the two people beside the pool.

12

Under his breath Mike said "Oh, Christ!" and got over to the steps and started down them, hissing sharply, trying to attract the younger man's attention and stop him. It was an asinine time for him to show up. Apparently he had gone to the *excusado* and now was looking for Sadie. She was in no real danger, but he sure as hell was. Unfortunately, before Mike was halfway to the pool Robert Sanders had turned the corner at the shallow end and was heading up the walk toward the girl struggling with the big man. As Sanders neared them, he slowed. His voice was cautious, but penetrating.

"There you are, Sadie Flippo. I lost you. You promised me the next Charleston."

There was a second of silence. Then Machia relaxed his bear-hug on Sadie and looked over her head with annoyance. In the patronizing tones of a man on his own ground and supremely sure of himself, he said, "Señor, you can see—this dance is taken. Some other time, eh?" Sadie shoved his enveloping arms away, extricated herself and smoothed her dress, fuming.

Ignoring Machia, Robert Sanders said, "What about that Charleston? I'd settle for a Watusi. Or a frug. Even a black-bottom."

Machia thrust out his jaw angrily. Then he gave a hard, surprised laugh. This time his tone was not condescending but insulting. *"Oye, gringo. Es sordo?* You deaf? The lady is busy. You beat it, eh?"

In a shrill, angry voice Sadie cried, "That's what you think, you drunken oaf! Mr. Sanders is a friend of mine. You can beat it yourself!"

"Mr. *Sanders?"* Machia said with surprise. "Mr. *Robert* Sanders? O-ho! I have hear of this gentleman. This is indeed a great honor, Señor." His words were edged with contemptuous laughter as he bent from the waist in an exaggerated bow. He straightened and extended his hand.

Robert Sanders had no desire to shake hands with the man. Somebody once said that the average American would shake hands with the devil before he thought about it. It is called the Rotarian instinct. In this situation it was an unfortunate trait. Machia reached for Robert Sanders' responding hand, then grabbed it hard, and lunged backward.

With a laughing roar Machia cried, "In the place of a dance, how 'bout a little swim, Señor Sanders?" Jerking the smaller man off balance he pivoted, and in the same motion propelled him sideways, irresistibly toward the pool. The lights

79

from the club shimmered like streaks of quicksilver on the water. Robert Sanders didn't have a chance. He grabbed futilely at the air, then he hit the water with a flat splash, shattering the quicksilver into splinters of light.

Sadie yelled furiously, "You idiot sonofabitch!"

With a shout of laughter Machia hooked his arm around Sadie's waist. "Now *we* will dance the frug, eh *gringita!* You and me, eh? While Señor Sanders takes his bath!" With a drunken whoop, he lunged down the poolside toward the club lugging Sadie on his hip like a sack of meal. Struggling, Sadie gritted through her teeth, "Let me go, you insufferable ass!"

Blowout pressure built in Mike's arteries instantly. He started toward the pool at a run, several thoughts flying through his brain at once. What he was going to do could get him a bullet in the ear. The old man would probably bust him back to gunnery sergeant. Nevertheless, he was going to knock some teeth down the throat of the eminent *Coronel* Lupo Machia, and just as fast as he could get to him!

He never got there.

Breaking the surface of the dark water, Robert Sanders' face was a phosphorescent blur. He laid out in a strong crawl stroke toward the shallows, keeping right up with Machia, now fully occupied with Sadie, who was clawing and spitting like a tiger cat. The young American came up the pool steps with a rush, spraying torrents of water. Then he swung around and blocked the walk, before Machia reached the corner of the pool.

"Ho-ho, *gringo!*" Machia said savagely. "How you like the water? You wish to go again, maybe?"

Moving toward him, blowing water out of his mouth, Robert Sanders said, "It was real nice. Now I want you to try it."

With a violent laugh the big man gave Sadie a shove that sent her sprawling on the grass. He stood a head taller than the American, whose suit, pasted to his body, made him look almost a boy by comparison. Robert Sanders moved toward him easily, almost casually. Sadie screeched like a banshee, but neither man paid her any mind. When Machia's fingers, outstretched like a wrestler's, nearly touched him, Robert Sanders hesitated. Then with a quick upward feint of his head, he ducked in like a flicker of light. Brushing under Machia's arm he drove his shoulder into the big man's thighs. In the same lightning motion he grabbed Machia's booted ankles with hooked wrists and jerked them from under him. Machia fell heavily on his back. His head cracked the concrete like a block of wood. Quick as a cat Robert Sanders was on him. He grabbed Machia's legs and clamped a foot under each arm. With a strong backward twisting motion he swung the half-stunned man, head out, in a wide arc over the pool. Their shadows jumped and flew across the lawn and water in fantastic shapes as they whirled. On the second turn Robert Sanders let go and Machia sprawled through the air. He splashed into the surging water on his back.

At the end of the pool Mike let out a shout that was amazed, delighted and profane. Machia exploded from the murky shallows like an angry sea lion. Trailing wreaths of water from his head, he barged through the waist-deep water, emitting furious trumpeting sounds. When he mounted the steps Sadie was screaming and chattering like an angry bird. Mike stood watching as if frozen to the ground. This was another man's show, and he was too late anyway. Only Robert Sanders appeared unconcerned. With the edge of his finger he flicked water from his forehead. He faced around as Machia came up the steps.

Dripping rivers of water from his ruined uniform, Lupo Machia moved toward the American, his shoulders bunched with fury. Robert Sanders waited for him, hands loose at his sides, his head slightly forward. In the very mildness of his manner there was something formidable. Machia stalked to within a pace of him, his arms hooked, wordless sounds coming through his nose. Trembling with rage he stopped. For an instant Mike was sure they were going together.

Then Machia couldn't carry it through. It wasn't fear that stopped him. He was a shrewd man even when drunk, and this was a ridiculous, impossible situation in which he could not afford to be trapped. Attracted by the commotion, people would come pouring out of the clubhouse any minute. The Chief of Staff and real power of the junta would be found soaked and wrestling on the pool's edge like a schoolboy. The loss of face would be intolerable. He hit Sanders hard, contemptuously on the chest with the back of his hand. His voice was a maddened snarl.

"You want to play rough, *gringo?* Okay!"

His tone left no doubt he would have Robert Sanders' heart. But he could wait for it. He jerked around savagely and strode past Mike as if he didn't see him. The sucking sound of his boots made ludicrous music as he marched toward the clubhouse and disappeared under the portico.

Then Mike moved around the corner of the pool. Sadie saw him and cried his name. In spite of himself Mike exploded with laughter. "Goddam, man, this is no time to go swimming!"

With the slightest laugh Robert Sanders shrugged. "The sonofabitch pushed me in."

"Mike, that was Lupo Machia!" Sadie cried shrilly, running up. "What will he do?"

"Change his clothes, first, I expect."

"Be serious, Mike! You know that man! What are *we* going to do?"

Mike said, "If you really want my opinion, our next move should be to take out more life insurance."

Looking Robert Sanders up and down, Mike shook his head. Standing there dripping, squeezing water out of his necktie, the fellow looked a mess.

"There are eight million people in this country," Mike said. "And you picked this particular one to throw in the swimming pool. You must be some kind of a genius."

Sadie said firmly, "Well, he's got to get out of here. That's for damn certain."

"And where," Mike asked dryly, "would you suggest he get *to?*" Staying out of Machia's clutches in Maragua was not all that easy, if Machia wanted you.

"I don't give a damn where!" Sadie cried. "Clear out of the wretched country if necessary."

"You're talking sense now," Mike said.

"Folks," Robert Sanders said with mild annoyance, "there are no planes leaving here tonight. And if it's all right with everybody, I'd like to get some dry clothes."

"Check!" Sadie Flippo said decisively, assuming command of the situation. She grabbed Robert Sanders' hand and started toward the club. "You go around that side, boy," she said, pointing. "Wait for me by the gate at the entrance. Mike, you come with Sadie."

Because he couldn't think of anything that sounded better, Mike shrugged. "Huckelty-buck. Might as well be shot with a pretty woman as a hag."

Splitting off as they approached the club, Robert Sanders disappeared into the shadowy shrubs at the end of the building. Sadie ran up the terrace steps, her voice vibrant. "Wasn't he simply terrific, Mike! Rescuing me from Machia like that! A second time!"

"It put me in mind of two stud airedales fighting over a bitch poodle," Mike said, running after her.

Sadie said, "This man has possibilities."

They entered the salon, now sparsely occupied by a scattering of diehards hanging on for one last drink, Rusty Cobb and Archie Pringle, both well stoned, among them. These two were dancing vaguely to a cha-cha and commiserating one another on the hardness of life. Archie, vice-consul at the Chancery, mother-henned American tourists. He was a pudgy old-maid type with bags under his eyes and a little red mouth that perpetually pouted.

Sadie slapped him on the back as she went by. "Party's moving to El Gallo, sport. You coming?" Without missing a beat of the music Archie and Rusty cha-chaed right in behind her.

Mike looked at Sadie in amazement, trying to keep up with her as they swept out of the salon. "The *what's* moving to *where?*"

"I'm giving a party," she said, smiling at him, "for Robert Sanders. To celebrate the tossing of Lupo Machia into the swimming pool."

"At El Gallo?"

"At El Gallo."

"Are you crazy?"

"It's the last place they'll look for him." Sadie flashed Mike a smile of delicate scorn. "If this makes you nervous, you run on home, Captain, sweetheart."

Mike stormed angrily after her down the stone steps. When the attendant brought the blue Cadillac around, Archie and Rusty fell into the back seat. Sadie slid into the front seat on the driver's side, but Mike shoved her roughly over and got under the wheel, then gunned the car out of the drive. At the gates on the *avenida* he stopped. Robert Sanders was standing in the shadows of one of the pillars. Sadie opened the door. He got in beside her, then they rolled smoothly out into the street and turned toward the city.

When they were sailing down the wide *avenida* with the wind blowing across them, Mike said tiredly, "Sadie, let's us rethink this proposition. I like a party as well as the next one. On the other hand, I *know* that by now Machia has put out a pick-up on this gentleman. It's a certainty. We've damn well got to put him on ice in the Embassy till somebody can figure out what to do with him."

He might as well have been talking to himself. Sadie was laughing raucously, like a ten-year-old, clapping her hands. "That was the finest thing I ever saw! Robert, you were marvelous!"

Robert Sanders said, "It was completely stupid. All of it. Why did that jackass want to throw me in the pool?"

"People—" Mike said wearily. "Somebody's gonna get shot tonight if we don't serious-up. I'm taking this man to the Embassy."

At this point Robert Sanders seemed to hear for the first time. "Not me," he said. "Just drop me off anywhere. I'm going to the hotel and get some dry clothes."

"Mike," Sadie said with exaggerated concern, "do hop out at your place, darling. I *don't* want to get you in trouble. You might lose your good conduct ribbon." She gave him a sweet little pat on his cheek.

From the back seat Archie Pringle sat forward, sticking his head between Sadie and Robert Sanders. In his gravelly voice he crooned a Spanish love ballad— *"La ultima noche que pasé contigo . . ."*

"That's *lovely,* Archie," Sadie said.

"Folks—" Mike said.

One of Archie's hands drooped over Robert Sanders' shoulder, felt his wet suit, and he stopped singing. "My word, you worked up a real sweat, old boy! Tropics bad for dancing, what?"

This tickled Sadie and she let out a new spasm of laughter.

"Folks—" Mike said again, then he muttered, "Oh the hell with it!"

Breezing through the dark, palm-lined streets with the soft night air blowing in his face, with Sadie close to him, Mike began to feel a little of the pointless, heat-seeking recklessness that throbbed in her. What Scotch hadn't done to unhinge his sober judgment, which the situation desperately needed at this moment, the faint scent of Sadie's perfume and the warmth of her bare arm across the back of his neck completed. He began suddenly to feel more like a boot hungering for a fight than a hashmarked veteran with a serious problem on his hands. The taste of imminent action began to inflame him, as of old.

"All right, you motherin' idiots," he muttered. "We'll go to El Gallo. There's nothing like rhumba music for a funeral."

13

El Gallo de Oro sparkled through the trees as they rolled into its wooded park. The rambling casino was outlined against the dark sky with twinkling lights along its eaves and gables. A fuzzy glow from red, green and blue bulbs festooned the entrance archway, reminding Mike of the gates of an amusement park when he was a kid.

Underneath the portal an attendant, costumed like a Moor, opened the car doors. The occupants climbed out and trooped into the casino and went up the deep-carpeted stairs. Pulsing waves of music, solid, groin-stirring sound with a fine beat, met them as they ascended. Miguel always had a band that was good and tough.

Sadie and Robert Sanders went up ahead. Mike's eyes fastened on the swaying of Sadie's hips, upon the backs of her knees, on her fine calves and slim ankles as she mounted the stairs. This and the throb of the music fed the old excitement stirring in his viscera. He knew it was an illusive, siren thing he followed, with nothing at the end for him but empty air, unless it was a bullet, but he didn't care.

Robert Sanders moved easily beside Sadie, lightly supporting her elbow. He was wearing his other suit—Sadie had made a quick swing by the hotel to let him change. It was an inexpensive suit off the rack, but Mike grudgingly admitted that on him it looked good. Some men could look well-turned-out in dungarees.

Dancing at El Gallo took place on a small floor at the bottom of a tiered, carpeted bowl. On the raised bandstand at the end of the room the Tico-Tico Boys, in flamboyant ruffled shirts and tight pants, capered and shook, dealing out a fast rhumba. The place was half full. A few well-bred couples twitched expertly to the aphrodisiac rhythm in the semi-darkness. Candles flickered in opaque glass chimneys on the banked tables, suffusing an exotic glow over the room. Marching ahead of Sadie's party, Miguel led the group down through layers of cigarette smoke to a table on the lowest tier, the best

87

in the house, for Sadie had the presence of a young queen and, as Miguel well knew, the money. With a clap of hands that brought waiters running, he seated them, showing an attentiveness that told the importance of these guests to the cash register.

Sadie threw him a dazzling smile. "Champagne, *cholito*. Dom Perignon, of course. But *rápido!*" Almost as soon as they were seated *mozos* with napkin-wrapped bottles were pouring the expensive sparkly stuff into the glasses. Robert Sanders put his hand over the top of his glass. Mike heard him mutter "Coca-Cola."

In all his years of dealing with men of all conditions, Mike had not seen one who appeared so completely detached as Robert Sanders. He gave the impression of a man who has been reduced in some crucible of pain to the basic elements of which a man is made, and the rest discarded. There was in his manner none of the civilized posturing detectable in most men, none of the sophisticated artfulness that flickers like the shadow of bat wings across their faces.

But this Coca-Cola bit irked the hell out of Mike. It was too much. Those deep dissipation lines in the forehead and the yellow-purplish color around his eyes hadn't been acquired at any Boy Scout camp. Already slightly tight, Mike drained his Dom Perignon in a gulp, then glared at Robert Sanders with a look of anger. Who did he think he was kidding?

Over the rim of her glass, held lightly to her lips, Sadie watched this performance with huge enjoyment. The champagne gave a glitter to the deep amethyst of her eyes that matched the delicate diamond pieces fastened to the lobes of her ears. When she took down the glass there was a glitter on her lips as well. She smiled a pleased minx's smile at the two of them.

Glaring at Robert Sanders, almost as if throwing out a

specific challenge to him, Mike said, "Can I have the pleasure of the first dance, Mrs. Flippo?"

"It would be an honor, Captain Hodak," said Sadie with a twinkle.

Mike got up and stalked around the table. Sadie arose and stepped lightly into his arms. The look of high amusement on her face as they moved out onto the floor did not improve his disposition. But his ugly mood couldn't last. The Tico-Tico Boys were knocking out a slow rhumba. Under his hand Sadie's waist was narrow and supple. He felt as if he could almost encircle it with the thumb and big finger of one hand. No sensation he had ever known was comparable to dancing with her. He wasn't conscious of his large feet or thick limbs, and there was no weight to her at all. Only the electrifying touch of her hand in his and the sinuous feel of the hollow of her back as she moved with the music. Her hair against his cheek had the natural fragrance of cleanness, the scent of a young beautiful woman bathed in plain soap and water, that was more intoxicating than any perfume.

"You're pretty surly tonight, *amigo,*" she murmured as they danced. "Is your ulcer flaring up?"

"I haven't got any goddam ulcer. But when I see a bird-brain friend of mine making a fool of herself, I don't go around hee-hawing like a happy jackass. What have you got in mind with this brush-ape, anyway? He's a solid loser, Sadie."

"Don't be so negative, *amigo,*" she said lightly, dreamily ignoring his reproach. "This man makes meaning for me. To-night has stars and skyrockets in it. If you bark at them, they'll go away."

Grimly Mike said, "Lupo Machia's gunsels will show up here before long. And they won't go away. I can't bark that loud."

89

Sadie seemed not to hear him. She said, "This night has promise, *amigo*. I feel I'm closing in on reality. It's exciting! The day is an ugly dream. Only the night has essence, substance!"

Mike muttered an obscenity. But the pulsing music, the timbre of her voice close to his ear and the clean, devastating scent of her hair dismantled his common sense. He said, "That's a bunch of crappola. But if you say it, I got to believe it."

As they glided around the floor, time seemed to stop and hover in a state of golden iridescent pleasure for Mike Hodak. Then his fool's paradise was shattered.

"Mike, darling."

"What, sugar?"

"We're not being very nice to our guest of honor, are we? Don't you think we should—?"

"Go back to the table? I can take a goddam hint. You don't have to knock my brains out."

Sadie laughed again and drew her arm tight around him and hugged him. Then they parted and he steered her toward the table.

The waiter with the Dom Perignon went round and around. Plates of exotic food were set before them, scarcely touched, then taken away. Archie Pringle babbled endlessly, and his accent, which grew thickly British as the champagne flowed, became almost unintelligible. At one point, leaning over to Mike, he opined with great seriousness: "Seein' you dancin' with Sadie reminds me of *Beauty and the Beast,* old boy. Jolly frightful, what? Different though, what? In the tale the beast turns into a handsome prince. You're not under an evil spell, are you, old chap? Just naturally ugly, what?"

"Screw you, Mother Pringle," Mike said, unamused.

Archie roared with laughter and choked and got deeply red

in the face. Rusty Cobb pounded him on the back, then she reached across and squeezed Mike's hand and looked at him with sympathy. She understood how he felt about Sadie.

"Archie is a motor-mouth," she said. "Ignore'm."

Rusty was a kind and sincere person. She drank too much, and she was tight now, but that was par for most Americans, male and female, in these circumstances at this hour. It went with the Foreign Service life—a party every night—and it was a poor substitute for having roots and a home. The champagne gave her complexion a ruddy, outdoorsy look. She was a big girl and could hold a lot of booze, but she wasn't fat or sloppy. In fact, her figure had a very nice shape to it. One hundred and ten per cent girl, all freckles and white meat, Archie called her. Her family were ranchers in West Texas and she could throw a leg over a cow-pony and ride all day without tiring. She had green eyes and light-reddish, rather frizzly hair, which she wore behind her ears in an offhand boyish style. She wasn't pretty. But she was good-looking, and she was nobody's fool. There was natural sympathy about her eyes and mouth. And from one or two tentative encounters Mike knew she was quite passionate in a wholesome, hell-for-leather sort of way. He received the impression that one day she would literally wrestle the right man down and smother him with love. And no doubt the right man would like it—if he could stand up to it.

Now she plucked lightly at Mike's sleeve and blinked her big green eyes at him. "When are you going to dance with *me*, old buddy?"

"The next time they play a goddam march," Mike said, still smarting.

Rusty stood up. "I can't wait that long. Archie is stoned and I need to be danced with."

"Aw, Rusty, I can't dance. I didn't go to dancing school."

"You can stand still like a Maypole. I'll dance around you. Come."

Mike got up and they moved onto the floor. They were poorly mated dancing partners; their knees hit at every step. Rusty would have made two of Sadie. Still, when Mike looped an arm around her waist he knew he had hold of a lot of woman. It wasn't unpleasant.

After a while Rusty said, "It's a shame that homely people can't fall for other homely people."

"Begging your damn pardon, who are you referring to?" Mike said.

"Seems like both beautiful *and* homely people fall in love only with beautiful people. That leaves the homely ones in a bad fix, doesn't it?"

"If you're gonna get insulting, I'm leaving," Mike said.

"I'm talking about all us mud fences, lover."

"You're not homely, Rus."

"Plain. Same thing in a female."

"Archie says I'm a beast."

Rusty drew back and looked at him thoughtfully. After a moment she said, "You kind of are. Until you get to know you. I know you, and I think you're beautiful."

The soberness with which she said this tickled Mike and he laughed loudly.

Rusty said, "Oh, it's not so funny. My point is: the sharp-looking cats win first prize. And what do the nice, homely cats get? Honorable mention, but no Tootsie-roll!" She said this last caustically, almost angrily, and so saying took a firm grip on Mike and swung him around so that he was looking over her shoulder right at Sadie and Robert Sanders, who were floating past on the wings of a fast samba. Rusty said, "Exhibit A. Unquote!"

Mike winced. Watching Sadie and Sanders dance together was fascinating and painful. The band shifted gears and charged into a frenzied cha-cha. Robert Sanders knew how to dance. There was nothing contrived or practiced in the way he moved. He led his partner with a rhythm as natural as breathing, held her lightly, turned her loose and caught her again, under perfect control. Sadie was like a young dream Terpsichore, come to life at his touch. People around them began to move away and make room as the two warmed to the throb of the music. The tempo accelerated like a quickening heartbeat as the band caught the excitement.

The pair whirled mindlessly, as if in the eye of a hurricane, totally unaware of the people around them. Rusty released Mike and pulled him by the hand to the table.

"They are beautiful," she murmured.

A drunk at a ringside table leaned far out and kissed his hand. *"Qué rica!"* he cried and fell out of his chair. The excitement clicked around the room like electricity.

The Tico-Tico Boys in their ruffled shirts tightened the beat. They were hopping all over the bandstand now, clavos, maracas, drums, cowbells, guitars, all clashing wildly as the cha-cha leaped into an abandoned mambo. The couple on the floor danced as if they were alone in the world. It was violent, elemental, like a primeval love dance surging toward an orgasm. As Robert Sanders whirled Sadie across the floor, flinging her out at arm's length, her skirt, flaring like a ballerina's, revealed the wispy briefs at the top of her bare, flashing thighs. The sandals on her small feet, hardly more than heels and soles bound on with golden threads, heightened the allurement. Caught again in his firm embrace, her head lightly turned, her eyes closed, she seemed to abandon herself to the music as though it were an ecstatic fever.

93

Jealousy and anger and a strange, tortured thrill churned inside of Mike Hodak. Gritting his teeth he turned in his chair and looked away. As he did, his eyes swept up the carpeted stairs to the topmost tier and focused on the figure of Lupo Machia.

The man stood with booted legs planted wide apart, like polished tubes. In his fresh uniform of dark olive material he reminded Mike of nothing so much as a hawk poised on a limb glaring down at a pair of mice capering on the forest floor below. A semicircle of staff officers hovered behind him. Machia's white teeth gleamed in a humorless smile. He slapped his gloves lightly into his palm. Mike groaned and wondered how badly the man needed the AID grant from the United States. At this moment he hoped the need was desperate.

The music swirled to a crashing stop. The room burst into applause for the American couple who, unaware, had been putting on the floor show. Sadie fell away from her partner; then, laughing, glowing and breathless, she came across the floor with Robert Sanders, hand in hand, toward the table.

Then everyone was talking at once, except Mike, and he was watching Machia and his officers saunter down the stairs to a table halfway across the room. He could almost feel the heat of their eyes as they took in Sadie's party.

Mike's brain was working fast but not coming up with any good ideas. He only knew that the situation was explosive and that something had to be done. He said, "Let's get the hell out of here. Some of us peons work for a living."

To his surprise nobody objected to the proposal but Archie, who had his nose down in a flute of champagne, and he was ignored.

When they were out into the street sliding through the darkness again, picking up speed, Mike felt quick relief, though he knew this sense of security was false and temporary. The night air blew cool and sobering against his face. He kept looking into the mirror for the lights of the tail he expected would surely be following. He was not disappointed.

14

A pair of headlights in the mirror stuck with them through the traffic of Calle Panamá and swung in behind them again as Mike turned on Avenida Sucre and headed toward Miraflores. The lights were not steady, but moved, now apart, now back together.

"All right, you mothers," he said raising his voice harshly to be heard over Archie's singing. "There's two motorcycles tailing us. They're not an escort of honor. I'm gonna lose 'em if I can."

"Su-per!" Sadie cried. "You can do it, Mikecito. Go, man! Dig!"

"How revolting," said Archie in bass tones from the back seat.

Grimly Mike said, "Sanders, you be ready to jump when I tell you. Sadie will go with you. You'll have about five seconds to get out of the car and into the bushes if we're lucky. This is not fun and grab-ass. It's got to do with your life."

"That's clear enough," Robert Sanders said. "What do I do then?"

"You'll be within a few blocks of my house, if I can arrange it. After the motor jockeys pass, go there; Sadie knows the way. Roust my boy Nestor and take my car. Drive to the Embassy. Wait for me there."

"Gee," Sadie cried. "This is just like Secret Agent on the telly."

"You better sober up, little sister," Mike said glumly. "Hang on. Here we go."

He put his foot down hard and the big car surged ahead, pressing its occupants back against the seats.

"Fifty . . . fifty-five . . . sixty-five . . . ! Go, daddy!" Sadie screamed. "It'll do a hundred and twenty!"

"Shut up," Mike muttered, herding the car through and past the thinning traffic of the *avenida*. In the mirror the two motorcycle lights dropped behind. As he approached a heavily-traveled cross street Mike saw the traffic light turn against him. He held his thumb down on the horn ring and went blaring through the intersection on a late amber. This was good. It would slow the motorcycles.

"Neat! Neat!" Sadie cried, clapping her hands.

Quite relaxed, Robert Sanders glanced across at Mike Hodak's rugged, worried profile and said, "What happens when we get to the Embassy? Matter of fact, why should I go to the Embassy at all?"

"Goddamit, Mac, let's fight one fire at a time, okay?"

"Ours not to reason why," Sadie caroled happily. "Ours but to doo-be-doo-be-doo!"

Mike figured he now had about three blocks' lead on the motorcycles. There was a clear space in the traffic ahead.

"Stand by," he said. Suddenly he braked the car and put it into a hard, tire-punishing left turn into a side street. Houses with low walls and gates and shrubbery along the sidewalks flashed by. Halfway down the block he jammed the car to a squealing halt that piled both Rusty and Archie into the floor of the rear seat.

"Jump!" Mike said.

Robert Sanders was ready. He had the door open and was out, yanking Sadie after him like a rag doll, then Mike hit the accelerator and slammed the car ahead, again. All in the space of five seconds.

At the end of the block he turned left, and as he did, he saw the motorcycles roar into the side street on a hard slant off the *avenida*. He squared the block and got back on Avenida Sucre and headed again toward Miraflores and the *malecón* and the ocean, slowing his speed a little as the blocks rushed by. He told Rusty to get over in the front seat, which she did, throwing her leg over, almost taking his ear off with her high heel. Archie remained on the floor in back, moaning.

"Godamighty, Mike," Rusty said, shaken. "What in the mothering hell is going on?"

"Just sit there and keep your mouth shut," Mike said, holding the painfulness of his ear.

After another block he slowed further and let the motorcycles catch up with them. An excited *soldado* gunned up beside him and waved him angrily to the curb. When Mike eased to a stop the two motorcyclists slewed their hot motors around, dropped them and came running to the car, one on each side.

Mike found himself looking into the hole of a .38 revolver.

"Where are you going that requires such speed, Señor?" the man said breathlessly.

"Officer, I have a sick man here," Mike said, very gravely, thumbing the back seat. "See for yourself. I'm trying to find the Clinica Americana and I've lost my way."

The *soldado* whipped a flashlight from his belt and shined it in the rear floor. Archie moved and groaned appropriately.

"And where are the other two, the man and woman?" The man demanded, angrily, flashing the light in Mike's face again.

"Another two?"

The *soldado* jammed the muzzle of his revolver hard into the soft flesh under Mike's chin.

"Oh, *those* other two," Mike said, swallowing and nodding rapidly. "You mean that girl and the fellow she was with. They decided to walk. You know, a little exercise, fresh air. And—" He shrugged, winking at the motorcyclist, "Who knows what else?"

The man made an ugly sound and holstered his revolver angrily.

"Very clever, Señor. We will find them, don't worry. Now about this so-called sick man. We will escort you to the *clinica*."

As the two went back to their motors, Archie raised up from the floor and said, "I'm feeling much better, thank you. Just drop me off at the Golden Cock."

Reaching around with an arm, Mike shoved Archie flat in the floor. "You're a sick sonofabitch and you better act like it. We're going to the hospital."

In the still, after-midnight darkness Mike pulled wearily and harrassed into his driveway. He and Rusty had seen Archie through a complete physical examination by an officious intern at the *clinica* under the watchful eyes of one of the motor *soldados*. Afterward Mike had had to cuff Archie a couple of times to get him into a hospital gown and a bed for overnight observation. Then he drove Rusty to her apartment and went straight to the Embassy, where he learned from the night watchman that neither Sadie nor Robert Sanders had showed up there.

When he reached his house, Nestor opened the door for him in his nightshirt.

"You had a pleasant evening Señor?" the boy said, smiling sleepily.

"Señora Flippo," Mike said harshly. "Did she come here with a man? They were to get my car and go to the Embassy."

"Oh, yes, *Capitán*, they come. And they take your car. But not to the Embassy, I don't think. She say they are going to the *playa* . . ."

"To the *beach*? To swim?"

"But of course, Señor," Nestor cackled, winking. "What else could they do at the beach at this hour?"

15

Cursing the day he first laid eyes on Sadie Flippo, Mike Hodak drove fast out of the city and headed south on the narrow highway that paralleled the coast. He asked himself repeatedly, as the kilometers flashed by, why he was tearing out on this fool's errand. He received no satisfactory answer. He was not Sadie Flippo's guardian. She was over twenty-one and it was no business of his if she chose to foul up her life with sorry characters like Lupo Machia, and now, this stray alley-cat, Robert Sanders. Yet, here he was barreling down the road at 1 A.M. in frantic search of her, as though she were his wayward daughter.

There are many beaches along the coast south of San Felipe, but he headed for a particular one—on a hunch—a special beach that he and Sadie had discovered. The road cut through the darkness of irrigated fields, and after a way it crossed a swift stream that boiled whitely over rocks as it rushed down toward the sea from the mountains to the east.

Twenty kilometers out of San Felipe he turned off the highway, seaward. As the car followed the windings of the dirt road the terrain became rougher. Sand dunes encroached into the cotton fields. Here and there gigantic volcanic rocks jutted through the surface, as though they had been flung there by some cataclysmic subterranean upheaval when the earth was young. The road wound for a while through this eerie landscape and then he could see and then hear the ocean as it broke with hissing phosphorescence at the shoreline.

He and Sadie had found the place by accident one Sunday months ago, while exploring and beachcombing along this stretch of coast. It was so inaccessible that picnickers from San Felipe hadn't spoiled it. They named it New Moon Bay, and it was truly a small, perfect crescent of white sand, guarded at its points by jutting masses of rock. They had entered the beach along the narrowest strip of sand at one tip of the crescent, built a small fire and then had idled along the water's edge, talking, until it grew dark and the tide had come in. Then they found that the strip of sand over which they entered had disappeared, under rough breakers crashing against the rocky headland.

Faced with the prospect of a cold night on the beach until the tide went out again, they spent an hour probing the cliffs of lava rock that loomed behind the beach. Finally they discovered a scalable path upward over the top, which led them back to their car and the comforts of civilization. In the following months they had returned to this beach a number of times, using this hidden pathway over the cliffs, known only to themselves. It was for this place that Mike now headed.

Once at New Moon Bay, sitting by the embers of a small driftwood fire, her knees drawn up under her chin, wrapped around with her beach robe, Sadie had said to him:

"Anyway I look at it, I'm a big, round naught."

"You're not a naught, Sadie. You don't know what you are. But you are something, and you're trying to find out what it is. That's more than most people do, their whole life."

"If I'm not a big, round naught, then I'm a bunch of little round naughts strung together, adding up to zero."

"Aw, you do a lot of good. Don't low-rate yourself."

"I'm the worst kind of do-gooder. I give something it doesn't hurt me to give—money—which I didn't make and have too much of, anyway."

"Money is necessary. You don't have to give it. You could keep it all."

"The amount I can give is calculated by a high-priced tax accountant who determines just how charitable I can afford to be this fiscal year. That's a pretty poor substitute for real charity. This is the sin of the rich. When I give down to the hundred-cent dollars, my charity dries up, immediately. It's called fiscal charity. It's not one of the 'shalt nots' only because Moses never heard of the graduated income tax."

"Sadie," Mike sighed, "you are a bird."

Mike talked about himself these times, too. Sadie drew him out, with real interest, gently in the main, but sometimes imperiously.

"What do I want out of life?" he said once. "Sure, I've

thought about it. **Plenty**. That's how you get in trouble—thinking."

He poked the dying fire with a stick and reached over and pulled a can of warmish beer out of the picnic basket. Puncturing the top with the opener, he blew at the foam that rushed out of the hole and down his fingers.

"For a long time I just wanted to be the toughest, best Marine in the Corps. In a big war there's no time to think, or much reason to, for that matter. You have the feeling that what you're doing, right here, is important. You don't know why, exactly, but you're a part of a big thing, and you figure somebody's running the show that knows what he's doing."

"Quite an assumption," Sadie said dryly.

"No, a big war is simple. You got only one problem—win it. You don't worry about right or wrong. You take it for granted you're the good guys and the people on the other side are the bad. Nobody asked you to worry about this, anyway." He paused and spat into the fire. "I got to know two or three of their people. I mean the bad guys. They actually thought *they* were the good guys."

"So who were the good guys?" said Sadie, looking at him with a flat gaze.

"We were, naturally. Aw hell, sometimes I think the whole thing is a trap—that we're just suckers trapped by our own meanness and stupidity. On both sides." He sighed. "When I sit down and really try to figure it out, all I ever end up with is a headache. Anyway I go I always come back to this: I can't hardly see Jesus, under any circumstances, manning a fifty-caliber machine gun."

"Mike," Sadie said, "you are a bird."

Sadie sat barefoot and cross-legged on the blanket facing Robert Sanders. Reclining on one elbow, the young American looked out across the small fire he had built, toward the ocean, a dark moving expanse faintly burnished with the light of a high white moon. Sadie still wore her wispy green Chanel frock. Robert Sanders, barefoot also, had shed his coat and tie and rolled up his pants legs.

Sadie said, "You have fine-looking feet, Robert."

Robert Sanders almost smiled. He wiggled his toes and looked down at them.

"They're serviceable."

"They have character."

"You judge a man by his feet?"

"I judge a man by where his feet take him. Why did yours bring you here?"

He did smile at this, and his face was boyish and relaxed and happy-looking. It was the first time she had seen him really smile. He flicked some sand at her, as if he were shooting marbles.

"Here we go again," he said. "A woman is never satisfied. You can't just admire my pretty feet for themselves. You got to understand them, too."

Sadie made a house of her fingers and gazed over them at him.

"Robert, I'm not a complete dumbbell. You're mixed up in something naughty, and Colonel Machia wants to kill you. What is it?"

"You really have been watching too much TV, Sadie. If he wanted me, he could have taken me at the night club."

"He wants you. But he thinks he's conned Uncle Sugar out of an AID grant or something and he doesn't want any dust-up over an American citizen to queer his deal—until he gets the boodle. Mike says it's all but set. When it is, you're marked for extinction. Especially after tonight at the swimming pool."

"Aren't you afraid of him, Sadie? I mean, on account of me? He's cold-blooded as a snake."

Sadie held out one hand and gazed at her nails. "Colonel Machia admires me," she said aloofly. "He also thinks I'm a harmless idiot. They don't pay much attention to women down here. Except in bed."

After this they were silent for a while, listening to the sound of the surf. Robert Sanders lay back on the blanket, his fingers locked behind his head as he gazed up at the silent stars. Sadie stretched full length on her stomach across the blanket from him and worked her fingers and toes into the sand.

After a while she turned her head and looked at him across her upper arm.

"Robert—I'm fascinated. I'm a sucker for mysterious characters. Please tell me you were a young banker who lost his head in Las Vegas and embezzled his bank's money and fled to South America. Then I won't be fascinated any more, and I'll get over you. Are you married?"

He did not answer for several seconds. Then he said, "I was. Not any more."

"Tell me about her. Were there—are there—children?"

"I don't want to talk about it, Sadie. It's none of your business."

Rising suddenly, arching her back like a cat, Sadie switched around in a cross-legged position. Her skirt rose high on her thighs and she tucked it angrily into her crotch.

"Dammit, man, you've got to talk about it! I—I'm trying not to fall in love with you. I may already have!"

Robert Sanders took his hands from behind his head and rubbed them over his face. Then he sat up and worked his fingers hard into his forehead for a while. He looked around at Sadie, then back at the embers of fire framed between his knees.

"Sadie," he said in a low voice, "I'm a dead son of a bitch. Don't fool with the dead."

Instinctively Sadie reached out her hand and touched him. "That's not true, Robert. You're young and lovely and alive. You're going to get out of this thing. I can help you."

There was no timbre in his voice as he spoke again to the flickering fire. "That's not the problem, Sadie. I died a long time ago. A long ways away. Don't fool with the dead."

Sadie made sudden cat claws at him with her fingers. Her voice quivered. "You're *not* dead! Don't say that again! You're only asleep. Semi-comatose over some silly man thing, probably. I'll wake you up. Let's go for a swim. The ocean is cold. It's brutal and shocking."

"I've got no swim trunks."

"Isn't that a coincidence? I haven't, either. Skinny-dipping is the best, anyway. Will you be embarassed?"

She scrambled to her feet and shook out her hair. Then, reaching behind her back, she pulled down the zipper of her dress.

"How long, Robert, since a beautiful woman got naked in front of you?"

She stood until he slowly looked around and up at her, then she hooked her thumbs under the pencil straps of her dress and lifted them from her shoulders and let the dress fall slowly to the ground. He watched her, transfixed, hypnotized by her amazingly peaked bare breasts as the chiffon slid over them, at her narrow, flat belly with its deep navel eye, at the flare of her hips and the dark pubic mound visible beneath the wispy briefs. Without hesitation she stuck two forefingers under the top of her pants and brushed them down over her hips and thighs and let them fall to her ankles. Then with one foot she kicked them into the fire, which consumed them with a flare of flames.

She stood then before him, completely nude, legs slightly apart, arms at her sides, her hands open.

"Wake up, Robert," she said softly. "If you won't come with me, I'll swim out to sea as far as I can. Then I'll sink down in the seaweeds and drown. I promise you I will. I don't mind dying. But I would die crying, if I had made a fool of myself."

Robert Sanders let his gaze travel slowly up and down her, penetratingly, his eyes shining from the fire. He got to his feet and faced her. A quizzical smile played on his face. With the back of his hand he stroked her cheek, then the underswell of her breast. Then he gently knuckled the tip of one puckered nipple.

Then he began to unbutton his shirt and unfasten his belt.

16

The lights of the Cadillac flashed up and down, slashing the darkness as Mike fought the wheel, picking a twisting way through the rough waste of sand and rock. Then, topping a rise the big car nosed over and down and the headlights outlined the dark shape of the Corvette—his car—parked and empty under the greenish-black escarpment looming ahead. His hunch had been right. On the other side of the rough ridge of hardened lava, in the privacy of New Moon Bay, he would find his "friends."

And what did he propose to do when he found them? He rolled to a stop in the soft sand beside the smaller car, shut off the motor and sat for minutes, pondering this. What would he say? "I just happened to be passing by and thought I'd drop in on you"? He would feel and sound like an idiot. Yet, he reminded himself, he did have an official responsibility—to help this jackass Sanders evade the hounds of Lupo Machia, and stay alive long enough to get out of the country. It appeared that the man had no interest whatever in being thus aided, and Mike Hodak had no enthusiasm for helping him. He told himself that duty was duty, but he knew he was really just seeking an excuse to go barging into this little beach party uninvited.

He got out of the car, clicked the door shut softly, then picked his way across powdery sand, through the dark rubble of rocks. Where the sand played out under the black shadows of the cliff he found the familiar trail that snaked steeply upward through breaks and crevices in the escarpment. He had speculated that some solitary Chimu fisherman must have discovered and used this passage to the sea centuries ago.

Scrambling up through lichen-covered boulders damp with sea mist, Mike reached the end of the trail. Then, breathing hard, he hunched his way farther upward through a narrow up-tilted chimney between two great slabs leading to the very top of the cliff. Sadie always scooted up this backward, on her rump, to save her knees. At the top he would be able to look down the steep twisting path to the beach. Where the narrow passage ended, in the open blowing air above the sea, he paused to get his breath. Leaning against the rocky parapet, he was afforded a full view of the whole beach below—a perfect crescent of sand, pale mauve in the moonlight, edged with the perfect white scimitar of the surf.

Below him in the foreground he saw the glow of a small fire, then as his eyes focused, the dark rumpled square of a blanket and a scatter of clothing on the sand. The girl and the man he sought were not there. For minutes he scanned the beach, slowly, methodically, in the manner of a forward artillery observer, straining his sight into the darkness from one point of the beach to the other, then back again. Back and forth, forth and back. They were not there.

Then, before he saw them, he heard them. Rather, he heard Sadie. He could not mistake that voice amid all the sounds of the world. It was a shout on the wind, a sound of breathless, hysterical laughter. Then he made out her form, faintly at first, small as a doll in the distance, rising out of the foaming surf directly ahead. She came running, half-stumbling and laughing across the beach. And then he saw the man coming out of the dark sea, following her. Mike's scalp shriveled. The blood in his chest and throat thickened, almost choking off his breath. They were both naked.

Dripping water, bodies glistening in the moonlight as if retaining the phosphoresence of the surf, they ran toward the fire. There was no doubt now they were both naked, for Mike could see the dark eyes of full young breasts, swaying, as Sadie ran, and the small, sharp vee of pubic hair, black as a bird's beak—and the man, as he caught up to her at the fire and pulled her roughly around, was sprigged up like eternal springtime.

A sound that was more a howl than a cry escaped Mike's throat and was lost in the wind as he gripped the rocks before him, peering down at the pair below. For moments verging on madness he crouched, shaking, poised to leap over the parapet and down the rocky trail, roaring out his lust to kill with his bare hands.

On the beach, clinging together, the pair sank slowly, turning, to the blanket. Then the man covered her, and Mike Hodak could not watch any more. He ducked his head to hide the sight from his eyes and he beat his forehead against the solid rock, repeatedly, sobbing, until his forehead was bloody. Then he released his grip and slipped back down the rough throat of rock, toward the trail leading to the cars.

17

It was nearing daylight when Robert Sanders entered the deserted lobby of Hotel Bolívar. The sleepy night clerk stared at him, startled, before turning to get his key. As he waited Robert Sanders brushed at dry sand clinging to the back of his hand. Then he took the key and went to the elevator.

In the birdcage lift he sighed, heavily. His face was thoughtful and troubled, and he was tired. At the third floor he went out of the lift and walked down the dim corridor, to his room. There he stopped and inserted the key.

The instant he opened the door he saw light inside the room. In a reflex action he pulled the door shut and started to run back down the hall toward the fire stairway. He had not left a light burning. Of this he was certain. That meant somebody was inside, waiting for him.

In the same split instant it sank into his brain that through the crack in the door he had seen Mike Hodak, seated in a chair in the corner of the room, looking at him. When all of this registered, Robert Sanders stopped, blew out a big breath, then went back to the room. He shoved open the door and entered. Then he closed the door behind him.

"What do you want?" he said.

"Not much," Mike Hodak said, glancing up.

"Are you arresting me?"

"I'm not a policeman," Mike said, returning his gaze with a stony glare of hatred. There was dried blood on his forehead. His hands gripped the arms of the chair. Both men were tense and bone-tired.

"Then kindly get the hell out of here. I'm going to sleep. I'll talk to you tomorrow."

"Tomorrow will be too late."

Compressing his lips, breathing out hard through his nostrils, Robert Sanders took off his coat, threw it on the bed and started unbuttoning his shirt.

"You beat anybody I ever saw for minding other people's business."

Mike Hodak hauled himself out of the chair and walked across the room toward him.

"All right, I'll make it short and sweet," he said. "There are two international flights out of San Felipe every day. One goes north at three-ten, the other goes south at five. I don't care which way you go, but you're gonna be on one of them, tomorrow."

Robert Sanders gave an irritated, incredulous laugh. He pulled out his shirttails and ripped off his shirt. Reaching, he grasped the door handle and opened the door.

"Very well, Captain, you said it. Now, good night."

With a strong motion Mike drove the ham of his fist against the door and closed it hard. His voice was gritty, his eyes hard and humorless as zinc.

"Don't mess with me, Mac. Are you gonna cooperate or not?"

"You're really worked up over this fairy tale Colonel Machia told you about me, aren't you?"

"I couldn't care less what you're up to here with Rafael Benavides. Sadie Flippo is something else."

"Sadie?" Robert Sanders cocked his head in surprise.

"She was doing all right till you showed up. You can't just blow in like a horny sailor making a liberty and ruin her."

"Ruin her?" Robert Sanders said. "What's to ruin?"

"That's about what I expected you would say," said Mike Hodak, unbuttoning his coat and removing it. Without taking his eyes off the man, he laid the coat across the desk chair. "Sadie's got problems that you wouldn't know or care about, but she was holding her own. Now, are you going to get on that airplane by yourself, or am I going to have to put you on it?"

Robert Sanders drew his spread fingers across the muscle ridges of his bare belly. The look in his eyes hardened.

"I'm not going to get on anything going anywhere until I'm ready. And I'm not ready. Is that clear?" His words were edged with challenge. "What do you propose to do about that?"

The two big men looked at one another coldly, calmly, for seconds, then Mike Hodak said:

"Well, for openers, I'm gonna whip your ass."

He started the punch from his pocket. The overhead light sparked off his ring as the fist streaked through the air and caught the younger man, flush, below the cheekbone. It made a solid, crushing sound, the sound of bone striking bone thinly cushioned by living tissue. The force of the blow knocked Sanders violently across the bed and onto the floor beyond in a sprawled heap.

His thick shoulders bunched like an enraged bull's, Mike cursed him. "That was just a sample, lover boy. Get up and I'll give you the main dish."

For a moment he thought the man could not rise and he felt disappointment, for a blood lust was upon him. Then slowly Sanders hauled himself to his feet and onto the bed and started across it on hands and knees, shaking his head. His eyes were glazed. A trickle of blood had started from his nose.

As Sanders dismounted shakily from the bed and stood to his feet, Mike stepped back and set himself. Then something made him hesitate. You don't rack a man, even a man you hate, when both his arms are hanging limply, as if paralyzed, at his sides.

"Get your hooks up, sonny boy, just like they taught you in boxing class," Mike said contemptuously, savagely. "Double up your fists—"

He never finished the sentence. A star exploded between his eyes as though he had been kicked in the head by a mule. He didn't even see the punch coming; the man was that fast. The blow hurled him half around and draped him across the desk with his head ringing. Righting himself and letting out a shout of rage and surprised laughter, Mike rolled around into a crouch, guard high. He had been suckered into a trap. This jackass had fight in him, and he could hit! Fine and dandy! Now it would be a genuine pleasure to knock his brains out. Weaving behind his guard for a moment until his head cleared, Mike moved in cautiously.

Feinting with a left, he came out of his crouch with a jet-whispering right hand that had two hundred and twenty pounds behind it. His fist crashed into Robert Sanders' jaw, spraying saliva in the air and dumping the man heavily on the floor against the bed.

Then, instead of the exultation he expected, a strange, ugly feeling rippled through Mike Hodak. *The idiot had not moved a muscle to defend himself.* He had not raised his guard, as men instinctively do when attacked. Instead he had—or so it seemed—deliberately held his arms down, rigid at his sides, so that hitting him was like striking an armless man, or a baby, in the face with your fist.

Robert Sanders sat dully on the floor for nearly a minute, wiping blood from his nose with the back of his hand as Mike Hodak stood over him, breathing hard in a fury of perplexity. Then the younger man again climbed painfully to his feet, much more slowly this time, and faced his attacker.

"Get your goddam guard up!" Mike hissed. "I'd just as soon hit a woman!"

The star burst behind his eyes again, with dazzling brilliance. This time Mike saw the fist coming at him, but too late to do anything about it. It was too absurdly quick and unexpected. This was beginning to be *ridiculous,* like playing patty-cake with sledge hammers! Finding himself sprawled on the floor, canted back against the wall, he looked up in stunned, slackjawed amazement at three pulsating images of Robert Sanders. These gradually quit revolving and congealed into one in his jarred-up retina.

Rolling, lurching to his feet, fighting to focus his vision, Mike stared at his adversary with maddened puzzlement. Robert Sanders' nose was bleeding profusely now. Blood was smeared all across his face.

"You crazy bastard!" Mike gasped. "What's the matter with you?"

In all his travels he had never encountered a man such as this—who would not defend himself, but who struck back at you like a triggered spring of coiled steel.

Mike moved in on the man again, circling warily now, eyeing him over his knuckles. Suddenly he shot out a hard straight left, but instead of hitting with it, he purposely grazed the younger man's cheek. Robert Sanders' arms were still held rigidly, almost quivering, at his sides. He did not move so much as an eyelash.

Brow furrowed in ridges of perplexity, Mike stepped unsteadily backward. Then he set again and loosed a hard right cross that deliberately flicked the man's ear. Robert Sanders did not duck or dodge. He stood as if rooted, only slightly swaying. Mike stepped back then, out of range, breathing hard.

"Getting tired?" Robert Sanders murmured through deadened lips.

"Put up your guard and I'll show you who's tired!" Mike gasped. "Put up your goddam guard!"

"You tend to your side." Robert Sanders said. "I'll take care of mine."

Mike stared at him, unbelieving, for several seconds more. Then he threw up his hands and backed clear away, totally confused.

"I don't hit a crazy man, if I know it."

"Do you really think I'm crazy?"

"If you're not crazy, you're the stupidest sonofabitch I ever met!"

Robert Sanders stared at him, limply, strangely, as though pleading with him, to hit him once again. There was an uncertain glitter in his eyes, as if he were about to cry.

"You think I'm yellow, Captain?" he said.

"*Yellow?*" Mike Hodak shouted, rubbing his head, beginning to doubt his own sanity. "You're a fuckin' nut! That's what you are! Or else I am!"

Robert Sanders lifted his hands, cupped, almost pleading. His voice was barely audible. "Captain Hodak, please—let me alone."

Mike Hodak rubbed his hands over his hot, sweaty head as if he were about to go mad, or vomit, or both. This man, this day, this night—everything together—had been too much for him.

He swept his pulsing gaze around the room until he saw his hat, where he had dropped it on the floor. Picking up the hat, he jammed it on his head. Then he grabbed his coat from the chair and barged unsteadily out the door, leaving it open behind him as he headed down the hall, talking to himself, cursing and mumbling over and over, "The sonofabitch is crazy! He really *is* crazy!"

18

Mike did not remember his mother, and so when he was very small he invented a mother, in his mind, out of sheer necessity. One who came to him in the dark loneliness of his cot and lay beside him and rubbed his back and smoothed out the small knotted muscles of dread between his shoulders, and told him he was a good boy and that she really would come one day and take him away with her.

Even after he grew to manhood and became one of the earth's wanderers he still dreamed sometimes of this invented mother. He wondered what his real mother had been like. He did not even have a picture of her, but he could not imagine that she was pretty. Still, he had a feeling that he would have liked her.

He was not dreaming of her this morning when he was

awakened by Nestor's small brown hand, but of being caught in a crashing military disaster, an ambush from which there was no possible escape. He returned to consciousness in the grip of a skull-cracking, almost unbearable hangover. It was more than the booze. He had taken on bigger loads many times. It was the remembered sight of Sadie running naked across the dim beach with Robert Sanders in hard pursuit.

On top of that, there was the maddening, unreal episode of his fight, only it wasn't a fight—exchange of head-shots, with Sanders in the hotel room. He couldn't digest the fact that Sanders had deliberately let him rack him, without lifting a finger in self-defense. Mike had known a fighter who killed a man in the ring and afterward vowed never to hit another man as long as he lived. This was nothing like that. Sanders had got off the floor and knocked hell out of him, twice! And he could hit! With baffled fingers Mike felt the hot swelling on the side of his head.

Tearing away the tangled sheet he got out of bed. He then stalked across to the mirror and glared with aching fury at his image. Whereas he was normally merely ugly he now looked like a freak. He cursed loudly, passionately.

Who was this Robert Sanders anyway? What possessed a man of his obvious abilities to bring him to this off-track spot on the globe on the absurd mission he apparently had undertaken? In his state of mind Mike was ready to believe that Sanders' appearance in San Felipe had been arranged by some ambitious department head in Hell, whose job was the torment of low-rent sinners of minor importance.

When he tried to fit his Panama onto his swollen cranium it would not go. At the door Nestor stood watching, holding his breath to keep from breaking into wild laughter.

"It's not so funny, you little bean-headed bastard," Mike

116

said. He flung the hat back into the closet and stormed bare-headed out into the morning.

The General arrived at the Chancery promptly at nine. When the receptionist relayed this intelligence back to Mike, he unglued his poisonous stare from the doorknob and walked down to the Ambassador's suite. On the way he passed Rusty Cobb at the water fountain. The *mono* was riding her hard this morning also. She had two fingers pressed flat to her temple and gave him a silent look of loathing as he passed. Mike shrugged, feeling it was purely impersonal.

Sitting beside the Ambassador's desk scowling at the floor, Mike recounted to the old man most of what had happened since they had parted last night at "El Coontry." As Mike talked the General kept cutting his eyes back to the purplish lumps on his aide's head and breaking out in little whiffles of laughter, which he suppressed with considerable effort.

"You say Sanders threw the beggar in the *swimming* pool?"

"That's what he did, General. Like a blasted sea-bag," Mike said dolefully, remembering the General's parting words to him at the Club, and feeling that he had failed miserably in his duty.

General Gatch shook his head with a faint smile of admiration, but he covered this with a grimace and compressed his large mouth thoughtfully. "That puts our young man in the soup, what? If he wasn't there already."

"Machia will keep a tail on him and let him run loose until it suits his convenience. Then he'll pick him up and that'll be the end of Mister Robert Sanders."

"Mm. Yes," the Ambassador mused. "We'll have to explain a few facts of life—and death—to the young man. I invited him to come in for a chat at ten."

"He won't be here, General."

"Oh? How do you know?"

"I don't *know*. But I'll bet on it, because he's blown in the head."

"Oh, come now, Gunner."

"No, sir, that's the truth. He looks all right, he talks all right. But he's a pure cuckoo."

"How the hell do you know that?"

"General, I'll certify to this. Believe me," Mike insisted.

The old man eyed him doubtfully. Then he shrugged and decided to accept the diagnosis provisionally.

"Assuming he is, what do you propose?"

"If you want to help him, and I personally don't give a rat's ass whether we do or not, we'll have to do it for him. He won't help himself."

The General pursed his lips again, pondering this a while. He played a thoughtful arpeggio on the desk with his big fingers, then a full chord, decisively.

"In that case, see that he comes to the booze-party for Clap-saddle tonight. Maybe the young lady can help you get him there. We'll detain him as our houseguest and fly him out to Panama tomorrow, in the Lockheed. Whether he wants to go or not. The plane is due for an engine check, anyway. I leave the details to you."

Mike said, "Aye, aye, sir," and got up to depart.

At the door the General stopped him.

"And Gunner—"

"Sir?"

"This time don't screw it up."

Without pleasure Mike rang Sadie's number. He dreaded the sound of her voice this morning. When it came on the wire, his own voice was stiff and strangely formal. Sadie sounded like a sleepy child awakened from a wholesome nap, as if last night had never happened. Mike did not enlighten her about his absurd encounter with Robert Sanders in the hotel room. She would find out soon enough. Mike's right hand was swollen and skinned across the knuckles. Sanders was certain to have corresponding marks on his face.

Sadie's tawny yawn and stretch came over the wire. She said, "Oh, dear. Yes. Yes, I am coming to the General's party for the new colonel—Quicksaddle?"

"Clapsaddle."

"Yes, dearest Mike, darling. And thank you for your help last night. Very solid performance, as usual."

"Will you be seeing Robert Sanders?"

"As a matter of fact, I will," she said lightly. "Archie is going down to Lima for a week. Local leave. He's letting Robert use his house while he's away. Much better than the hotel. I'm taking Robert out and helping him get moved in, after lunch."

Mike refrained from expressing his opinion of this colossally bad idea, which he knew was Sadie's own.

"Will you kindly invite him to the party tonight? The General wants him to come."

"I think that would be very nice."

"And see that he gets there?"

"Yes, I suppose. You sound awfully serious and business-like this morning, *amigo*. Are you hung over?"

"This is serious business, Sadie, and I haven't got time to spar with you. If you care about your friend staying alive, see that he comes to the Embassy tonight."

"Mike—oh, I will, of course. But I don't like the way you sound, Mike. Are you unhappy with me?"

"Why should I be unhappy with you? And what difference would it make if I was? I've got to go now, Sadie. Just do what I told you."

He hung up, feeling very depressed and angry with himself and the world. Ten o'clock came, then ten-thirty; Sanders did not appear, as Mike was sure he would not. In a dark mood he got up and left the Chancery and walked toward the Hotel Bolívar. The morning was bright and humid. As he crossed the plaza a squad of fat pigeons rubbernecked along beside him, looking for a handout. Mike kicked at them as he cursed the miserable circumstances that made it necessary for him to concern himself with the fate of a man he wished he had never seen.

At the hotel he learned that Sanders had gone out at an early hour and had left no message. Head and heart pounding, Mike went to a nearby *botica,* bought a box of Mejoral, then stopped at a sidewalk café under the arcade and ordered mineral water and coffee. As he swallowed the aspirin a *mozo* poured a stream of thick black liquid into the tiny cup. Nauseated, Mike let his gaze wander away. Halfway down the arcade his aimless vision stopped with a jerk, focusing on the figure of Robert Sanders.

Three shops away, bareheaded, hands in pockets, the young man leaned against the wall of the ancient building, one foot perched on a shoeshine box. His face was thoughtful as he contemplated the small boy who, in a frenzy of motion, was imparting a high polish to his shoe.

As Mike watched, another boy, equally dirty and ragged, approached Sanders from the flank. With a flourish this one fanned out a sheaf of lottery tickets and in a whining singsong began to explain the fabulous rewards of the *sorteo.* Sanders frowned at the boy and waved him away. Undiscouraged, the urchin circled and attacked from the other flank, his voice rising to a shrill insistent pitch as he shook the soiled tickets under Sanders' nose. With a gesture of annoyance Sanders made as if to backhand the boy, who dodged instinctively and withdrew a safe distance where he squatted on his haunches and glared at Sanders like a small hungry animal, muttering curses at him.

With a final spit on the shoe and a sharp pop of his dirty rag the shine boy finished his job, then hopped smartly to attention, holding out a blackened paw for his pay. Sanders drew a money clip from his pocket and extracted a bill. He studied it a moment, then he motioned to the lottery boy. At the sight of the money the child arose and went toward him, as if drawn on a string. Holding up the bill Sanders scissored his fingers as if to cut the paper in two. Pointing to the boys in turn, he indicated that each was to have half. The dirty faces cracked open in big smiles. Seizing the bill, each holding tight to his part, the two boys raced off to the kiosk on the corner to get it changed.

Observing this little drama, Mike growled contemptuously, though the unguarded display of soft-heartedness puzzled him.

In San Felipe it is said that news of a tender heart travels through the ragged brotherhood by mental telepathy. Robert Sanders had not gone halfway down the block before the pack was upon him: a small mob of dirty boys with shoeshine boxes and lottery tickets, an ancient crone selling artificial flowers, a toothless old man with a tray of carved peach pits, a little girl with a basket of candied fruit rinds. They materialized from nowhere, racing and hobbling around the corner, across the plaza, converging on Sanders from all directions, their voices piercing the morning air like the cries of hungry gulls. In moments they completely barred his passage down the arcade.

121

Fearing the situation would grow into something that would attract the police, Mike left money on the table, glanced around for a *libre* taxi and started down the arcade with the thought of extricating this stupid American from his stupid plight.

His concern was unnecessary. A small forest of arms reached up at Sanders, plucking at him, shaking things in his face. The babble of shrill voices drowned all other sounds. Then something, perhaps a tiny hand snaking into his hip pocket, made Sanders turn, and Mike saw, to his amazement, that the man was laughing. The thing he did next made Mike mutter with admiration. Like everything else he had seen him do, this was perfectly timed and executed.

Sanders drew a fistful of small change from his pocket. Cupping his hands over the semicircle of heads, he tossed the coins up and caught them a few times so that all could see. Then, with a shout, he flung the coins up and backward over his shoulder. They fell in a ringing shower all around Mike's feet. With a screech the little mob scrambled after the scattering, rolling silver and copper. Urchins and ancients alike scratched and fought on the pavement around Mike, like a bunch of starved animals after food. It was Mike, now, who was completely immobilized.

He stood thus, in amazement, as Robert Sanders ran lightly to the end of the arcade, just as an ancient streetcar, plastered with bullfight posters, screeched around the corner of the plaza and headed up Mercaderes. Without breaking stride the young man bounded into the street and onto the rear platform of the car as it picked up speed and disappeared behind the end of the building.

The next thing Mike saw was a black Chevrolet pulling away from the curb next to the square. It angled sharply into

Mercaderes after the trolley. He recognized the man on the near side, the one with the pitted smallpox face, as one of Lupo Machia's plainclothes exterminators.

After he had extricated himself from the tangle of wrestling beggars, Mike strode to the end of the arcade, rubbing at the growing tension in the back of his neck. Then he turned up Mercaderes toward the Plaza de Armas and the *Comandancia* as he decided to play another hunch. What the hell, nothing had worked so far. He might as well drop in on Colonel Machia—on some pretext he would have to think of between here and there. The quickest way to find out how tiger feels is get in cage with him—old China-duty saying. News of the signing of the AID agreement in Washington was expected momentarily. That would make a hell of a difference in Robert Sanders' picture. He had to know something.

He was approaching the entrance to the old *Comandancia* building, frowning at the sidewalk, tidying up the lie he would tell Machia about the reason for this visit, when he heard the clatter of rifles snapping to present and a sharp command: '*Atención!*' Then Machia came rapidly down the entrance steps just as Mike reached them.

Though it was non-Navy-reg in mufti, Mike drew smartly to attention and saluted. Machia stopped and faced him, scowling. Three aides, following, almost ran over him.

"*Buenos días, mi coronel,*" Mike said in what he hoped were tones of sincere cordiality.

Machia looked him over with utter contempt. "*El ayudante del Embajador Estadounidense, no?*"

"The same, Colonel. Mike Hodak, aide to the U.S. Ambassador."

"So?"

"Colonel," Mike said with great earnestness. "The matter

we discussed yesterday. The Ambassador is concerned seriously. It will be taken care of. Don't worry. We'll get that bird Sanders on his way by tomorrow, at the latest. I assure you of this."

Machia sneered at him: "I cannot imagine what you are talking about, Captain. Perhaps you will communicate officially in writing. Through channels, of course."

Mike stared after the man, with nothing else to say, as Machia turned and got into his waiting car. Before the door was closed, the Maraguan leveled a granite gaze at the Marine.

"Captain Hodak," he said. "During the remainder of your stay in this country, if you are wise, you will keep out of my sight. The next time I have the misfortune of seeing you, you will become, officially, *persona non grata.*"

"He can't do that," the General said hotly. "Declaring my aide PNG is an insult to me personally, the son-of-a-bitch!"

"Don't sweat it on my account, General," Mike said. "I've screwed things up royally. It might help if I checked out, quiet like."

"Never!" the old man roared, outraged. "You're not leaving till *I* tell you to leave."

They were riding to the airport in the Embassy limousine to meet Lieutenant Colonel Thomas Clapsaddle, U.S.A., and family. As they traveled through the streets the Ambassador reiterated heatedly his decision to detain Robert Sanders tonight and fly him out of the country, against his will if necessary. The hell with Machia. He recognized the problems involved. They had nothing official to go on. Sanders doubtless would resent being shanghaied out of Maragua by force, possibly to the extent that he would complain to his Congressman. Machia would be enraged. So what? The hell with it. Rolla Gatch had never been one who hesitated to take action called for by the circumstances merely because there was danger of getting into official trouble. It was one of the simple, direct qualities that made him a great General of Marines.

Though pleased by the old man's ire, Mike remonstrated mildly.

"General, this ain't the USMC. You got to remember that. We're State Department now."

"Yes," the General grunted. "There are still some celery-heads up there who think we can buy friends with handouts. We've given Maragua millions of dollars in the last ten years, and they hate our guts." He added, musing darkly, "My daddy was a country banker. In time he came to know everybody in town, on a very intimate basis. Pocketbook level. Before he died he told me something I never have forgotten. He told me the only people who never forgave him were the ones he had saved." The General pondered this a moment, then he added, "Countries are much like people. Proud, stupid, mean, ungrateful, and unreasonable as hell."

The big plane sparkled in the sun, banked and flared its flaps, then nosed down toward the end of the runway. A small crowd milled about in the fenced enclosure outside the terminal building—a sizable contingent of Embassy personnel and wives, a couple of Maraguan lieutenant colonels from the General Staff dripping with gold aiguilettes, a reporter or two and a couple of photographers.

When the Pan Air plane taxied up and swung slowly around, its turbo-prop engines whistling shrilly, the General and Molly came out of the terminal and stood waiting in the center of a respectful little clearing in the crowd. In a moment the plane hatch opened and the steps unfolded, then the pilot cut the engines. Lieutenant Colonel Thomas Clapsaddle and his wife and daughter were the first out.

They were rumpled and tired-looking. Clapsaddle was a tall, rawboned man, sandy-headed and sunburnt. He had what the General called a fresh "white-sidewall" haircut and he looked more like an Oklahoma wheat farmer than a multi-decorated hero of Korea and Viet Nam. His wife, almost as tall as he, was also sandy-colored. She led a knobby-kneed little girl by a leash attached to a harness around her chest.

In a moment they were down in the crowd, shaking hands with the General and Molly. Mrs. Clapsaddle, embarrassed, tucked at her hair, which was flying in all directions. Mike's first thought was that military attachés must be in very short supply in Washington. Later, when he knew him better, he revised this appraisal and came to think of Tom Clapsaddle as someone he would like to pull combat duty with, and that was about the best you could say of a man.

The greetings and introductions went on for fifteen minutes. The newspaper people took some pictures and asked many questions in rapid-fire Spanish, which Mike fielded and answered, to the Army man's relief. Then the General brought the welcoming ceremony to a close.

"Colonel, we're delighted to have you and your ladies aboard. Captain Hodak will take charge of you and get you settled in the Country Club. Spend the rest of the day unwinding. We're having a smallish reception at the Embassy tonight, to introduce you to a few people you'll be living and working with. A car will pick you up at seven. Until then, ta-ta."

After Mike had checked the new arrivals into their rooms, had advised Mrs. Clapsaddle on her dress for the evening,

126

assured her of the reliability of the baby-sitting *ama*, warned against the drinking of tap water and the eating of uncooked fruits and vegetables, briefed the Colonel on the ceremonies of the big holiday Monday and so on, he left them and headed for home. His head hurt. Too much booze, Sanders' hard fist, other people's problems piled on top of his own—together they made him almost wish he was a PFC again with nothing to look after but a Browning Automatic Rifle. At this point, if everybody's affairs went to hell in a handbasket, he was going home, take a couple of aspirin and sleep an hour. A man could take only so much at a time.

Nestor met him at his front door. The smile on his mild brown face was the best thing Mike had seen all day. He felt like putting an arm around the little fellow and giving him a hug, just because he was an optimistic man. Then Nestor shattered the incipient tranquility and Mike felt more like kicking his tail for him.

"Señor," Nestor said. "There are someone important to see you in the *sala.*"

In anger Mike said, "You know better than that, Nestor! Why in hell did you let anybody in?" He went storming past the little man toward the living room, prepared to escort some brassy rug peddler out into the street.

"Señor," Nestor said, following close behind. "He says it is a matter *muy urgente*. And that he is your friend. He told me so himself."

As Mike strode across the reception and down the two steps into the living room he absorbed a distinct jolt. There in a chair in the corner of the room sat Robert Sanders.

19

On top of all else that had happened in the past forty-eight hours the sight of Sanders sitting there, calm and relaxed, left Mike momentarily speechless. His muscles tightened instinctively, as though he expected the man to spring from the chair and come at him with that murderous right hand. His skull began to throb as if it had a memory of its own. Behind him Nestor murmured that this was the señor—the friend—about whom he had spoken.

The gently spoken words relaxed his tension slightly. Mike said, "Well, I'll be go-to-hell."

"Hello, Captain Hodak," Sanders said. "Hope you don't mind my dropping in." He lifted a glass of Coca-Cola from the small table beside his chair. "Nestor has taken good care of me."

Mike, completely baffled, looked at the man. Sanders spoke as casually and amiably as though he were accustomed to dropping in like this and making himself at home. There was not the slightest hint of last night's fiasco. And he appeared as rational as you could want a man to be. The only visible sign that anything was amiss was the dark strawberry mark on his chin and a slightly swollen cheek. It injured Mike's pride to see what really minor damage two of his best punches had done to the man.

All hope of a siesta was gone now. Mike muttered for Nestor to bring him a drink, then he crossed the room, sank down on the couch and stared at Sanders, bemused. In moments Nestor reappeared with a martini on a tray. Mike took it down in a swallow. The chilled hotness braced him sharply.

"Is good?" said Nestor.

"Like scorpion piss," Mike said, growling his throat clear. "Get out."

"Nestor is quite a fellow," Sanders said as the little *mayor domo* left the room, chuckling.

"All right, my friend," Mike said. "Let's have it."

It was a moment before Sanders spoke, and when he did it was almost as if his words were enclosed in parentheses.

"You're wondering why I'm here, naturally. Well—this is not a social call."

"Now I'm sorry to hear that," Mike said. "I thought we could have some tea."

Robert Sanders frowned into his Coca-Cola, then he put the glass down and squinted at Mike.

"Last night you hinted—" he gently touched the strawberry on his chin "—that I should pull out of here. Assuming, of course, that I didn't read too much into your subtle suggestion."

"Well, now, I didn't mean to be so obvious," Mike said. "The way things stand, I just thought you might be happier elsewhere."

Sanders almost laughed. "Okay, Captain. Let's knock off the *shitezvous*. You want me to powder out of here. All right. I want something, too." He cupped one hand, then the other, as if hefting two weights to see if they are about equal. Then he shrugged. "It's this simple. You help me—I'll leave."

Scowling at the man suspiciously, Mike said, "That sounds simple enough to be fatal. What do you want?"

"You know already."

"I don't know anything. But if I had to guess, I'd say it had to do with Rafael Benavides."

Sanders gazed at him for long, hesitant seconds, as if debating with himself for the tenth time. Then he decided that he had no alternative but to lay it on the line.

"Correct."

So that *was* it. Though he had felt sure, Mike still found the admission startling.

He grunted, "You're a high trader, friend. This involves holes in the head."

Sanders smiled. "Not for you, Captain. You're a practical man. I think we can make a deal. I want to free Rafael Benavides. I can't do it alone. The people I came to work with are dead, as you well know. You can help me—without risk to yourself."

Mike got up and walked around the room, beginning to feel addled again. Seeing Nestor's eager brown face peering at him from the hallway he flung his martini glass across the room at him. Nestor speared the glass neatly out of the air, uttered a curse of self-admiration and went gliding toward the pantry.

Turning back to his guest Mike said, "If Rafael Benavides spends the rest of his life in the Colombian Embassy, I won't lose any sleep. But that's not the point. If he was my own brother, I wouldn't help you. Because you can't swing it. And I don't believe in getting myself killed when I haven't got at least an outside chance of winning. What are you, anyway, a professional martyr?"

"You won't get killed," Sanders snapped with an edge of contempt in his voice. "I just want you to help me communicate with Benavides. Nothing else." He sat back, put his fingertips together and blew thoughtfully over them as he watched the big man. Then he went on: "Maybe you don't know that I'm being followed everywhere I go now. They'd cut me down before I got within a block of Benavides. You can be sure the telephones are tapped. Mail is out of the question. Somebody's got to carry my message to him, personally."

Nestor entered without a sound. Mike took the drink from the tray and waved him out of the room.

"That wouldn't fool a retarded idiot, me running in and out of the Colombian Embassy like a Western Union boy. Machia already thinks I'm mixed up with you some way."

Sanders considered this for a moment. Then he reached into his inner coat pocket and drew out an envelope which he tapped lightly against his knee.

"There's a reception at the Colombian Embassy tonight," he said. "Some wheel from Bogotá. Finance Minister, I think. It's in the bulletin."

Mike grunted. The *Boletín Diplomática* was a little flyer carrying news of social events, ceremonies, arrivals and departures and the like in the diplomatic colony. Sadie must have given it to him.

"So?" he said.

"So it would be natural for you to attend. No one will know that you weren't invited." He looked from the envelope to Mike. "Machia's people wouldn't dare stop you. You could deliver this, easy."

"No deal," Mike said shortly.

"Look," Sanders said, almost laughing again. "I'm paying you a compliment. I'd be killed if this envelope fell into the wrong hands. I don't know anybody else down here I'd trust with my life."

Mike uttered an obscenity. He got up and strode across the floor. Then he stopped and faced the younger man. "Like you say, let's knock off the horseshit, shall we, Sanders? You got no right or reason to trust me. I hate your guts. It's *that* simple."

"That has nothing to do with it," Robert Sanders said. "If you made a deal with me, I know you wouldn't sell me out."

"And why should I make a deal?"

"It would be the easy way to get rid of me. If you deliver this envelope, I'll be gone Monday." He shrugged. "If you don't, I'll have to stick around a bit."

His words were so simple and matter-of-fact that Mike, all but dumfounded, found himself half believing him. It was almost as if they were playing poker, with Sadie as the stake. The threat was implicit.

"That's all I have to do, deliver the envelope?"

"Not quite. After Benavides reads the letter, he'll give you an answer to bring back to me. It will be just—'yes' or 'no.' Nothing more. That's it."

Mike paced nervously across the room and back. One of the clear impressions he had gained was that this man wasn't a bluffer. Another factor was that if he went along with Sanders' proposal, ridiculous as it was, he wouldn't be interfering with the General's plan to ship the man out of the country. At the same time this would be insurance, in case the Ambassador's strategy didn't work out.

He stopped in front of the young man and said, "How do I know I can trust *you?*"

Looking up at him Sanders said, "If you don't trust me, don't do it. It's that simple."

This apparent lack of guile enraged Mike Hodak.

Addressing the air he said, "Goddam sonofabitch!"

The next moment he held out his hand for the envelope, thinking that this was the stupidest act of his entire life.

With a grin that was almost boyish, Sanders got up and laid the envelope in Mike's open palm.

"Thanks, Captain," he said. Then, as if this concluded all of the business he had come to transact, he walked around the big man and headed for the door.

Following him in a daze of anger and confusion, Mike stopped him at the entrance.

"Sanders. What in *hell* is this all about? Why do you want to free Rafael Benavides?"

Sanders hesitated. Then he turned and Mike was looking straight into his eyes. The joking was gone, and for an instant it was as though he saw through the eyes into the tortured depths of the man, as if the brash, opaque screen with which he faced the world had suddenly been pulled aside, revealing naked despair. Mike had seen this once before. There was no doubt that he had touched something close to the secret of the man.

Then the opaque screen rippled closed again.

Sanders said, "Just say I don't like cages."

For a long time after Robert Sanders had gone down the geranium-bordered walk and out of sight up the street toward the *avenida,* Mike stood in the doorway, elbow on the door frame, a hand upon his aching head.

The Chevrolet with two of Machia's thugs in it crossed his field of vision, Cadillacing up the street after Sanders. This did nothing to help the throbbing.

Standing beside him, his face abeam with admiration, Nestor murmured, *"Es un hombre formidable. No, Señor?"*

Mike came out of his trance and said, "Mind your business and answer the goddam telephone."

The call was for him. He took up the instrument and immediately recognized the buffoon voice of Alvaro Rodriguez, chief customs inspector at the airport, although that worthy was doing his best to disguise it.

"*Oye, Capitan,*" Alvaro spoke in a frightened whisper. "Thank you for the *cigarillos,* eh? You know who is this?" Before Mike could answer he added quickly, "Don't say. Others may be listening. *Oye, Capitán.* The *gringo* you ask about the other day. I have bad news on him, eh? A matter of gravity. Orders from the *Comandancia* itself. All emigration *oficiales* are alerted to prevent him to leave San Felipe, by any means whatever. Special guards has been posted."

"When did this happen?" Mike demanded. There was no reply. He spoke sharply into the mouthpiece and jiggled the bar, but the line was dead. Replacing the receiver carefully in its cradle, he reflected that small friendships can pay big dividends.

Sitting on the stool by the telephone he cracked his knuckles for half a minute. It helped him think. Then he called the Chancery and got Rusty Cobb on the wire. Would she go to a reception with him before the party for the Clapsaddles? He described it as a duty detail, but didn't say where. He knew it would look more routine and be less likely to arouse suspicion if he was escorting a lady when he went into the Colombian Embassy. Rusty sounded a little cool, but said that she would go if he wanted her to, seeing that it was duty.

Next he told Nestor to put on a pot of water for tea. Then he told him to go to the *botica,* three blocks away, for aspirin.

"There is plenty aspirin in the *cómodo, Señor.*"

"That's old aspirin. I want fresh aspirin. I have a strong headache. *Váyate!*"

He wanted Nestor out of the house, because the thought which came to him when he had been talking with Sanders had now clarified itself. He had only committed to *deliver* the letter to Rafael Benavides. He had not said he wouldn't read it, first. It was sealed, but it could be unsealed. A military commander who goes into action with poor intelligence is half defeated at the outset.

As he ran the envelope back and forth in the soft plume of steam from the teakettle, Mike felt a slight twinge of conscience, but he justified his action on the grounds that this could be the means of saving the crazy fool's life. If he knew what the man planned to do, he would have a better chance of keeping him out of Machia's hands. The whole business had taken a critical turn. The plan to shanghai Sanders and fly him out in the Embassy plane, which seemed simple and direct a few minutes ago, had now become a very risky undertaking, if not an impossibility. Under the circumstances Mike felt he must know exactly what Sanders had in mind.

The envelope came open easily. Mike took it into the *sala* and sat down to read. He drew out two large folded sheets of hotel stationery, covered with Sanders' open boyish handwriting. The message was astounding:

Dear Mr. Rafael Benavides:
    The bearer will tell you who I am, and that I am capable of doing what I propose.
    Your loyal friend and supporter, Carlos Sanchez, in New Orleans, arranged for me to come here. He sends warm greetings. He has had some success in stirring up sympathy for your cause in the American press. He is not doing too well with the TB, I'm sorry to say.
    I arrived too late to work with Gongora and the others—an unfortunate breakdown of communications. They were brave, but very clumsy.
    I am here for one reason, to get you out of there. If you are willing to take the risk, there is a fair chance we can succeed. You will have to trust me and do

exactly what I tell you. No complicated plan can succeed. These people are smart and are looking for tricky stuff. The only thing that will work is something simple, bold, and perfectly timed.

This is the plan. On Monday—the big holiday—a parade will go down Avenida Sucre about 2 P.M. You must be ready to move, fast. Be at the front door, ready to go, from 2 P.M. on.

Shortly after two someone will create a disturbance in the crowd directly in front of the Embassy. When this starts, count to fifty by ones. Then walk directly into the street. Don't run. Act casual. Work your way through the crowd to the center of the street. Then get into the nearest car. Remember this. It is important. No matter what it is, get into the *nearest car*. You will have to trust me to take it from there. I'll be wearing a gray suit with a blue handkerchief in the breast pocket.

I think this will work. If you are willing to try it, send me the answer "yes" by the bearer. Otherwise send "no." Don't say "yes" unless you mean it, because I will be there, and the fat will be in the fire.

I do not sign this for obvious reasons.

That was all.

20

At seven o'clock Mike called for Rusty at her *pensión* and they took a cab to the Colombian Embassy. Seven is a glamorous hour in San Felipe. A soft dusk flows over the city then. Lights are coming on in cafés and shops; people come out into the plazas and the tempo of the streets picks up like an expectant heartbeat.

Rusty seemed to blossom with the approach of darkness. She had put some sparkly things in her hair. Her eyes reflected the lights of the neon signs along the *calles*. She was vivacious and friendly, having recovered from her earlier pique.

Mike found it comforting to have her beside him as they lurched along the crowded streets. He was thoroughly unhappy over this fool's errand he had undertaken—partly because he had read Sanders' letter and now really was a kind of accomplice, and partly because he hadn't made an immediate full disclosure of the whole affair to the General. However, this was a show he had taken unto himself as his sole responsibility, and he was determined not to involve the old man if he could help it.

That was because the matter had now gone beyond official business. It had become a thing of vital personal concern to Mike Hodak, because he knew that somehow Sadie's future hung in the balance. He could not even guess at the outcome of the tangled mess. He could only hope that in the untangling Sadie would not succeed, finally, in destroying herself.

Rusty linked her arm through his and drew close to him. In a bright, warm voice she said, "Where we going, Mike? Not that it matters."

"Colombian Embassy. Reception for some joker from Bogotá."

"Colombian Embassy!" Rusty said. "Isn't that where Rafael Benavides is?"

"It is."

"Jay-*zu!*" she said excitedly. "How about that? Boy!"

"Rus," Mike said, frowning, "do me a favor and keep this

little outing to yourself, will you? For the time being? It's a touchy situation. Top secret. You know what I mean?"

"Sure, Mike, if you say so. I can keep things real confidential. I love to." Rusty sounded impressed, but Mike felt uncomfortable. He distrusted all women.

By the time they reached Avenida Sucre it was almost dark. Special floodlights, erected on Machia's orders, stood at the corners around the Embassy. They illuminated the streets with a bluish glare. Machia was thorough. Darkness never fell on Rafael Benavides' sanctuary. It was said that the Colombian Ambassador blindfolded himself with a black silk handkerchief upon retiring, in order to sleep.

They were arriving a half-hour late. Mike planned this purposely, hoping they could enter a house already full of guests animated by their first drink. Then chances would be good it wouldn't be noticed that he and Rusty were party-crashers. A limousine was standing at the front gate discharging other late arrivals. At the street intersection a policeman held up a white gloved hand, signaling their taxi to wait until the limousine had moved on. Then he whistled them forward.

"Get out your *cédula,*" Mike murmured to Rusty, looking ahead through the windshield. Rusty rummaged furiously in her purse for her identification card and Mike touched Sanders' letter under the waistband of his trousers. It felt hot as mustard plaster against his stomach.

An officer flanked by two *soldados* with carbines at port met them as they climbed out of the cab. Brusquely Mike gave the officer their names and shoved the cards at him for inspection. After a moment the officer handed the cards back, saluted, then stood aside to let them pass into the Embassy gate.

In the entrance a *mayor domo* bowed them into the hall,

138

then ushered them on into the high-ceilinged salon that opened on the right. It was a large room dimly lighted by small bulbs in wrought-iron chandeliers. The walls were paneled in darkly polished wood. The whole place had the close, aromatic smell of a cedar chest.

To Mike's increased discomfort the room was not as crowded as he had hoped. The guests were gathered in small groups talking in subdued tones. Inside the door Mike and Rusty were greeted by the Colombian Ambassador, whom Mike had met on several occasions. The Ambassador's wife and the guest of honor, a portly, financial-looking gentleman with a black mustache, stood beside him.

Mike did not miss the puzzled frown on the Ambassador's face before it was smoothed out with practiced diplomatic aplomb. He felt very awkward, but there was nothing to do now but bull the matter through.

Shaking hands he mumbled some polite but unintelligible verbal garbage and started into the salon. Rusty, however, stopped and began jabbering her fractured Spanish at the Ambassador's wife, turning on the charm, full force, saying how she had *so* looked forward to visiting the Embassy which had given sanctuary to Rafael Benavides and on and on until Mike, sweating, finally clamped his fingers into her arm and led her away.

There was no point in wasting time now. He lifted a drink from a passing tray and put it in Rusty's hand.

"Mix and mingle," he said under his breath. *"Try* to keep that big Texas mouth shut, and don't go away until I come back." So saying he drifted casually through the little conversation groups and found his way into a passage leading out of the rear of the salon. Halfway down the passageway he ran into a *mozo* who bowed and inquired, *"Baño,* Señor?"

"*Sí*," Mike said, "*baño.*"

With a nod the servant led him around the corner and showed him a door, slightly ajar, leading to a rest room. Mike motioned for the man to follow him and went in, closing the door behind. Fixing him with a dangerous look Mike said, "I want to see Rafael Benavides."

Immediately the man became alarmed. He threw up his hands and began to protest. Putting a finger to his lips Mike drew a fifty-peso note from his pocket and held it directly in front of the man's eyes. It was probably a month's pay to him. It seemed to hypnotize him instantly.

"I have a message for Señor Benavides, from his friends," Mike said. "He will want to see me." Remembering the name in Sanders' letter, he added, "Tell him I bring a message from Carlos Sanchez."

The sound of the name seemed to relieve the *mozo*. His fingers snaked around the bill and he backed through the door, whispering, "The *señor* will wait here, *por favor.*"

In less than five minutes he reappeared, indicating with his eyes that Mike should follow him, which he did, down the passageway, through a pantry, up some dark narrow back stairs to a wide and dimly lighted hall on the second floor, also paneled in dark wood and smelling of camphor and cedar. At a door near the end of the hall the *mozo* stopped.

"Señor," he said in a hushed voice, full of real concern. "Rafael Benavides is not strong. I beg you to be gentle, and as brief as possible." With this he quietly turned a knob and opened the door to admit Mike into the room.

It was a library. The walls were lined with leather-bound volumes from floor to ceiling. At the end of the room on an oval table stacked high with books a brass lamp provided the only light which cast deep shadows into the corners. An old man sat behind the books, writing. He wore a green eyeshade and an old brown bathrobe. Mike stood a full half minute staring at him before he realized that this was the famous Rafael Benavides.

Presently the man looked up from his writing and saw him. Then he arose and came around the table, his hand outstretched. He was older, much older than Mike thought he would be, and quite frail. His once powerful bone structure was a gaunt skeleton now, a fragile framework for the sallow mantle of skin that covered it, like an old garment. When Mike saw how feeble he was, a feeling of relief passed over him. The man was obviously unfit for any such hairbreadth undertaking as the letter under his belt proposed.

"You bring a message from Carlos Sanchez," Benavides said, grasping both of Mike's hands in his soft fingers. He shook the hands repeatedly as he talked. His voice was soft, but intense. "Tell me, tell me, how is he? Is he well? Are his spirits high? Is he not discouraged?"

Looking at the old man, Mike felt a wave of sadness. So this was the champion of *el pueblo,* the symbol of hope for the downtrodden, the torchbearer of freedom for the sandalfoot, the cotton picker, the cane cutter, the taxi driver. This old hulk, this doddering ancient! This is what the man Góngora and the others spilled their lives on the street for. What a shame, what a damned pitiable waste!

Then as he stood there looking at him, staring into the keen old eyes, he began to sense, imperceptibly at first, then with a feeling that enveloped him like a warm draft of air, the greatness of the man. Almost immediately Mike had the feeling that the old man had already identified himself with him, that he felt all his aches and sorrows and understood all of his hopes and hidden fears.

The old man's nose was large and hawklike. The sagging skin of his face was the color of yellow ivory. Swatches of wiry gray hair stuck out from under the green eyeshade. It was really an ugly old face, yet it was most appealing. It was as if he generated a kind of magnetic field around him. Mike felt at once the selflessness of the man, the thing about him that made the lottery vendors and the street sweepers and the old women of the *barrios*—all the *pobrecitos*—love him. It was the same thing, perhaps, that had made him a failure as a president. One sensed almost immediately that here was a man totally incapable of artifice, of sacrificing principle for expediency, of condemning the weakness of any man, because he understood too well the weaknesses of all men. For several moments Mike stood there holding hands with him, perfectly at ease under the old man's spell.

Then Benavides spoke again, "When did you leave Sanchez?"

Mike snapped out of his daze. "I haven't seen Sanchez, señor. I only bring greetings from one who has lately been with him."

The old man took him by the arm and led him to a chair near the table. "Sit down, sit down, please." He sat in a chair facing Mike, hands on bony knees, his knees almost touching Mike's. "Now," he said, his eyes sparkling, "tell me about my friends."

"I understand Sanchez has not been too well, but is better now," Mike said. "He is working hard and meeting with some success. His spirits are high."

"Ah, that Carlitos!" Benavides exclaimed, throwing up his hands. "He is a magnificent boy. The indomitable human spirit! Is it not a thing of wonder?"

Mike reached inside his shirt and extracted Sanders' envelope. "This, señor," he said, handing it over "is the reason I am here. It is a message from a friend of Sanchez, and though you do not know him, a friend of Rafael Benavides, as well."

Taking from the table a pair of spectacles, the frames of which had been repaired with adhesive tape, Benavides put them on and with painstaking care opened the envelope. For long, silent moments Mike watched his face as he read. When he finished, he started over and read the entire letter again. There was not the faintest flicker of expression. When he had finished the second reading, he folded the letter carefully, replaced it in the envelope and laid it on the table. Then he removed his glasses and turned his fathomless blue eyes upon Mike.

"This young man—he is a young man, no?" he said. "He is what we call in Spanish *muy valeroso,* is he not?"

"He is young and *muy valeroso.*"

"Is not the spirit of man a wondrous thing!" he marveled again. "How I should like to see him and talk with him! Will you not carry for me to him a greeting of *mucho cariño?*" He shook his head and smiled. "The world will not die while there are young men like this."

Mike knew that he had to go. Rusty was downstairs, undoubtedly shooting her mouth off. He was an hour overdue at the party for Clapsaddle, and the General would be looking for him and growling like a mistreated lion.

Mike stood up and said, "I better shove off now. I'm glad I met you." Then, though he hardly thought it necessary, he motioned toward the envelope on the table and said, "I'm supposed to take back an answer to the sender."

With an exceedingly calm and benign smile the old man nodded his head. "Please convey to the young man my extreme gratitude, and tell him that my answer is—yes."

143

Mike was thunderstruck. "Your—what?"

He repeated, "Tell him my answer is yes."

"Hell's fire, Señor, do you know what this letter says?" Mike spoke with visible agitation. "Do you read English all right? You want me to translate it for you?"

"I read English quite well. I understand what the letter says." He reached out a thin, blue-veined hand and touched Mike gently on the knee. "I also understand your concern and your doubt. I'm a pretty old customer. Too old, too feeble, perhaps you're thinking, to make such a valiant attempt as this." He gave Mike a smile that seemed to have actual warmth in it.

"Let me tell you, young Señor, that few old men have this opportunity to be valiant. How better could I spend my remaining strength? Shall I dribble it out peseta at a time, here in my comfortable prison? Or shall I invest it, perhaps all of it, in an act which may put a little courage into the hearts of the *pobrecitos* of this unhappy land? The answer, of course, can only be—*yes*."

Standing at the door, deeply affected by the old man's simple speech and staggered by this new development, Mike said, "You didn't ask his name."

"Would it help to know his name?" the old man replied with a smile. "The letter rings true. You do not have the look of a traitor. That is enough for me." Then he added, almost wistfully, "If I do not know the name, it will not be possible for anyone to wring it from me . . . though they are masters of torture."

21

Over a period of time Mike Hodak had become hooked by more than Sadie's overpowering physical desirability. Without in the least intending to he had become painfully involved in the management of her morals and deeply concerned with her dark, nihilistic slant on life. As though these things were any of his concern. Once, for example, in one of her deep lows, Sadie became tight at a luncheon party at the club. She was getting herself involved with an amorous Argentine polo player who recognized opportunity when he saw it, when Mike rescued her—or, to be more exact, abducted her. Seeing the situation develop he wrapped a couple of sandwiches in a napkin, stuck them in his pocket then told Sadie she was wanted on the phone. Next, with a firm hand, he escorted her straight through the lobby, out the front entrance and down the steps to his waiting car.

He drove south out of the city and down the coast road with Sadie screaming at him and threatening to jump from the car at every kilometer. After a time she began to sober and settle down a little, and she started to cry, angrily, accusingly, as if Mike were the cause of all her troubles.

Before he knew it they were at the turnoff for New Moon Bay. He figured that would be as good a place as any to eat the sandwiches and finish the sobering process.

They sat barefoot on an old shelter half and looked out

over the sparkling afternoon sea. To induce Sadie to eat, Mike broke off bits of his sandwich and poked them into her mouth. A flight of gulls came winging down the beach. Sadie stood up and began to fling pieces of her sandwich to them. The sea birds returned, circling and screaming as they swooped to spear the bread from the sand with their sharp beaks. One bold one came close enough to catch a morsel in midair. This seemed to cheer Sadie. She laughed and tried without success to repeat the feat until the sandwich was gone. Then she sank to the shelter half and stretched out, face down, her arms and brown slender legs extended, as she rolled back and forth, crying "Oh-oh-oh-oh!" After a time she sat up and brushed her dark hair from her eyes.

She looked at Mike. "Have you any notion—any idea at all—why we're here?" she demanded.

"Here?"

"Not *here,* stupid man. I mean *alive,* born, existent?"

Mike looked at her with a pang of sadness and longing. "I don't reckon I ever worried about that one. But seeing as we *are* here, I guess we ought to try to make the best of a tough situation."

"Oh, I don't buy that jolly old crap at all!" Sadie said, snapping her eyes at him. "Why should we make the best of it? Why not make the *worst* of it? Whoever's running this miserable show, this so-called life—if anyone is—that'll teach 'em! The hell with it! Fuck everybody! Fuck the whole world!"

She said this last with such intensity, her fingers made into cat's claws, her white teeth clenched, that she trembled all over.

"Sadie, Sadie," Mike said mournfully. "It don't help to talk dirty. You're supposed to be a lady."

"And that goes for you, too!" She spat the words viciously. "Fuck you too, Sergeant Hodak!" She stuck her thumb to her nose and waggled her fingers at him.

In a flash of fury Mike slapped her hand away from her face, hard. He resisted a strong impulse to back-hand her on the return swipe.

"Don't talk to me like that, little one," he said with a heat of pure anger that made Sadie begin to sob. She sat bent over, weeping into her hands for minutes. At length she sat up and brushed the backs of her fingers over her eyes. She blew upward, fitfully, at a strand of hair falling over her brow.

"If I must be salt," she said tremulously, "I want to be the bitterest, saltiest salt there is."

Mike gave a groaning sigh and shook his head again as he looked at her. "You can be, if you keep on working at it. But you have a choice, Sadie. You know that, don't you? You have a choice."

That night when Mike returned home, exhausted, half smashed emotionally and with alcohol, he pinned Nestor to the wall with a thick finger. His voice was rough.

"You know what we are, Nestor? We're nothing but a bunch of bugs at the bottom of the sea, eatin' each other."

Nestor nodded seriously.

"This is true, Señor. This is very true—most of the time."

Mike sneered and poked him with the finger. "What d'you mean, most of the time?"

Nestor returned the sneer with a wistful smile that had warmth and sweetness in it. "Now and then we remember we are not bugs, but men—and try to act so. That is only reason why we are here, is it not, Señor?"

Mike patted the little man's cheek with his big hand.

"*Chico,* you are a friggin' philosopher if I ever saw one. I wish I could believe you."

Mike arrived with Rusty at the party for the Clapsaddles one hour late. The Embassy, brightly lit and full of people, gleamed like a big jewel box through the trees. Rusty was peevish because Mike had dragged her away from the Colombian Embassy just when she was getting to know people. There was this fabulous young Colombian. . . . Mike paid her no mind. His visit with Benavides had stirred him profoundly. Talking with the old man was like being in the presence of the pristine stuff that mankind was made of before it became adulterated with the world's meanness and selfishness. Rafael Benavides made him feel acutely his own sorriness. Now a sense of guilt was growing in him, that he had let himself become instrumental in a weird scheme that would lure the old man out of his sanctuary, probably to his death.

As the two crossed the black and white squares of the vestibule they found the party in full motion. The state dining room to the right and the spacious solarium straight ahead were crowded and festive. Waiters hurried in and out with trays of drinks and food. Music came from the terrace beyond the solarium.

As they entered the latter room they ran squarely into the General, holding court to an admiring circle of girls from the Chancery. Tall and handsome in their midst, he was putting it on for them, in his most gallant and charming manner. When he saw Mike, he drew in his chin and withered him with a stony scowl. "It was good of you to come, Captain. Young ladies, you are acquainted with my part-time aide-de-camp?"

"I'm sorry, General," Mike said. "I got tied up."

"I can vouch for that, Mister Ambassador," Rusty chimed in eagerly, trying to be helpful. "I've been with him."

"I am sure it is enlightening to be tied up with a man of Captain Hodak's talents," the General said, his voice spiky with innuendo. The girls all giggled. Mike, flushing, threw Rusty a look that told her to keep her mouth shut and beat it. Then he stalked off in search of a drink.

A big swallow of Scotch soothed the sting of the General's caustic greeting. In any case there was not time to sulk. He bumped into and visited very briefly with Clapsaddle, meanwhile scanning the crowd. Then he felt a sudden lift of spirits, for through the hubbub of the room the unmistakable sound of Sadie's laughter reached his ears.

Taking leave of the colonel he homed on the sound and found Sadie in the center of a group of men. Mike thought of a bunch of peacocks crowding one another, spreading their fans, as they tried to strut and prance in the same space before a winsome young peahen.

When she saw Mike, she smiled at the gentlemen and escaped their encirclement, leaving them talking to each other.

"I've been looking everywhere for you," she said intensely as they moved onto the black-and-white checkerboard of the hallway.

"So you found me."

Ignoring his sullen tone Sadie stopped and confronted him, fixing him with her eyes. "Where is our friend? He hasn't come."

"Our friend?" Mike feigned a look of puzzlement.

"Don't get funny with me, Mike. Where is Robert Sanders? He said he would be here. He told me he had been at your house and would see you again tonight. What's going on? Where is he?" Her tone was sharp, suspicious.

Mike was about to tell her that he hadn't taken Robert Sanders to raise, when, over the top of her head, through the grillwork doors of the entrance he saw a cab pull to a stop and a man get out. Seconds later the man was bowed into the hallway by the waiting *mayor domo.*

Answering Sadie's question, without words, Mike turned her around.

When Sanders saw them, he stopped. He and Mike exchanged wary glances. For a moment no one spoke. Then Sadie broke the silence. She said, "Hello, Robert Sanders." The sound of the band on the terrace floated into the hall. It was playing *"Bésame Mucho."* Sanders glanced at Mike again, then at Sadie. Then he said, "This dance for me?"

His fingers felt for her waist as they came together. Then they moved out across the black and white squares. It was as if, suddenly, nothing existed beyond themselves. Mike imagined he could see a change come over Sadie, a kind of sea change as she looked at the man, a calm radiance, as though this was what she had been waiting for, all of her life.

Watching them, awkwardly, he felt all at once like an intruder. With a mutter of profanity he turned and walked into the drawing room.

Some time later Rusty Cobb saw Sadie go into the powder room and followed her. She found Sadie nervously combing her hair before the mirror.

"Sadie—"

"Hello, Rusty Cobb."

Rusty was feeling her drinks. She leaned back against the door, arms folded over her ample breasts, her wide green eyes very serious.

"Sadie, do you realize what you're doing?"

Retouching her lipstick Sadie gave her a short look. "What kind of a remark is that, Rusty Cobb?"

"I'm talking about Mike. And this hard-luck Romeo named Sanders."

"So, what about them?"

"Mike loves you."

"So I love Mike."

"Yes, I know. Everybody loves Mike. Like a big brother. Like a good old true-blue friend who's always there when you need him. That's not the way he loves you. And you're playing around with his feelings as if you didn't give a damn."

Anger flashed in Sadie's eyes. She turned and faced the other girl squarely.

"Look, old dear. I haven't asked Mike for his love or you for an opinion. Mike feels a certain way about me. I feel a certain way about him. I can't help the way either of us feels."

The big girl from Texas said flatly, "Then quit leading him on. Love him the way he loves you, or turn him loose."

Sadie's claws began to show. "What if I don't? You going to scratch my eyes out? What's your interest in this little deal, anyway?"

"Never mind what my interest is," Rusty said. "I hate to see a good man hurt for nothing." She opened the door, then stopped and leveled her green eyes. "And don't worry about me scratchin' your eyes out, sweetie. If I ever take in after you, I won't scratch. I'll wring your neck like a bantie chicken."

"Bully for you," said Sadie.

A half-hour later the party reached its peak and began to disintegrate as the first guests drifted out and departed with gay and slightly tipsy farewells. Robert Sanders came up to Mike in the drawing room. Sadie was not with him. He offered Mike a cigarette, which Mike declined, then lit his own, inhaled deeply and blew white ash from the end with a sharp jet of smoke. It was an impatient, nervous gesture.

"What about the letter, Captain?"

"I said I would deliver it."

"So?"

"So," Mike said. "That's what I did."

Sanders' eyes widened perceptibly, and when Mike added nothing to this, purposely riding his nerves, the younger man said sharply, "All right, let's not fence, Captain! What did he say?"

"He said yes." The words came out with a leaden flatness, as if Mike felt he was uttering fatal intelligence. Sanders looked at him with disbelief. Then the expression on his face underwent a series of rapid changes, a fleeting frown, a look of amazement or possibly fear, then it broke into a broad smile of surprise that was almost boyishly jubilant.

"By God! Are you sure?"

"Never a doubt about it. Señor Benavides also said you must be a pistol. He sent you good wishes."

Sanders gripped Mike's arm impulsively, his eyes intense. "That's great, man! That's terrific!" He turned and started away, lost in his own whirling thoughts. Mike put out an arm, blocking him.

"Just a minute," he said. "I've done my part."

Sanders' smile was brash and confident. "We made a deal, Captain. Don't worry about it." Then he pushed the arm aside and was gone.

Mike did worry, however. He worried fast, about what his next move would be. The fast conclusion was that he now had no alternative to making a full disclosure to the General.

By the time he had worked his way back to the solarium the old man and Molly were accepting thank-yous from a small mob of departing guests. The evening's bourbon had had its effect and the General gave his hulking aide a benign look which said that all was forgiven, but somehow this didn't make Mike feel any better. When the wave of guests had straggled out, the General said, "Turn to, Captain. Job to do. Go collar Sanders before he gets away. A little chin-chin, you know."

"General, you and me better talk first."

"Look sharp, Mister Hodak. There he is now." The General pushed Mike aside and beckoned to Robert Sanders, who had wandered into the room from the hallway. "Ho there, my friend. Come over, come over." He held out his arm and drew Sanders into the circle. "You know my lady. Molly, you remember this young man." Molly and Sanders exchanged smiles. The General went on. "We're glad you could be with us, old boy. It takes a little mixing around to get the feel of a foreign country. Everything going to suit you?"

At that moment the Clapsaddles strolled up. "Well, there you are," the General called. He turned to Sanders. "Here's someone I want you to meet. My new military attaché and his charming bride."

Clapsaddle stepped forward. In his deliberate, country-man's manner he thrust out his hand.

"Hello, Sanders," he said clearly.

Something about the way he did it was startling. Mike looked quickly from one to the other. Sanders' lips parted slightly. He licked them and untold things reeled through his eyes. For seconds the outstretched hand hung before him in the air. There was a tortured silence. Then with a sudden, jerky motion Sanders grasped the hand.

"Hello, Major."

"Lieutenant Colonel," Clapsaddle said. "I was promoted since I saw you. This is my wife. Edna Mae; this is Robert Sanders."

"How do you do," Mrs. Clapsaddle whispered.

153

"Well, what the devil!" the General said. "The blighters know one another! Small planet, what? How about that, Moll?"

"Mister Sanders and I were in the same division," Clapsaddle said, not taking his eyes off him. "In Viet Nam."

"Well, I'll be jigged!" said the General. Mike kept watching Sanders. His face had taken on the pallor of deep shock, and around the eyes he had the look of a man who has begun to hemorrhage internally from an old lesion. "I will be jigged!" the General exclaimed again. "That calls for a drink. A toast to old shipmates met up in a foreign port. Splice the mainbrace, Mister Hodak!"

Three couples and a stag with hats and wraps, all very gay, barged up just then, shattering the tension with loud, effusive expressions of gratitude. Good-byes caromed all around. One bold, slightly tight female kissed the Ambassador playfully on the cheek. Mike was cut off from Sanders and before order was restored the party started breaking up in earnest. Whole troops of people crowded around, laughing, shaking hands. Detaching himself from the throng, Mike circled, looking for his man. Then out of the corner of his eye he glimpsed Sanders' back as he went through the front doors, beyond the black-and-white foyer.

By the time Mike reached the entrance, Sanders was striding rapidly through the driveway gates onto the *avenida*. Before Mike was halfway to these gates the man had flagged a cab and got into it. Mike arrived at the street, muttering and cursing, in time to watch the taxi disappear in the traffic streaming toward the heart of the city.

As he re-entered the house, Sadie met him at the door, her eyes flashing angrily. "Where did he go? Why did he leave? What are you cooking up, my friend?"

154

Moving around her and heading back to the solarium, Mike said, "He took off like a scalded dog. I don't know why. And I'm not cooking."

The three men, General Gatch, Clapsaddle and Mike Hodak sat in the Embassy library behind closed doors. The last guest had departed and now servants moved through the empty rooms clearing away party debris. Molly and Edna Mae Clapsaddle had retired upstairs to collapse and regroup. Later they would come down and rejoin the men for a light supper.

The General sat with one elbow resting on the library table, stroking his jowl with a finger. The light from the table lamp cut across his florid face as he listened to the strange story Clapsaddle was unfolding.

The General had begun the meeting by outlining concisely for his new attaché the problem which this man Sanders had created by his arrival in San Felipe. Sanders was accused of complicity in a Populista plot to rescue Rafael Benavides. The American Ambassador wished not only to avert an ugly incident involving a U.S. citizen—in the event Machia's accusations were well-founded—but in any case to keep the young American alive and get him out of the country.

At this point Mike interposed the intelligence, gained from Customs Officer Alvaro Rodriguez, that all exits from Maragua were now sealed against Sanders' departure. Something stopped him from revealing the other disturbing bit of information he had acquired this afternoon; that Sanders was actually planning an attempt to rescue Benavides during the junta anniversary celebration on Monday. Something told him he had better learn what Clapsaddle had to say before making this revelation.

In a quiet voice the General summed it up: "You can see

we're pretty much in the dark about the man, Colonel. We planned on having a showdown with him tonight. Your appearance on the scene disturbed him, obviously, since he fled forthwith. Frankly, that leaves us—stumped. I will appreciate any light you can shed. Maybe it will indicate a line of attack out of this mess."

Clapsaddle studied his big rawboned hands for a moment, then glanced up and said, "I'll tell you everything I know, General. Under the circumstances, I consider it my duty, though it surely isn't a pleasure." He spoke in solemn tones. Mike hitched his chair closer in order to catch his words. Strangely he felt a kind of dread to hear what the man was going to say, as though he were about to hear a doctor pronounce a fatal diagnosis upon a friend.

Clapsaddle began: "Lieutenant Robert Sanders first came to my attention over a year ago, in Viet Nam. I was Acting G-4 of my Division at the time. We had been involved in a search-and-destroy operation northwest of Dak To for three weeks. A pretty rough one. It's funny. I read about Sanders before I met him. A citation recommending him for the Silver Star medal had been approved and processed through my section a month before. He had done some very outstanding work in an earlier operation south of Pleiku. Probably saved his platoon from being wiped out when we couldn't get back to them with helicopters or air support for two days because of weather. In spite of a painful wound in his buttocks he formed his men into a perimeter, dug 'em in deep and when they were being overrun, called for artillery fire right on top of his position. That had been done before, but it still took a lot of nerve. And he called for it a second time, and we gave it to him. Laid it right smack on top of him. When the weather cleared and we finally got back to them, we counted thirty-nine dead VC around the perimeter. We lost only three men, and only one of these from our own stuff, that we were sure of, though all of our people were well shook up, as you can imagine."

The Army man paused and looked from one Marine to the other. The General and Mike nodded. This was the account of a commendable piece of professionalism in their trade—a trade in which the ability to improvise and the guts and boldness to take the calculated risk were sometimes more important than the "book."

The Colonel went on: "I was impressed, and when I looked at Sanders' personnel jacket I realized I knew him. Not personally, but about him. I played a little football in college at Texas A&M, and I've kept up pretty well with the Southwest Conference since then. Sanders was first-string defensive half-back for two years at the University of Texas. I saw him play a couple of times. A little light for the job, maybe, but damned good. So, after the decorations were handed out I went around and looked him up. Invited him to eat at the Division mess. I had a little hooch stashed away, and we spent the evening together. Talking football mostly. He seemed to be a hell of a nice guy, though rather quiet and reserved. He talked about his wife, as I remember. Showed me a picture of his baby, who had been born since he'd been in Viet Nam.

"Later, thinking back over that evening, I remembered that he was kind of nervous, quite tense, in fact. Something about him was always moving, fingers, jaw muscles, face muscles. I attached no importance to this at the time. Out there, as you well know, everybody has the jerks of one kind or other. Considering what he had been through, it wasn't unusual."

He paused and looked down and ran the fingers of one hand up and down his forehead for a moment, as though he were reluctant to go on. Neither the General nor Mike broke the silence.

"In a short time, too short, the Division was given another mission. Orders were prepared and issued. Unit Commanders were briefed, all up and down the line."

He paused and closed his eyes and rubbed his chin and neck with his fingers as if thinking how to phrase what he had to say next.

"The night before we were to jump off at daybreak the next morning—Robert Sanders turned in his suit. He just folded up and refused to go back into combat."

Clapsaddle broke off and looked from one face to the other, almost angrily, as though what he had to tell them made him feel ill. The silence was funereal. These were three career professionals. In their iron-clad caste the act which the colonel had just pronounced was the one unpardonable sin a man could commit—and the only one for which there was no acceptable excuse, or penance, or retribution.

The General began to make clucking noises in his throat. With a freckled hand he shaded his eyes from the desk lamp. Clapsaddle compressed his lips and continued:

"Sanders walked into Division HQ about midnight. It was muggy and raining. He was bareheaded, wet and unarmed. I looked up and saw him standing there, and at first I thought he was sick. He shook his head and said he wasn't sick. He told me very simply that he was through fighting and killing people, and that he wasn't going back into combat.

"Well, we worked on him for an hour—everybody, including the Division Commander. We tried everything—pep talk, reason, threats. Nothing had any effect at all. He just sat there, staring at the ground as if he wasn't hearing us, or else didn't give a damn what we were saying."

Clapsaddle kneaded his brow for a moment, then with a gesture of finality he said, "We had a war on our hands and couldn't waste any more time on him. He was turned over to the Medical Officer and psychoed out of action."

He glanced at the General. "Acute psychoneurosis—that's what the doctors call it. It can disable a man as effectively as shrapnel. I'm sure you've experienced it in your commands."

The old man took down his hand and gave a short grunt. "Some. Couldn't afford much of it."

In a voice without expression Clapsaddle wound up his story:

"The man was hospitalized for a couple of months, then he was released from the service. In view of his previous record, no other action was taken. He was considered a battle casualty."

"Someone told me he was divorced a few months after he returned to the States. Then I heard one other thing. A friend of mine at the Pentagon told me that Sanders had applied for active duty again. A very curious request. He asked for extra-hazardous duty. Said that he desired to volunteer for any assignment, in the space program, or whatever, that might result in some benefit to the national interest, but wouldn't ordinarily be undertaken because of the risk involved. Sort of a Kamikaze offer. In view of his history, the request was turned down, of course.

"This business with Rafael Benavides—if there's anything to it—is, I suppose his way of trying to make up for what happened in Viet Nam. An attempt to get back his self-respect."

22

After the Clapsaddles had left and Molly and the General
were surveying left-over whiskey stock and cigarette burns in
the carpeting, Mike wandered back to the library. He was
deeply depressed. He felt, in a way, as he had felt once when
he was a child upon discovering an older boy he admired
taking money out of a blind newsvendor's cigar box. For,
unconsciously, Robert Sanders had begun to assume dimen-
sions in his mind of somebody extraordinary, almost heroic.
He hated the man's guts, and he thought him some way
warped. But still made of genuine metal. And, in spite of
himself, he had begun to admire him. Now his thoughts were
painfully confused. Mike was too much a Marine to view the
ugly incident in Sanders' past with philosophical tolerance.
The canon law on which he had been catechized since youth
was all contained in the Marine Corps Manual, and the basic
tenet of this, the only religion he knew, was that cowardice
was a loathsome, unspeakable thing.

The one consoling thought that came to him was the certainty that there was nothing more to worry about, so far as
Sadie was concerned. Sadie was many things, maybe, that
were not good. But, as the saying went, she was *legítima*. If
Sanders had robbed a bank, she would help him hide the
money, but she wouldn't waste the time of day on a man who
had chickened out. When she learned about him, she would

write him off. Mike felt sure of this. And, most strangely, he felt bad about it.

Ever since Clapsaddle had finished his story Mike had been groping to think of something, feeling way back in the dusty corners of his memory. Then he remembered. After a short search in the library shelves he found a copy of *Moby Dick*. He took the volume down and sat at the table under a cone of light from the lamp. Leafing through the pages he found, finally, the passage he sought. It was written by a man who said what he felt, and what he was sure that the General and Clapsaddle must feel, better than anyone had said it, before or since. He read slowly, tracing out the words with his thick finger:

> . . . It is a thing most sorrowful, nay shocking, to expose the fall of valor in the soul. Men may seem detestable as joint stock companies and nations; knaves, fools, and murderers there may be; men may have mean and meager faces; but man, in the ideal, is so noble and so sparkling, such a grand and glowing creature, that over any ignominious blemish in him all his fellows should run to throw their costliest robes. That immaculate manliness we feel within ourselves, so far within us, that it remains intact though all the outer character seems gone; bleeds with anguish at the undraped spectacle of a valor-ruined man.

He was staring at these sad, majestic lines when the General came into the library. The old gray Marine entered quietly and closed the door behind him. He had an acey-deucey board under his arm.

"I envy any man so composed that he can read a book at a time like this," the General said with asperity. "What in God's name would it be—a funny book?"

Rising, Mike turned the book around on the table and put his finger on the passage that had drawn him to the library. Grunting, the General read, then closed the book and shoved it out of the way. Placing the acey-deucey board in the center of the table, he sat down and began to arrange the men, the reds and the blacks, in their places for battle.

Mike once calculated that he had played in excess of ten thousand games of acey-deucey with Rolla Z. Gatch, some of them on stacked ammunition boxes in a dripping jungle under Jap artillery fire. Mike had won a very small percentage of these, for the old man was a masterful player. To the General, however, acey-deucey was not so much a game as a tranquilizer, an analgesic that gave temporary respite from mental pain and tension. The board and box of buttons were as much a part of his gear as razor and soap.

This night Mike's mind was not on the game at all. The General growled and upbraided him. Twice, with exasperation, he made him recall a stupid move and play it over.

When the third game was well under way the General spoke casually, without looking up: "You don't want to be too hard on your young friend, Gunner. But for a lucky combination of genes or some damn thing, there go I—or you."

The mild pronouncement took Mike by surprise. He put down the dice cup and looked at the General in puzzlement. A common working courage was the first requirement of Rolla Z. Gatch's chosen occupation, and for that matter, of life itself. There had never been any allowance in his creed for weakness in a man's fortitude. Or any acceptable excuse when it faltered. True, his fighting days were behind him now, and he was old and mellowed by all he had seen. Still, the sympathetic, conciliatory tone of his voice now was surprising.

With a sharp complaint the old man snapped him out of his

daze. "Goddammit man, wake up and play!" Mike shook the dice, rolled and moved. The General grasped the dice in his big freckled hand, rolled them, and went on talking in a low, thoughtful voice.

"Courage, also, is partly a matter of early conditioning. Through minor experiences in childhood most men learn that it's better to undergo the pains of being brave than to be safe and cowardly. Numerous small catastrophes are usually involved before the lesson is well learned."

With a precise move he knocked off one of Mike's men and sent him to the boneyard.

"Play up, Captain. In the big experiences, like Sanders', the penalties for not having learned the lesson can be quite severe. Stigma and other punishments for cowardice, including the firing squad, are not designed to help the poor devil who falters, or to reconstruct him, but to scare hell out of the rest of us. To give us a college education in bravery, in a hurry, so we'll be more afraid of the penalties of cowardice than we are of the perils of being brave."

With a flourish he knocked off two more of Mike's men. Then he went on: "It's a pity that's the way it's got to be, because the ones who have faltered, who've chickened out and suffered the agony of disgrace, would likely be among the bravest people we had thereafter—if there were some way to rehabilitate them without breaking down our rather barbaric system. They know the terrible consequences of being branded cowards, and would be determined to prove they are not. Too bad it's a once-and-be-damned proposition."

The game was over and Mike was skunked. He sat back from the table and glowered at the old man, gloomily, doggedly. He said, "Maybe so, General. But for every man that folds up and runs away there are a hundred or a thousand that tough it out. Good kids, scared to death, that go out and do their jobs. You got to give them some credit for that."

As he stacked the red and black discs neatly into the box the old man nodded. "Quite true, Gunner. Most of us have somehow learned how to be brave though scared witless. This is commendable."

He got up rather stiffly. He looked suddenly old and tired. "But remember this, Captain," he said. "Every man can be bought . . . every man has his price of terror." He paused, looking down at the table, then mused softly, more to himself than to Mike, "Sometimes I think our passage through this vale of crocodile tears . . . is a process of learning the unreality of terror."

He slipped the checker box into his coat pocket and tucked the playing board under his arm. Then he leveled his blue eyes at Mike. "As long as a man keeps trying, it's important to see that he doesn't run out of chances." He started away. Without turning around, he grumbled, "You're a lousy acey-deucey player. I don't know why I keep on playing with you." He went through the door and left it open behind him.

23

Mike walked around the corner and down the block and across the street to his place, and went to bed. He felt very bad; too tired, too keyed up, too sunk in depression to sleep. For a long time he lay with his hands under his head, watching the pale patterns of moonlight on the curtains moving in the slight breeze. He was thinking that somewhere in a dark bed Robert Sanders must be turning helplessly in the depths of a tortured memory. There was no place a man could go to hide from himself. Mike thought again of the agony he had seen behind the man's eyes when something blew open the shutters that hid his secret. He thought again of the encounter in the hotel room. The mystery of that was cleared up now, and Sanders, like a man skinned alive, stood raw and fully exposed before the world.

A long while later Mike got up and dressed in the moonlight. He had no plans for going anywhere, or at least he admitted none to himself. It was simply impossible to lie on the bed any longer like a cocked crossbow. He went out of the house and walked down through the dim, moonlit *calles* under the palm trees, following no particular route, but going always in the general direction of Archie Pringle's house.

Archie's place stood on a corner facing a small plaza with flowers and a statue in a very old part of the city. His house was an architecturally perfect Spanish Colonial town-house, rendered in miniature. It had been built, so the legend went, for the mistress of a rich *hidalgo* in the days of the Viceroys. Its walled patio, beautiful tiled floors and carved cedar woodwork had been restored by Archie, who modernized the place into a little gem of a bachelor apartment with eighteenth-century atmosphere and twentieth-century plumbing.

Strolling into the silver-shadowed plaza, Mike went along its walks of crushed shell. He peered into the darkness looking for a light behind the barred and shuttered windows of Archie's house, but there was none. He was halfway across the plaza when he saw the car, a dark shape under the shadows of the palms along the street.

A cigarette glowed red inside the car and he stopped. He

felt almost sure this was the same Chevrolet that passed his house in the afternoon. It required no Indian scout to read the sign. Machia's men were on the trail, and Sanders was inside the house.

Treading softly, he carefully retraced his steps out of the silent plaza. In the next ten minutes he walked south one block, then two blocks west through dark streets, then he cut back north one block and presently came cautiously up a street approaching Archie's house from the rear. Pausing in deep shadows, he looked ahead toward the plaza. The car was still there, and the cigarette inside glowed faintly at regular intervals. One of its occupants was a nicotine nut.

Archie's house extended a distance along the side street. The building then elled inward while the high wall enclosing the patio continued on to the rear of the property. Mike could make out a heavy door set in this wall. The door, he knew, led into a laundry yard, then through an archway into the patio. Tattered fronds of a large banana tree inside the patio extended over the wall. These leaves reflected a faint glow from a light somewhere beyond the wall. The same source of light, Mike mused, undoubtedly illuminated his unhappy "friend" in his nocturnal anguish.

The streets were deserted at this hour. There was no traffic, no sound. Turning up his coat lapels to hide his white shirt, and shielding his moon-reflecting face with an arm, Mike moved silently across the street and stopped at the door in the wall. It was made of heavy timber strapped with iron, and was locked. For moments he stood in the black shade of the doorway, wondering why he didn't just go on home and mind his own business. He was in the process of doing that, when, halfway down the block, he passed a pile of rubble, refuse from a house-remodeling. Scraps of lumber, tin and broken plaster made up the pile. He felt around among the rubble until his hand came upon a piece of two-by-four perhaps three feet long and sawed to a point at one end. He eased it carefully from the pile.

The idea that grew out of this discovery was too tempting not to try. With the length of two-by-four in hand he retraced his steps along Archie's wall until he passed the door and stood under the overhanging banana tree. Without thinking, he found himself bracing the thick board against the wall, pointed end pressed into the ground. It made a crude but serviceable step. When he placed a foot on the square upper end, he found that he could ease himself cautiously upward and reach the wall top with his fingers.

The tops of patio walls in San Felipe are studded with sharp spears of glass, shards of broken bottles, jars and panes which were imbedded in the wet mortar when the walls were built. The practice is supposed to discourage thieves, at least stupid thieves. A brief reconnaissance with his fingertips revealed to Mike that this wall was so armored. Stepping back down to the ground, he took off his coat. Folding it lengthwise, he stepped up on the two-by-four again and looped the coat carefully over the top of the wall as a protective mat. Then he bounced lightly on the step to be sure it was solid, poised, and with surprising agility for a big man, sprang upward. Catching the wall top with his fingers, he chinned himself, then hooked the heel of one foot over the ledge. Then he fought his way upward, managing with a temendous effort to gain the top and throw himself across it. Through the padding of his coat the shards of glass gouged into his belly but did not cut him. A moment later he dropped down into a soft flowerbed on the other side and leaned back against the wall, breathing hard from the exertion.

The patio was a small square garden of tropical plants and climbing flowers, set into the ell of the house. Across a terrace were leaded glass doors leading into the *sala*. Through this doorway came the faint light Mike had seen from the street.

Moving silently onto the terrace, Mike tried the door. It opened. He entered and surveyed his surroundings. He was in a room of pleasing proportions, furnished in the austere, carved-wood-and-leather furniture of the colonial period. A single iron chandelier overhead cast shadows that deepened in the corners of the room. For a moment he didn't see Sanders. Then a noise drew his glance to the large chair facing the cold fireplace at the end of the room. As he watched, an arm and a hand holding a bottle of whiskey appeared from behind the chair. The occupant of the chair set the bottle down hard upon the tile floor.

"Sanders?"

There was no answer. Then Robert Sanders lurched out of the chair and wheeled around it. He held onto the chair with one hand to steady himself. His jaw was slack, his eyes glazed, his face a sagging mask. He was deeply drunk.

"Get out of here," Sanders said in a thick voice.

Ignoring this, Mike crossed to the small bar, which Archie kept well-stocked. "I guess I'll just have myself a little drink," he said.

"Get out," Sanders snarled, "or I'll throw you out."

"Take it easy," Mike said, splashing Scotch into a glass. Then he moved to a chair, a modern piece made of reeds and wrought iron and fashioned in the shape of a clam shell. Settling into this, he set his glass on the floor and loosened his tie. "When I finish the drink you can throw me out," he said mildly, "if you think you're big enough."

For seconds Sanders stood swaying in the half light, head

lowered like a bull ready to charge, his eyes working to focus. For that short space Mike half expected the man to come at him. Then Sanders whirled and flung himself down into the big chair again. His hand went over the side and grabbed the bottle.

In the ensuing silence Mike sipped his drink dismally, frowning as he reflected upon this universal signal of defeat, when a man's misery becomes too great to bear—the blind, stumbling flight into the delusive refuge of alcohol. After a long time he gave a slight start when the hoarse voice behind the chair broke the utter quiet. The words came bitter and mocking and slurred together.

"No doubt Clapsaddle filled in background for you. Didn't satisfy you? What'd you come here for?"

For several seconds Mike did not answer, but sat rubbing his fingers over the hills and valleys of his nose. Then he said, "I've been asking myself the same question. I'm damned if I know."

24

When the night was over he had Robert Sanders' story, torn out by the roots with the man's own hands. Mike wondered, with suspicion of guilt, if the real reason he had come here was not to gloat over the humiliation of this stranger, who had taken so easily, almost off-handedly, the thing he wanted so badly and could never touch. But no, he told himself, he was here because it was duty, and maybe even because he wanted to help a poor bastard who was in a deep hole, and alone. Still, he knew it could have been the other thing.

Sanders' story didn't come all at once, and there was no order to it, for the drunken recollections snarled and mumbled at Mike during the long night were the tortured confessions of a man at the limits of agony, unconnected, half-delirious explosions of anguish that lapsed, toward morning, into stupor and silence.

There is something as delusively attractive as alcohol about spilling human troubles into other human ears, even when the trouble is beyond human help. There is in the simple act of telling some temporary relief from pain. So it was that once started, Sanders' words spilled out of him until it was all said, and Mike had seen the man laid open to the raw, palpitating heart.

When the wandering tale began, the younger man spoke in a low, rasping voice, as though each separate word sickened him. Did the Captain have any conception of how it felt to become nauseated, physically ill at the sound of a military band? Did the Captain know what it was like to hate men he had never seen before, when he found out they had been out there, too, and had stuck out their time? No, of course he didn't. A stupid question. Well, he Robert Sanders, could tell him: it was like a foretaste on earth of everlasting hell to come.

This crazy talk came from behind the high back of the cedar-and-leather viceroy chair. Hidden from Mike's view, Sanders plunged on, scathingly. The Captain couldn't possibly appreciate little matters like that, because he was a brave Marine. All Marines were brave. He saw it in a picture show. Did the Captain know that he, Robert Sanders, was the son of a brave Marine? Well, he damn sure was. His father was killed on Guadalcanal one month and five days before he, Robert Tillman Sanders, was born. A real genuine hero he was, too. At least that is what he had been fed, along with cod liver oil and Wheaties, when he was a kid. Sometimes he wondered if it wasn't all just a bunch of conglomerate family crap. Just as likely his male parent had been cringing and crying in a stinking swamp when the Jap bullet zapped him. That was one advantage of being zapped. It made heroes out of cowards.

His voice became quieter then. It took on a far-off sound, and for a little while he seemed to gain clarity.

"I was raised by a house full of split-tails. Three women. My mother, her sister and their mother—my grandmother— and me, under one roof. *And* the household deity, my father's ever-present ghost. Wonder I didn't go nuts. Picture of my father in every room, kind of like a shrine. His bravery and red-blooded Christian American virtue grew so big I began to think he was a saint—too *good* to live. Found out when I was eighteen or nineteen that he married my mother a week before he went overseas, after his girl turned him down. Guess he figured he had to marry somebody."

As long as Robert Sanders could remember he had been his mother's big man. He never cried—she did enough of that for both of them—though he felt like crying plenty of times. But he didn't. He had a 5 A.M. and 4 P.M. paper route, hustled groceries at the A&P on Saturdays and in the summers. People said he was fine boy, and he began to believe them. In fact he began to believe that if you kept on going along, holding in the tears, being a fine boy, someday you'd turn out to be the President of the United States. Or at least president of the gas company or the First National Bank.

He earned the Eagle Scout rating. That just naturally went with the kind of boy he was. He was strong, had good legs, and when he put on weight in high school and made the all-city football team, some businessmen got together and sent him to college. It was a patriotic civic enterprise, helping such a fine youngster, son of a deceased war hero, etc. It also gave his sponsors a feeling they were racking up some merit-badge points with the Great Scoutmaster themselves.

At some break in this bitter recital Sanders had lurched out of his chair and retreated into a dark corner of the room where he wedged himself between a chair and bookshelf, glowering at Mike like a sick animal. He clutched the nearly empty bottle in one hand. His shirt was unbuttoned halfway down the front, and the sleeves were unbuttoned. The electric bulbs, like little candle flames, glimmered forlornly in the iron chandelier and cast shadows that masked the deep misery in his eyes.

"I didn't invite you here, Captain," he said in a sarcastic voice. "You asked for this. All right. I'm going to tell you things that'll make your flesh crawl with shame, because you're a brave Marine." The scorn in his voice wasn't meant for Mike; he was punishing himself, hard. He lunged on, winding back through his life.

He played football at Texas, knocked his brains out, and gave his sponsors something for their money they could understand and appreciate. Summers, he had a job as counselor at a boy's camp near Kerrville. During his last summer there he met a girl. At a camp dance. When he began to talk about the girl his voice lost its harshness, became almost gentle, as though he were talking about half-forgotten things he wasn't sure had happened.

She was a fine girl. Good-looking, down-to-earth. Her daddy was a hustling country boy who had got lucky, then rich, trading in real estate, and she wasn't impressed by it. Her family had a summer place on the Guadalupe River. She was a

Pi Phi and a Blue Bonnet Belle and all that at Texas, one of the big girls on campus, not because she wanted to be but just because she was a hell of a woman. Warm, lovely, funny and fine.

He made all-conference defensive halfback his senior year. Then, right after graduation, they were married. Big wedding in San Antone. He went to work for her old man, a mistake to begin with. Then the draft was breathing down his neck. With a little effort he could have got into one of those one-drill-a-week National Guard outfits or signed on as a reserve medical corpsman for week-end duty at the local air base. But the old household deity was breathing down his neck, too. He didn't enlist because he had some serious reservations about what we were doing in Viet Nam in the first place. But he didn't dodge it. He just stood stock-still and let 'em draft him. Do it the hard way and get it over with. Take his chances and hope for the best.

He came out of the corner. His head was down and the dim light put shadows in his face that made him look years older than he was. It was painful to watch him. Sanders walked to the patio door, taking the careful, overprecise steps of a proud man deeply drunk. He stopped in the doorway, steadying himself against the door frame with an arm. His back was turned and he stared out into the darkness as he went on talking.

He was a sergeant by the time he got to Viet Nam, and a good one. He was a good team player, gung-ho, *esprit de corps* and all that. He tried to buy what they were selling: that communism had to be stopped somewhere, and this was the place. A few months passed. He was platoon sergeant of a rifle platoon that was in and out of combat, mainly on recon patrols, dropping into an area by helicopter, making a sweep and hopping out again. They had a few brushes with Charlie, but it wasn't bad. Twelve months of this and he could go home and somebody else could take over the job of stopping communism.

He turned and faced Mike. "Then it got hairy. I mean dirty. This time they dropped us right in the middle of a North Vietnamese regiment. All hell broke loose. Platoon leader was killed in first fifteen minutes, and it was my baby. The weather closed in and we lost air support. Choppers couldn't come back to us. We dug in and did the best we could. I spent the longest night of my life about fifteen feet from a little brown bastard —lying on open ground, in front of our perimeter. He was hit bad. His bowels kept oozing out into the mud. He kept tucking 'em back in. It was raining hard. When it lightened or a flare went up, he and I looked at one another. He kept whining and jabbering at me. Couldn't have been more than seventeen. I didn't understand the words, but I knew what he was telling me. He was begging me to shoot him. Kept making his hands like a gun, then pointing at his head. Then he would put his hands together like he was praying to me. He was really begging. He was in bad pain and he cried in the dark, like a child. I knew he couldn't live. When a flare went up I couldn't take it any more. I raised my rifle. He saw me and nodded his head. Yeah, yeah! He smiled, like he was thanking me. So I shot him."

After this recital Robert Sanders swigged deeply on the bottle and began to laugh to himself. He sang bits of a tuneless, unintelligible song. The rest came in bursts of anguished, disconnected talk which Mike pieced together.

The choppers finally came for them, and they got out. He was given a battlefield commission and a Purple Heart for some splinters in his ass, and took over the platoon.

Back at base the gung-ho began to wear off. He had seven

174

months left to go and he knew he would never make it. He knew it in his bones. And he would leave another little hard-luck case to be raised by a house full of split-tails, or a new daddy, or somebody, and what was it all about anyway? What screwy kind of national logic had put him, Robert Tillman Sanders, who wasn't mad at anybody, in this stinking Viet Nam in the first place, ten thousand miles from all he cared about in the world? Nobody had bombed Pearl Harbor or sunk any of our ships. Nobody was attacking San Francisco or marching on San Antone. And how smart were those jokers up in Washington, D.C., who said it was the same as if they *were* marching on San Antone? And that if we hadn't jumped into this fight between the Vietnamese people we'd be in danger of losing our own liberty? How the hell did they know? They were just a bunch of theory-happy college professors. And they were fooling around with his *life!* The only one he'd ever have on this ball. The hell with that!

A conviction had been growing in him that we had made a monumental national goof. We had stuck our foot into something, and then had got sucked in up to our necks in a big war we shouldn't be fighting at all. The Commies in the Kremlin were rolling on the floor laughing about it, and we were too proud or hidebound or stupid to get ourselves out of it.

If somebody was coming over your fence, or even your borders, that was one thing. But if *they* were using *him,* and betting his life on it, to prove they hadn't made a bonehead move in coming over here in the first place—the hell with that! He should give his life as a campaign contribution to the next election? The hell with that old jazz! And now they didn't act like they had any real conviction about what they were doing anyway. They were caught in a trap and would lose face if they admitted it was all a mistake—and so he would go on shooting little pongee-colored bastards in black pajamas until one of them shot him. In order to make the world safe for the motor car, sports, TV, the filter cigarette, and that fine, light brew, which totaled up to the cultural and spiritual values of our hallowed American Way of Life at the latest reading. Bullshit! We had become a nation of slobs, and we surely got what we deserved in the way of leaders. Well, not for him!"

Frowning at the floor between his feet, Mike murmured, "I—don't know, Robert. You've been standing mighty close to the trees."

Not hearing him, Sanders rambled on. For the first time, in a rainstorm in a Vietnamese jungle, he had seen things clearly, in focus. The thought of spilling his guts on this muddy ground, out here ten thousand miles from home, suddenly became complete and preposterous insanity!

So when they tried to send him back, he quit. He just flat quit.

They put one of his good buddies, a boy named Knox off a ranch in New Mexico, in his place, and the war went on without him. The ranch boy was killed two days later.

Sanders rolled suddenly to a sitting position and glared unsteadily at Mike. His voice was gritty. "I am here, my good friend, because I had the sense to run away from combat. A dumb sergeant named Knox lost his life because he didn't have sense enough to run with me!"

Wiping his hand spastically across his face he mumbled, "I finished my military career in a blaze of shit! But I'm alive and he's not, the dumb bastard. Now who's better off? You tell me. Never mind. The rest is real pretty, too."

When he got home to his wife and curly-haired baby, they thought he was a real hero. He had medals. Her old man took him to the Country Club and bragged to his friends like *he* had been out there.

Along in here his voice dropped almost out of hearing. "How do you think it is to have a pretty woman's touch burn you? Like acid? Or to want to run away from your own little boy?" He staggered across the room and held onto the patio door again, then he went back to the couch. His voice began to moan, as though a cold wind were blowing through him.

The clarity with which he saw things out there had got all fuzzed up back home. He wanted to tell her about it, to explain. But how could you explain? All that out there—it was unreal to the people at home—like a TV show. His only allies and "soul brothers" were a bunch of hippies and "flower people" he wouldn't be caught dead with. He started drinking, to try to drown out the shame and confusion.

Totally in the dark, his wife was understanding, up to a point. When he couldn't take it any longer, he broke with her old man. Then a doubt began to creep into his mind. He began to wonder if he wasn't just plain old-fashioned yellow: chicken-hearted. This came near to driving him nuts. He took a job with an oil-well firefighter out of Houston. He looked across at Mike and laughed, softly, derisively. That was supposed to be real dangerous work. Couldn't buy insurance. This way he'd prove that what he did out there wasn't a lack of guts, but a matter of principle.

His wife didn't understand him at all, but he couldn't explain. Drinking like he was, she said he was throwing his life away, and theirs, too. Sanders shook his head sorrowfully as the memory crowded in on him.

"But she stuck with me. So I started shacking up with whores, and let her know about it, to see if I couldn't make her hate me. It worked real well. I didn't contest the divorce. She and Robbie were my life. I threw them away like garbage."

"You could get 'em back," Mike Hodak said.

"With what?" said Robert Sanders.

The oil-well firefighting wasn't the answer, either. It didn't prove anything. Too damned impersonal. Nobody was trying to kill him.

He stayed drunk for a long time after that. A year, off and on. Got to be a real rum-bum, booked for vagrancy in half a dozen jails. But whiskey didn't cure what was hurting him, and after a while it didn't even take his mind off the pain. He was too strong, physically, to drink himself to death. It would have taken too long. He got to know this crackpot Sanchez in New Orleans. Sanchez was a drunk, too. Told him about Rafael Benavides and the Populistas, in this country that Sanders knew only as a vague name in a geography book. It looked like what he had been waiting for. They didn't pay him anything. He'd have paid them for the chance.

Sanders stopped a while, then, in a hoarse, exhausted voice, he said, "Never thought I'd run into anybody . . . like Sadie. I could love her, Captain, if I . . ." He didn't finish the sentence, but heaved a deep painful sigh, then added, "And I didn't figure on meeting up with . . . anybody from out . . . like Major Clapsaddle."

He hauled himself to his feet and turned up the bottle, spilling whiskey down his shirtfront. Swaying, peering at Mike through raw eyelids, he snarled with sudden viciousness. "Now go home, brave Captain. You've heard all there is to hear. Go home, goddammit!" Mumbling an obscenity, he fell back on the couch and rolled over, and covered his head with his arms.

After a while Mike hauled himself out of the giant clam-shell chair and went to the bar and poured another Scotch. It went down like lye-water. He walked slowly around the edges of the room, feeling bitter to his bones and wondering why he drank the swill. At the open door he stopped and spat copiously into the dark patio. He felt helpless, the way a man feels who is trying to console somebody whose child has died. Still, he had to do something. It was one of those junctures in life at which it was impossible merely to shrug and do nothing. Because when you gave up on a man, you were over the hill yourself.

Setting his glass on the carved mantlepiece, he walked over and shoved some ashtrays and magazines out of the way and sat down on the leather top of the coffee table next to the couch. He sat gloomily for a long time, frowning at the form before him.

As he watched, a kind of writhing spasm went through Sanders' frame, as though he had been wracked with a sudden pain. Impulsively, Mike laid his hand on Sanders' shoulder and gave him a shake. It was a gesture that said, "When it can't get any worse, it's got to get better."

Then something the General had said, about every man having his price, came to him. It was something to begin with.

Galling his throat clear, Mike said, "You're taking it too hard, Mac." He spoke in a low voice, as he would have to a broken-hearted youth who fumbled his big chance in a football game. "You're just a man, and every man has a breaking point. There's not five cents' difference between any two of us. Most of us live out our lives without really being tested. Three-fourths of us would bust out if we were." The words sounded stilted and feeble in his own ears.

Sanders twisted his neck back and forth and spoke into the cushions in a muffled voice, "You just don't . . . understand the problem. You can't . . . run away. That's all. You can't."

The words had a set and worn sound, as though he had

been over all of this ten thousand times, had argued the case with himself until the heart had gone out of him and he could argue no more.

Cursing his clumsiness, Mike tried again. "So you cracked? Jesus Christ! Nothing is final as long as you're kicking. You know now that running away is worse than what you ran from. You wouldn't run again. Any man is entitled to make a mistake, if he'll learn by it."

Struggling up, Sanders howled, "I didn't *make* a mistake! You sound like a retarded Sunday School teacher!" With a sudden motion he rolled over, almost falling off the couch. Then he sat up unsteadily, facing Mike. Not more than a foot separated the two men. Sanders fought to focus his eyes. His breath was rank with alcohol. He said, "Talk! Talk! Talk is nothing. Action! That's the only thing. That's why I'm here."

A telephone bell cut the silence that followed these unanswerable words. Sanders kept looking at Mike, eyes swimming. There was little doubt who the caller was. The phone kept up its insistent ringing, as though Sadie had the power to inject her own intensity into the sound. Sanders didn't move except for the slight swaying of his body.

The caller did not give up easily, and after some time Mike said, "The damn phone is ringing."

Sanders said, "Let the sonofabitch ring."

Finally it quit. Then Sanders spoke again, his head down between his hands. His voice was cold and lifeless. "I should have known . . . it wouldn't be . . . better here than anywhere else. . . ." His words faded into incoherence. He rolled over and turned his back to Mike, burying his face in the cushions.

Off and on during the rest of the night he mumbled other things, most of which Mike could not understand. Once he broke out laughing wildly, or it may have been crying, Mike was not sure which. Mike had a couple more drinks, sunk in the giant clam chair, drinking the stuff because he didn't know what else to do.

One thing that Sanders said he did understand. Sitting up suddenly, Sanders pointed a weaving finger at Mike and spoke angrily, as though recounting an injustice done him.

"Knox . . . the lucky bastard. Peacefully dead. All over. Settled."

Mike felt like saying "How do you know it's peaceful? What makes you think anything is settled?" But before he could form thoughts into words Sanders had caved in and fallen back into the cushions.

During his long vigil the rest of the night Mike drifted off in a light restless sleep. Then the telephone bell woke him with a start. Outside the sky was beginning to gray. Dampness with an edge of chill came through the open door. He was stiff and cold.

The telephone rang a long time, demanding to be answered. When it finally quit Mike hauled himself up and went over and tried to rouse Robert Sanders and get him into a bed. After he had given him several shakes Sanders threw himself around in a spasm of motion and took a wild swing at Mike with his fist. Then he fell back heavily. The blow didn't connect, but Mike felt the breeze. Under his breath he said, "The hell with you," and went to the bedroom and got a blanket and threw it over the inert form.

Then he went through the patio and let himself out the wall door into the street.

It was getting light now. The smell of charcoal fires in kitchen braziers was coming in the air. Mike walked stiffly up the street toward the plaza, feeling the hard years he had lived.

The black Chevrolet was still there, and he walked right past it, too tired to care whether the occupants recognized him or not. They were Machia's boys, all right. One of them was asleep, his head back on the seat, his mouth open. The one under the wheel was awake. His face was deeply pitted with smallpox scars, and his eyes were haggard for sleep. As he saw Mike cross the street he gave a visible start and shook his partner.

Touching the brim of his hat, Mike said, *"Buenos días, jefes"* and walked around the car. He could feel their eyes on his back and hear their angry, startled talk as he headed across the plaza toward his house.

25

Mike Hodak slept fitfully and awoke with a headache. Splinters of sunlight coming through the blinds hurt his eyes. From the angle of the light he could tell it was past noon.

As he lay there, unable to go back to sleep yet too tired and depressed to get up, Mike asked himself again why he concerned himself with Robert Sanders. The man's troubles were not his. He had tried to help him and so had discharged his duty. Beyond this there was no reason why it should make a damn to him what Sanders did or what happened to him— except as it affected Sadie Flippo. And Mike felt sure there was no longer cause to worry on that score. A man has nothing to feed a woman with when his pride is gone. Yet all through his restless sleep Mike had tossed and fretted as though he had assumed personal responsibility for Robert

Sanders, and as a consequence had taken a share of the man's misery unto himself.

After a time he faced the inevitable and hauled himself out of bed. Half an hour later, somewhat revived by a cold shower and a cup of Nestor's strong coffee, he made his way on foot dismally along the tree-shaded streets toward the Embassy residence. On Saturday afternoon the Ambassador would likely be at home.

As he turned the corner onto the *avenida* he stopped. Across the street from the Embassy stood the black Chevrolet, occupied by Machia's two secret policemen. Their attention was focused on the big pink house. The one under the wheel spotted Mike. He punched his partner and pointed.

Mike was puzzled. He couldn't understand what they were doing here. Had they stopped tailing Sanders? For a second he thought they were now after him, but that didn't make sense. He walked casually past the car, ignoring the occupants.

As he turned up the drive under the palms a wave of emotion elevatored through his chest. Just beyond the front door stood Sadie's Cadillac convertible. He quickened his pace, narrowing his eyes and clamping his jaws. If Machia had put his goons on Sadie's tail some international relations were going to get fractured and probably a couple of skulls.

Entering the black-and-white foyer he saw the General. The old man was standing in the doorway of the solarium. For seconds the General glared at him indignantly, like a school principal confronting a truant. Then he turned and strode across the room to a small table on which an acey-deucey board was open and manned for play. With a silent command he pointed to the chair opposite. Mike hesitated, then with reluctant obedience he crossed the room and sat down. The General rolled the dice.

This was one day Mike was in no mood for acey-deucey.

But he was trapped and so he resigned himself to it. There was nothing he could do for or about Sadie at the moment anyway. She was somewhere around the house he supposed, probably upstairs with Molly, weeping over her fallen prince.

After they had played a while in silence the General spoke in sarcastic, slightly peevish tones: "It doesn't really matter that I don't know what the bloody hell is going on. After all I'm only the Ambassador. But I do think my associates would try to keep me posted, just as a matter of courtesy."

Mike grumbled something apologetic. Then he briefly recounted his night with Robert Sanders. He informed the General about Machia's bloodhounds, who even now were on a scent, right across the street. The General's clucking noises started up angrily. So they were, were they? Well, Colonel Machia was about to press his luck a little too far. Mike could tell that the old man was building to a general-sized rage about this.

The old Marine won the first game before Mike got a man off the board, and Mike reflected dismally that, on top of everything else, he couldn't even play a decent game of acey-deucey anymore. He wished again that he had never heard of this fouled-up country.

"Dammit, General," he said, throwing his dice cup onto the board, "I'd rather be back in Viet Nam, or Bougainville. Rain, rot and all. At least we were doing something!"

The old man's face brightened as the thought distracted his anger. A quick look of youth crossed the light blue eyes. "You can say that, because you don't have to go back. As I recall, you bellyached the whole way." But it was apparent that the thought appealed to Rolla Z. Gatch also. They were doing something in those times and places that had the taste of importance, and the hard edge of purpose.

184

After the second game was under way Molly came in and stood quietly behind Mike. When he became aware of her, he started to get up, but she restrained him gently and put her arms around his thick neck and gave him a hug. She said, "How's my boy?"

Mike said, "All right, Molly. I guess."

"He's been bitching because he's not immortal," the General said with ridicule. "He wants to go back and live the good times all over again."

With a twinkle Molly said, "What's wrong with that? I'd like it myself. Wouldn't you?"

"Play, please, Captain," said the General with a patient sigh.

His mind completely off the game, Mike rolled the dice and said to Molly, "How's Sadie doing?"

"Sadie? I wouldn't know. Is something wrong?" she said.

"She's here, isn't she?"

"Why—no, I don't think so. At least I haven't seen her. Not since last night."

Mike came out of his chair with a suddenness that flipped up the acey-deucey board, scattering checkers all over the floor. The General let out a pained roar, but Mike paid no attention. Grasping Molly's arms Mike looked her hard in the eyes.

"Are you *sure* she isn't here?"

"I haven't seen her," Molly said, a shadow of fear crossing her face. "I've been at home all day . . ."

Setting her aside like a small doll, Mike took off for the front entrance. Outside he ran the dozen steps to the Cadillac convertible. When he opened the door he saw the envelope, fastened to the red leather seat with Scotch tape. On the envelope, in Sadie's familiar, schoolgirl hand was the single word *Mike*. Ripping the envelope apart, he pulled out the folded sheet and read:

Amigo:
I'm sorry for all the bad times. Forgive me if you can.
This is the main chance for me. I'm going with Robert
Sanders. I know all about him. The past is not important.
What he can be in the future is all that matters. He
needs somebody and I can be that somebody. We are
flying out from Barranco. Please try not to hate me.
Sadie

For a moment Mike stood in stunned silence. Then he walked on legs of wood back to the entrance, staring at the note, leaving the car door open. The Chevrolet across the street had started up as he came running out of the door. The driver was revving the engine nervously. This sound brought Mike out of his fog. The two unshaven men were leaning forward, watching him, holding the car ready to go, like a high-strung horse at the post. Then the light broke on Mike, as through a sudden rift in the overcast. These men were there—because Robert Sanders had come here, with Sadie. What he couldn't now fathom was why the men hadn't followed the two of them away, when they left for Barranco.

Sadie's copper mining company had a landing strip at Barranco, and a Beechcraft. The Beech had plenty of range to fly the pair out of the country. With all normal exits closed to Sanders, that was one sure way he could escape, from Maragua and from Machia's lethal, pride-strung wrath. Provided they could shake Machia's secret policemen and get to Barranco.

But how? Here stood Sadie's car, and over there sat the two men who had doubtless been ordered to follow Sanders, and kill him if necessary to prevent his escape. Was it possible that he and Sadie were, at this moment, somewhere inside the sanctuary of the Embassy, without Molly knowing it? These thoughts churned at his brain as Mike turned into the house. He ran straight into the General, with Molly right behind.

Without a word Mike shoved Sadie's note into the old man's hand and went around him toward the kitchen. In the serving pantry he found Julio, the *mayor domo,* polishing silver. In harsh tones that brought a startled look to the man's face, Mike began to question him. Had he seen the Señora Flippo? Had he seen a man with her, a man with close-cropped brown hair? Had anyone come to the Embassy today that he didn't know? Anyone at all?

To all of these questions the *mayor domo* answered a pained, "No, Señor. No, Señor. No, Señor."

"*Seguro?*"

"*Seguro,* Señor."

Seizing the man by the arm, Mike hustled him into the big kitchen where the cook and a helper were disinfecting vegetables. He put the same questions to them and received the same wide-eyed answers. Then he sent the *mayor domo* racing up the back stairs to get the upstairs maid. When she came down, breathless and frightened, she swore that she knew no more than the others. All knew Señora Flippo well, but none had seen her since last night. No one had seen anyone answering Robert Sanders' description.

Striding into the solarium, he found the General waving the note in Molly's face and trying to explain the situation to her in the tones of an approaching thunderstorm. Mike was baffled and fit to start breaking things. Then, through the windows of the solarium, at the rear of the Embassy grounds, he saw the bent and bony figure of Zapo, the old gardener, kneeling in the grass along a walk, digging in a bed of caladiums. Mike charged through the leaded glass doors and out into the garden. When he approached the old man and called his name, Zapo looked up. He took off his battered straw hat, revealing the lank white hair, sweat-pasted across his skull. He didn't get up. It was understood by all that once Zapo was down, crawling among his flowers, he was down for the day. Often he had to be helped to his feet at night when his work was done.

"Señor?" the old gardener said.

"*Oye, Zapo,*" Mike said quickly. "*Has visto una señorita? Una gringa, muy linda? Con pelo corto?*"

"*Una señorita, linda? Pelo corto?*" A quizzical look came over the old, leathery face. Then his face cracked into a wide grin, revealing yellow stumps of teeth and red gums. "*Ah, sí, Capitán. Una señorita, muy linda.*" He beamed and shook his head with satisfaction. "*Linda! Linda!*"

"Where?" Mike pressed him. "When?"

"Here, *Capitán.*" Zapo moved a gnarled finger slowly along the stone walk leading to the rear gate of the grounds. "She passed by when I was working compost into the lily beds."

"When was that, Zapo? At what hour?" Mike said, straining against exasperation.

"At what hour?" The old man frowned, "I cannot be sure. It was after the anemones and before the caladiums. When the sun was—here." He poked a finger at the sky. Mike judged he meant about ten o'clock.

"Now look, Zapo," Mike squatted beside him and looked closely into the yellow-amber eyes. "Was the señorita alone? Or was there a man with her?"

"Oh, there was a man with her, *Capitán.*"

"What kind of man, Zapo? How did he look?"

The old man moved his head back and forth and rolled his

eyes. Then he gave a high-pitched giggle. "A fine *caballero*, no doubt, *Capitán*, but—*un poco borracho!*"

"Drunk!" Mike muttered angrily, getting up. "That's the bastard!"

"They went . . . there, *Capitán*." Zapo pointed to the rear gate of the garden.

Giving the old man a pat on the head, Mike ran down the walk, around the fishpool and through the rose arbor. Then he came to the tall, iron-barred gate that opened onto the back street. It was a quiet street lined with eucalyptus trees. He halted outside the gate. Throwing a glance up and down the street he saw it was empty, except for an *ama* pushing a baby carriage through the dappled sunlight.

The thing was plain, simple. Sadie had picked up Sanders at Archie's, in the convertible. Then she had brought him here to the Embassy. She had parked the Cadillac in front, to fix Machia's people on a point. Next she and Sanders had walked straight through the big house, through the garden and out the back gate, unnoticed by anyone but Zapo. Then they had taken off in another car, probably one she had borrowed from her sister and parked there herself, in advance.

All of this had happened, Mike guessed, four or five hours ago. Barranco was a six-hour drive from San Felipe. In another hour they would be buckled into the mining company Beechcraft, skimming down the mountain runway between the high peaks of the Andes and headed for—what?

As he ran back toward the house his emotions were getting out of hand, inflamed and swollen, full of fury, jealousy and despair. The General stood in the doorway. Unwilling to risk speech Mike merely looked at the old man and swept his arm toward the back gate. The General understood. Just behind him stood Molly, her eyes glistening with tears.

After a minute of walking around aimlessly in the solarium, Mike stopped and said, "I guess I'll go to Barranco, sir."

"What will you do when you get there?"

"I don't know. I'll probably be too late. But I guess I'll go."

The General put his arm through Mike's. Then he walked with him to the front of the house. His voice was deep and quiet, as though he understood that this was his old friend's personal battle. "However you want to play it, Mike. If I can help, let me know."

Mike flashed the older man a look of gratitude. Molly planted a quick kiss on his cheek, then he went out the front door. The keys were in Sadie's car. The gas tank was nearly full. As he powered the Cadillac out of the drive and whipped right down the *avenida,* he saw one of the secret policemen jump from the Chevrolet to the curb. That one would stay behind to cover the Embassy. The other man threw the old sedan into a whining start and knifed into the traffic after Mike as he sent the big convertible whistling toward the center of the city.

26

Losing the secret police agent was not easy. The man with the scarred face drove the Chevrolet through the streets like a Cossack. It was only after leaving the city and getting onto the open highway that Mike could pull away from him.

He purposely took the route away from the mountains. Heading south on the down coast road he let the big car out and was hitting a hundred when the first village beyond the airport came in sight. Slowing into the S-curve on the outskirts of the village he momentarily lost sight of his pursuer in the mirror. Moments later he braked into a skidding turn off the main road and rolled to a stop in the shadows of dirty pink houses a block down a side street. Less than a minute later the old Chevrolet went roaring through the village doing seventy.

Mike waited two minutes, then turned around and headed back the way he had come. Nearing the city he turned off to the right on a dirt road that cut through truck farms behind the airport. Presently he came out on the Barranco highway. Here he waited another five minutes, to make sure he was not being followed. Then he turned onto the highway toward the mountains and shoved his foot to the floor.

For thirty miles out of San Felipe the narrow asphalt road cuts straight through a flat patchwork of cotton and alfalfa fields, then it begins to twine like a black ribbon among the foothills of the Andes, which loom ruggedly in the distance. Soon he was climbing up the floor of a narrow gorge into the heart of the first cordillera. A stream rushed noisily downward over its rocky bed alongside the road. In the winding ascent he met a number of trucks hurtling down the mountains, driven apparently by madmen and crowded with Indian folk converging on San Felipe for Monday's fiesta. And for the pageantry and cheap *chicha* the Junta would provide.

Higher in the mountains he ran into clouds, gathered about the shoulders of the cordillera like a loose woolen shawl. For a time he was slowed to a creeping pace, as he felt his way up through the choking mist, headlights burning. Then *sorroche,* the altitude sickness of the Andes, hit him, hard. It was late afternoon when he emerged from the clouds and pulled up the last curving grade into Barranco.

The sun's rays struck his back at a flat angle, giving a watery light without heat. During the long drive he had not relaxed his grip on the wheel, feeling some vague, unreasoning sense of accomplishment in driving himself to this destination. Now, as he approached it, sick in his head and stomach, and very tired, he did not really know why he had come. The reason was Sadie, of course. But it was Robert Sanders, too. He had run away again. That should not have mattered to Mike. But it did. A few minutes later he topped the grade and rolled into Barranco.

The little mining town clung to the sides of a narrow mountain valley two and a half miles above sea level. The town was a miserable collection of stone and mud buildings strung along the long cobblestone main street. Walls of tortured rock rose in the near distance on two sides of the town to sawtooth ridges which blocked out direct sunlight except during the midday hours. No trace of vegetation relieved the somber rows of houses. The street terminated in a drab plaza near the end of the town. The atmosphere was cold and cheerless, like the air in an ice house.

The Cadillac rumbled over the cobblestones between the colorless façades. Indian women in flat white hats, thick woolen skirts and shawls moved along the street, sacks slung over their shoulders as they drifted away from the plaza where they had been trading since morning, for this was market day. At a corner Mike passed an old man fanning the coals of a small brazier. In a reedy singsong the old man cried *"Anticuchos! Anticuchos!"* The small chunks of bull heart cooked on skewers over the coals were said to have a strengthening effect upon a man's fortitude, and upon his love-making powers. The gamy smell of the roasting heart increased the intensity of Mike's *sorroche*.

It would not be difficult to learn of the two people he sought, if they had come here. The mining company office and smelter, and the small airfield, lay a half-mile beyond the town where the narrow valley, opening at one end, allowed planes to land and take off. Foreigners other than company personnel were rare in Barranco. The arrival of the strange *gringo* pair would be common gossip in the town within an hour.

No cars were in sight as he pulled into the plaza. A few Indian men in round derbies and *serapes* still loitered about the corners. The government hotel, an austere, museumlike structure made of huge boulders, occupied one side of the square. Parking in front, Mike got out and went through the portal into the dim lobby.

As he crossed the threshold, dizzy and breathless in the thin air, his gaze swept out through the arches of the patio, bathed now in the greenish light of mountain dusk. Then he stopped abruptly, his legs trembling. On the far side of the patio at a table sat the two people he was looking for.

He stood rooted for seconds, perhaps a minute, catching his breath, trying to compose his thoughts and figure out what he was going to do now, now that he had tracked down his quarry. For he hadn't really believed that he had a chance of overtaking them, before they flew out of the valley and lost themselves in the wide world where he would never see them again. He realized now that his headlong dash up the mountain was just a device, to let him absorb the impact of their leaving a little at a time.

Robert Sanders' back was toward him, his forearms resting on the table, his shoulders hunched forward and his head sunk deep between them. Sadie's bare head was a dark daub in the twilight. She was wearing a fur coat, collar turned up, for the mountain air was sharp. One of her hands, extended across the table, gripped Sanders' wrist. She was talking closely, tensely to him.

She must have felt Mike's eyes upon her, for her gaze flickered distractedly toward him several times before she finally saw him. She lifted her head and stiffened as recognition spread in her eyes. Withdrawing her hand she pressed it to her temple, as if seized with a sudden headache.

There was nothing for Mike to do now but go and face her. Feeling very much like a meddlesome fool he walked into the patio and crossed to their table. Dropping her hand, Sadie looked at him and said, "As long as you're here, you might as well sit down."

"Thanks," Mike said. He pulled up a chair and seated himself between them. The two turned on him, silently. Sanders' eyes were sullen, glazed. A bottle of pisco, half empty, stood on the table next to Sadie's coffee cup. An ashtray was filled with carmined cigarette butts.

Sanders needed a shave. In the fading light his beard had a reddish tinge. He was in bad shape. Not semi-delirious as he had been last night, but solidly, saturatedly drunk to his bones. Mike understood now about this young man with old man's eyes. This was the way he punished himself when he could no longer bear the thoughts in his head.

Sanders smirked at him unsteadily. "Hello, Scoutmaster."

There were smudges of fatigue under Sadie's eyes as she looked at Mike. A piece of hair fell across her forehead, like a sparrow's wing. The sight of him obviously upset her, but she said quietly, "I expected you might do this. I hoped we'd be gone by now. The field has been socked in tight all day. That's the only way out of this wretched place, except the way we came in."

At the end of the narrow wedge of valley in which the airfield lay, a barrier of mountain peaks was broken by the sharp saddle of a pass. When the mountain clouds piled up in the pass, there was no possiblity of flying out.

Mike said, "I just decided to come. I don't know why."

A squat *mozo* trotted out of the hotel and bowed to Sadie. "*Señorita, teléfono.*"

Sadie hit her palms together. "Maybe it has cleared!" She got up from the table and started after the servant. Then she stopped and flashed a warning look at Mike. "I'll only be gone a minute. Don't make any speeches till I get back." Mike said nothing, but followed her with his eyes as she disappeared into the lobby. Then he turned back to Robert Sanders, who was watching him, scowling.

Sanders' voice was rough, full of drunken challenge. "So what have you got to say to me, brave Captain-Scoutmaster?"

Mike didn't reply; he studied the knurled shape of his fingers on the table. Suddenly Sanders half rose in his chair. Reaching across the table, he grabbed Mike's shirt. There was a tremor in his voice. "I said, what have you got to say? You came here to say something. Say it!"

With a flash of anger Mike grasped the wrist and tore the grip from his shirt. Shoving Sanders roughly back into his chair, he said, "Keep them cotton-pickers to yourself, Mac. She said no speeches till she gets back. Anything I've got to say can wait."

Within minutes Sadie returned, visibly distraught. "The bastardly pass is still closed." She bit her lip, fighting back tears. "No chance to get out till morning at the earliest." Glaring at Mike, as though the delay was solely his fault, she cried, "If I don't get out of the lousy country soon, I'll blow a *fuse!*"

195

Mike indicated her chair. "Sit down, Sadie. You can't fight the clouds."

She looked at him angrily for another moment, then sank into the chair. In a tight voice she said, "Why did you follow me? If you have any noble thoughts of saving me from myself, forget it!"

With a surge of meanness Mike said, "This drunk gentleman and I made a little bargain yesterday. I went to considerable trouble to carry out my part of it. Seems like he forgot his part. Let's just say I came up here to remind him."

Sanders drained his glass, spilling drink over his chin. He set the glass down hard. Mike looked at him, steadily, but Sanders kept his eyes on the table. He mumbled, "I said I'd leave. All right, I'm leaving."

Mike said, "That wasn't quite the deal. The lady wasn't included."

Sadie broke in sharply. "I know all about your asinine little deal. I happen to have a stake in it now, and the Benavides bit is out! There'll be no brave suicides while I'm around."

Quietly, Mike said, "Sadie, you're helping this man commit slow suicide. He can't run any more."

"Don't be an ass, Mike Hodak."

Mike addressed himself to Sanders, speaking the words slowly, grinding them in. "You may think you're making a clean getaway, Mac, but you're not. When you get to where you're going, you'll find out you're not any different from what you are right here. Right now." He drew a deliberate circle on the table with his finger. "Nothing will be changed, except you'll be a little bit crummier from the trip."

"Oh, you are a preachy bastard!" Sadie cried.

"Maybe. So what are you trying to do? Save this guy. Fit Humpty Dumpty back together? You can't do it. That's a job old Humpty here has got to do *all by himself.*"

"Rave on, Captain," Sadie said, lividly. "Enjoy yourself. But I'm not buying any." Sanders' chin was sunk on his chest. His head moved unsteadily.

Unable to curb the angry flow of his words, Mike tapped Sanders on the arm. "And what do you plan to give the lady for a wedding present, friend? A sexy physique with no guts in it?"

Sadie hit the table with her fists and jumped to her feet. "That's a lousy thing to say!" Her voice quivered and tendons stood out in her neck. "You'd love to see him killed, wouldn't you? Your idea of a fine, manly ending to this story. Well you're going to be disappointed! Now go away! Leave us alone, you stupid, ugly man!"

Mike's face was solemn and white as he pushed back and slowly arose from the table.

"I said my say, Sadie. I am going now."

Sanders' head was down between his hands, as if someone had beat it down with a club. He seemed about to fall out of his chair. Mike looked from the man to the girl. She was in a sorry plight. He growled, "Looks like old lover-boy's gone limber on you. You've got a room, I suppose."

"We have rooms, and I can manage very well, thank you." The confidence in Sadie's voice began to crack a little. "Just leave us alone."

Mike walked into the lobby. From the room clerk he learned that the señorita had engaged the presidential suite on the second floor. Mike told him that the gentleman had been taken ill. Then he ordered coffee and sandwiches sent up to the suite. The clerk nodded, knowingly.

When Mike got back to the patio Sanders was on his feet, swaying. Sadie stood close to him, clutching the lapels of his coat, talking rapidly, pleadingly with him. It was as though she were clinging to something she desperately wanted to believe in and could feel slipping from her fingers. Sanders tried to turn away. With a clumsy motion he pushed her from him, but she pulled him back sharply. She started crying. It was plain to Mike that she had more than she could handle.

Going out to them Mike hooked his arm around Sanders' waist and drew the man's limp arm over his shoulder. "I'll take him upstairs," he said to Sadie. "Call it my wedding present to you."

By the time he had half-carried the man up the flight of stairs to the second floor Mike was gasping like an asthmatic. He felt grateful that the situation had not called for him to do battle in this undernourished air.

The suite was a corner sitting room with a bedroom and bath on each side. It had been furnished with dark, massive furniture with lion's feet and horsehair upholstery fifty years ago when the hotel was built. Judging by the musty smell of the place, it had not been aired many times since then. Mike dumped Sanders on the sofa and threw open the French doors onto the small balcony overlooking the plaza. The minor-key cry of the old man selling *anticuchos* came up through the deep twilight.

When he turned around, Sadie had disappeared into the bedroom on the right. He supposed she had seen the last of him she ever wanted to see. Sprawled on the sofa, Sanders looked at him with eyes of glass. Mike was reminded of a once-fine house abandoned by its occupants to ruin and decay. Somehow this rekindled his anger and made him want to punish the man even more.

Standing in the center of the room with folded arms, he trained a contemptuous gaze at the sodden heap on the couch. "Do not say *yes* unless you mean it. That's what the letter said, wasn't it? Well, he said *yes,* and Monday afternoon at two a

hell of a fine old man is going to walk out into Avenida Sucre
—and die—without a chance. Because somebody won't be
there to meet him. It don't matter a hell of a lot, because the
man is old and hasn't got long to go anyhow. The pity is that
the last thing he'll learn on this earth is what a bunch of crud
the human race is, after all."

Sanders said nothing. With bleared eyes he followed Mike
as he moved around the room. Mike walked to the open
doorway. The old *anticucho* vendor had brought his brazier
up across from the hotel and was crying his wares directly
below.

Mike jerked his thumb toward the darkness. "You know
what that *anciano* is selling? *Corazón de toro*. Heart of bull.
Cut out of the animal while it's warm and quivering. The
paisanos chew it and chew it; hold it in their mouth a long
time, hoping they'll absorb some of the bull's courage."

He stood over Sanders. "I'll send down and get a stick for
you, if you say so. Might be worth a try."

Sanders waggled his head and cursed Mike drunkenly. The
big Marine jeered, "What about it, Mac? It only costs three
pesetas. It might work!"

With a howl of anguish Sanders struggled up from the sofa
and lunged at him. Mike stepped back easily and let him pass.
Without breaking stride the younger man stumbled across the
room into the adjoining bathroom and began to vomit violently, as though he were wrenching up his guts. Before he was
done, Sadie opened the bedroom door across the sitting room.
Her face was white. There were dark circles under her eyes.
She had been crying.

Mike said, "Something he ate a couple of years ago has
made him sick."

Sadie closed her eyes and pushed taut fingers through her

199

hair. Her voice was a hollow echo of the misery in her. "I think we've died and gone to hell. This is punishment for our sins when we were alive."

Mike grunted. "We must have been some sinners."

At this moment Sanders staggered out of the bathroom. He was a wreck, eyes watering, vomit down his shirt. He stood weaving helplessly in the doorway. Then Mike took pity on him. He took his arm and steered him into the bedroom on the left. When Mike turned him loose he collapsed on the bed, heavy as a sack of wheat. Mike doubled the velvet spread over him and left him, out cold. When he returned to the sitting room a *mozo* had wheeled in a cart with sandwiches and coffee. Mike gave the servant a bill and waved him out. Sadie was clinging to the balcony doorway, gazing out into the darkness. Not knowing anything better to do, Mike pulled a chair up to the cart and sat down.

Biting into a sandwich, munching, he said, "How about a little chow? Nothing like mountain air for the appetite."

Whirling around, Sadie clenched her teeth and called him some names and combinations of names he hadn't heard in a long time. Then she rushed past him into the other bedroom, sobbing, slamming the door behind her.

Mike munched doggedly through half the sandwich, then tossed the rest of it back on the plate in disgust. He felt suddenly weak, as if all the strength that held him together had turned to water and leaked out. He wasn't angry any longer. But he was sad, beyond telling, for he realized that the bright thing, the youth and hope and joy that had come into his life, was gone, and that nothing like it would ever come again. He also knew that Sadie's bitter words were not really meant for him, but were outpourings of the self-contempt and grief and hopelessness that suppurated inside her.

He went to the bedroom doorway and leaned wearily on an upraised arm against it. For a long time he stood looking into the dark room at the inert form under the old velvet spread.

After a while he spoke quietly to Robert Sanders, as though the man could hear him. It was a kind of coda to what he had said before.

"You can't break and run every time the light shines on you, buddy," he said. "Somewhere, sometime you're gonna have to stop and dig in."

He paused a long time, then he finished what he had to say. "I'm not saying I agree with what you did out yonder. I don't. I guess I'll always be a Stephen Decatur man, myself. But if you really believe what you did was right, you'll never be worth your mother's labor pains until you walk right out in the raw daylight and own up to it, and take your lumps."

He sighed heavily and added, "That's all she wrote." He turned then and went slowly back across the room, loosening his tie. He sank down on the uncomfortable horsehair couch, stretched out, and in a moment, from sheer exhaustion, was asleep.

Sometime in the night he woke up, stiff, aching from the mountain cold. The door to Sadie's bedroom was closed. He hauled himself to his feet and slammed the balcony doors. Then he went into the room where he had left his drunken friend. Sanders wasn't there. He had fled, Mike had no doubt, to the consoling arms of his lady-love. Fighting the image of the tender scene from his mind, he guessed it was better to go to hell in company than alone. He was worn out and he felt sick. Rolling onto the bed lately occupied by Robert Sanders he pulled up the velvet cover and fell asleep.

When he awoke again, Sadie was leaning over him, shaking him. It was light outside.

"Mike, please wake up."

"I'm awake."

"Mike, where is he?"

Sitting up, Mike scrubbed his hand over his face. "Damned if I know. I thought he was with you."

"He hasn't been with me. Oh, Mike, what a fool I am!" She looked terrible and he imagined how she was going to look if she lived long enough to get old. Haggard, intense, but still somehow beautiful. She sat down on the bed and looked at him closely. There was pain and tenderness in her voice.

"You love me, don't you, Mike?"

Mike looked back at her for a moment, then he grunted, "You're the damnedest woman. You keep changing the subject."

On the edge of tears Sadie said, "I'm really sorry, Mike." Then she got up quickly and drew a deep breath and patted her cheeks sharply, as if to wake herself up. "We've got to find him, Mike. Please go and find him. He's way over the hill."

With the help of a ten-peso bill the morning clerk at the desk could remember that the night clerk had told him that a young *americano* had come downstairs in the night and had gone out. At three, or perhaps four o'clock in the morning. And he had been a trifle . . . unsteady. Unaccustomed to the altitude, no doubt.

Leaving Sadie in the lobby huddled over a cup of *café con leche,* Mike went out into the gray, cold light of the town, looking for Robert Sanders. A bell clanged in the church tower across the plaza and a few Indian women with covered heads moved toward the sound for early mass. Sadie had left her sister's Oldsmobile in the town's only garage, around the corner behind the hotel. It took less than five minutes for Mike to go there and return.

When he got back to the hotel Sadie looked up at him. The amethyst of her eyes was misting up again. She said, "You didn't find him."

Sitting down, Mike felt queer and lightheaded. His voice sounded like a faraway echo in his own ears. He shrugged. "The crazy bastard has gone back to San Felipe."

27

The ride back to the capital was, for Mike, a down-spiraling nightmare. Alternately he felt ginned up with elation, then he plunged into the depths of gloom. Robert Sanders' drunken nocturnal flight back to San Felipe was good. It held hope of the man's salvation. Yet Mike could not shake the thought that he, Mike Hodak alone, would now bear the guilt if the hounds of Lupo Machia found the man before he did.

It began to rain as soon as they left Barranco. The downpour lashed the top of the convertible, cut visibility and slowed his speed. Through the cold, dismal drive Mike tried to rationalize and justify his actions. In so many words he recited it to Sadie: whatever men were supposed to get done in this life they couldn't even begin until they had laid hands on the essential ingredient of their manhood—courage. If Sanders had not turned back now, he would have been a ruined man. Beyond fixing. It was his last chance.

The words rattled with hollow fraudulence in his own head. He felt he was trying to cover a crime with a fake nobility of motive. For Robert Sanders, who at this moment could have been winging down the mountain runway toward freedom and other chances, would likely be dead by nightfall, killed by Mike Hodak as certainly as though he himself had pulled the trigger. And when he was gone, this chance for Sadie, maybe the best one she would ever have, would perish also.

Gripping the wheel with sweaty hands, Mike vowed that this would not happen. He would find Sanders and stop him before he could carry out the stupid attempt. By going back, by choosing danger over safety, the man had proved everything he needed to prove. Covering Sadie's hand with his own, Mike made her the solemn promise that he would find Robert Sanders and give him back to her. There was no need to add that he would lay his own life on the line, as necessary.

His words of promise and hope stirred no response. Sadie rode beside him, her face half-concealed in her collar, her eyes straight ahead, as though her bid for life with meaning she could understand had flared like a sparkler, then died to a cold, burnt-out wire. The enormity of what he had done sank slowly into Mike, and the feeling of guilt became almost unbearable.

They wound down through clouds that drifted across the road like wet gray rags. At every curve Mike half expected to find the guard rail split and to see the Oldsmobile on the dark rocks below, smashed and burning.

It was afternoon when they sped into the outskirts of San Felipe. They had driven but a few blocks into the *barrios* when he realized something had happened. The streets were nearly deserted. That in itself was not unusual on a Sunday afternoon in San Felipe. It was something else, something sensed rather than seen.

As they rumbled over the rough cobbled streets they began passing soldiers, squat, inscrutable Indians from the *sierra*, leaning on their rifles at intersections. Nearing the center of town they began to pass small knots of people. They stood in doorways and on the narrow walks between the corners, talking closely, sullenly.

Without warning a truck loaded with *soldados* lumbered out of an intersection into the path of the Cadillac, causing Mike to jam his brakes. He sent a curse after the driver, heaved a big breath and started forward again. Something definitely had happened. He said so to Sadie, but she appeared not to hear him.

Minutes later they were sailing through the broad avenues of Miraflores. As Mike turned up the parkway toward the Clinton residence Sadie sat suddenly forward. Directly ahead, parked at the curb before the house, stood the Oldsmobile.

With relief Mike said, "That's your sister's car. Five will get you ten Sanders is on the seat, sleeping it off."

But he wasn't, and the car keys were in the ignition. Mike got back in the Cadillac and pulled it up into the drive. The Clintons' *mayor domo* came out of the house. The sight of Sadie seemed to upset him. No, he did not know how long the Oldsmobile had been there. He had not seen the young American.

Mike groaned inwardly, but again he assured Sadie that he would find Robert Sanders. He would take him, by force if necessary, to the Embassy and detain him there until they could figure a way to get him out of the country. Sadie looked at him blankly for a long moment. Then without a word she got out and went into the house.

Mike watched until she disappeared, then he gunned the car out of the drive and headed for his apartment. As he neared the old section of the city he found himself, unexpectedly, in heavy traffic. The street was jammed with old cars and trucks in slow procession, all strangely quiet. No horn honked. Many people on foot moved slowly along the sidewalks. Their faces were somber, unsmiling, their eyes dull with tragedy. These were the poor people of San Felipe, factory workers, domestic servants, common laborers. The men wore their Sunday clothes: black trousers and white shirts without ties. The women moved sorrowfully behind their men, their faces half-hidden in their black *rebosas*. It was as though the whole populace was in mourning. At every corner now there was a detachment of *soldados* heavily armed. The stream of people flowed around them silently, sullenly.

By the time Mike reached Avenida Sucre the street was choked with taxis and trucks and old jallopies. He fumed and cursed at the creeping pace. During one halt, he stuck his head out the window and bawled to the driver of an old Chevy alongside.

"What the hell's going on, *amigo?* Why all the *gente?*"

The driver was a ferret-faced man in a threadbare coat. He stared at him as if he did not understand the question. His face was streaked with tears. Mike hollered at him again. "Where is everybody going? What's it all about?"

The man opened his mouth and held out his hand toward Mike, but it was a moment before he could speak. When he did his voice was choked with emotion.

"You do not know?"

"Know what?"

"He is dead, Señor."

"He?" Mike demanded. Hair rose on his neck. "Who? Who is dead?"

"Who?" the man swallowed. The tears welled in his eyes. "The great one, Señor. Rafael Benavides . . . is dead."

Rafael Benavides had departed this life in the dark hours of the morning. It had happened, Mike figured, about the same time that Robert Sanders had pulled himself out of his drunken stupor and started down the mountain. Perhaps the anticipation of the adventure that lay ahead was too exciting for the great old heart, or perhaps, as the saying went, it was simply his time to die. At any rate, his liberation from the Colombian Embassy came sooner and in a gentler and far different way than he had planned.

The Embassy housekeeper had been awakened in the night by the sound of someone entering the library. Something alarmed her. She put on her dressing gown and went down the hall to investigate. In the library she found Rafael Benavides seated in his customary chair, his head resting on his arm on the table, as though he had been overtaken by an eternal weariness and had laid down his head and gone to sleep. A pen had fallen from his open hand onto a clean sheet of paper, which never received the thoughts he meant to set down before he died.

By daylight the news reached the *comandancia*. Orders were dispatched at once to the Embassy demanding immediate interment. Machia had no intention of permitting a public funeral for Benavides. This could grow into a demonstration of homage that could get out of hand.

Rather than make an international issue over an old corpse, the Colombian Ambassador had given in to the demand. There was nothing in the laws of nations to cover the case. At 8 A.M. six young Colombians, secretaries and clerks of the Embassy, bareheaded, clad in neat black suits, had borne the polished cedar coffin on their shoulders through the front gates to the waiting hearse. Benavides' aged sister, his only relative, veiled and weeping between the Ambassador and a priest, followed the simple cortege.

The infamous happenings of the next minutes were to shock and outrage all of Latin America from the Rio Grande to Tierra del Fuego. The moment the high-borne casket passed through the gate and out of the Embassy sanctuary, rough hands of uniformed *soldados* wrestled it from the pallbearers and carried it to the center of Avenida Sucre. There they dumped it heavily on the pavement.

The lid of the coffin was pried off with a bayonet. An officer jerked the old man's body to a sitting position. Those who witnessed the shameful scene reported that it was as though the old man was riding to his funeral in a small rowboat.

The officer ripped off the black tie and tore open the plain white shirt. An official physician knelt beside the coffin and placed a stethoscope against the bony chest. Machia crossed the street from his idling Jaguar and knelt to peer into the lifeless old face. Then, as if to assure himself personally that the old man was thoroughly dead, he grasped the cold wrist, feeling for the nonexistent pulse. Afterward, as a final indignity, an official photographer spent several minutes photographing the body from every angle. Then it was shoved back into the coffin, the lid was thrown across the top, and Machia and his minions departed in a roar of motorcycle noise, leaving the ashen-faced Colombians stunned, huddled around their Ambassador, who was holding a broken old woman in his arms.

The hearse proceeded rapidly under police escort to the necropolis beyond the farthest *barrios*. There the body was sealed in an unmarked cript before the city was well awake.

The news that Rafael Benavides was dead and buried traveled through the streets, slowly at first, like a fog sliding over the worn thresholds of the working people, stealing into their meager kitchens. Then all at once it seemed to burst over the city like a black blossom of anguish. It was said that one passing through the streets of San Felipe that morning could hear a sustained and muted moan of wordless grief rising from the city.

As the day passed, the people moved out into the streets, wandering and driving aimlessly up and down, stricken, in the throes of a helpless agony, denied even the pathetic remains of their champion to focus their grief upon. Slowly they converged on the Colombian Embassy and the central plaza.

It took half an hour for Mike to work his way through the clotted traffic to his house. Parking in front, he ran up the walk, thinking to change his sweated-out shirt, shave and get over to see the General as quickly as possible.

Nestor met him in the doorway. His good face was a mask of tragedy. Looking at Mike, the soft brown eyes suddenly overflowed, spilling tears down his cheeks.

He murmured, "Señor, he is dead."

"I know," Mike said, pushing roughly past him. The sense of loss had begun to work into him also. He went to the pantry, took down a bottle and splashed a drink into a tumbler. Nestor had followed and stood dumbly at his heels as though there were something Mike could do about it. Scowling at the youth Mike impulsively thrust the glass of whiskey into his hands and poured another for himself.

Brusquely he said, "I met Rafael Benavides. He was a good man." He lifted his glass.

Nestor drew himself erect and raised his chin. Looking past Mike as to a far distant place, he raised his glass and they drank together. It was the first drink of *whiskey americano* he had ever had and it went down the wrong way and strapped him into a paroxysm of gasping. Mike slapped him on the back until he was all right, then went into his bedroom. He whipped into a clean shirt, skipped the shave and took off for the Embassy.

He found the Ambassador in the library. The old man was sitting in a big chair, sunk in gloom. His complexion had the mottled look it took on when he was deeply disturbed. Clapsaddle was with him. Mike was glad to see the Army man there.

When the General saw him, his face brightened and he hauled himself to his feet. His tone was gruff but Mike could tell the old man was glad to see him.

The General said, "I figured you'd be gone over the hill for good. Where in thunder have you been? Things have fallen apart since you left." His voice became low and ponderous. "The old boy up the street checked out this morning."

"I heard about it," Mike said.

"Where's Sadie?"

"I brought her back."

He sat down facing the old man and recounted the whole story, of Sanders' scheme to liberate Benavides, of his meeting with Sadie and Robert Sanders in Barranco, of Sanders' precipitate return to San Felipe. The General leaned forward, listening, making the small clucking noises in his throat.

When Mike had finished, the General said, "Where is Sanders now?"

"I don't know." Mike heaved a heavy sigh. "My next job is to run him down."

The General rose and paced across the room. "Yes, and you better not waste any time. Machia is a vindictive sonofabitch. Even with Benavides dead he'll still cut Sanders down just for pleasure. If he can find him. The AID grant was buttoned up in Washington yesterday."

Throughout the rest of the day and until long after midnight Mike combed San Felipe from one end to the other, without finding a trace of Robert Sanders. The city was a turmoil of confusion. People milled about the streets, herded dumbly back and forth by the soldiers, like distraught, lost animals.

Sanders had not returned to Archie's house. Mike learned this from Archie's *muchacha*, who slept on the premises, but she promised to telephone the Embassy immediately if he appeared. The clerk at the hotel, who remembered him well, swore he had not seen him for several days. Alvaro Rodriguez at the airport said he had not been there. Mike telephoned the Clintons' house and asked for Sadie, but was told only that she was indisposed. He took this to mean that she had either knocked herself out with booze or goof balls, or both. Nobody there had seen or heard from Robert Sanders.

Later in the afternoon he went to his office at the Chancery, on the outside chance that a message had been left for him in his absence, but from the guard on duty he learned nothing. He was about to leave when he ran into Rusty Cobb in the corridor. She had her arms full of little boxes.

"Hello, Rus, what's up?"

"Mike! I'm so glad to see you. I wanted to—see you, before I left. I've been cleaning out my junk. I'm heading stateside. By boat, in the morning."

"The devil you are! What's the rush?"

She unloaded her burdens on a table and pulled him to a bench in the hall.

"Sit with me a minute, Mike. I want to tell you about it. I received a letter a couple of days ago. From a boy I grew up with. He's a goat rancher back home now. For a long time he's been asking me to marry him, and help him raise kids. That's kind of a joke—you know. Well, somehow, I never could see it before. That letter did it. It was really an ultimatum, now or never. So I'm going. He's a good guy—reminds me of you, except he's red-headed and lanky. All of a sudden I'm—real excited about it."

She said she was, but somehow the excitement wasn't there.

"Gosh, Rusty, that sounds great."

"It really is. But, Mike—" She looked him suddenly in the eyes. "Only one—thing—could make me change my mind. I've got a twenty-section ranch out west of Ozona on the Pecos River. It's yours if you want it."

Mike pretended not to understand what she meant. "Gosh, Rus, I wouldn't know what to do with a ranch. I couldn't tell a goat from a gopher. But I sure hope you'll be happy. I bet you will be."

"I will. I hope you'll be happy, too."

"Don't worry about me, kid. I'm always happy."

She looked at him for long seconds, then she smiled and patted his hand. "Good-bye, Mike. When you come through Texas drop in and spend a week with us. Thirty miles west of Ozona on U.S. 290."

She gathered up her little boxes and started to leave. Then she stopped and turned. Her eyes were sparkling with tears. "God bless you, Mike."

The rest of the day turned up nothing in his search for Robert Sanders. When he got home late, beat, in a black anguish, he pulled off his shoes and sank down on his bed. He was out of ideas, and exhaustion had drained the fight from him. Lying there, asking for sleep that would cut off the tension, he thought about tomorrow.

Tommorow was the junta's birthday, ironically called *El Día de La Libertad*. Machia would now be more determined than ever to stage a big, gaudy show—to get the people's minds off their sorrow over Benavides. Mike would have to break out his dress blues and suffer silently through the whole farcical, despicable day. It was a diplomat's duty.

As he was spiraling off to sleep a shocking thought emerged from the confused pictures in his weary brain. Was it possible that Robert Sanders was holed up somewhere, in hiding, waiting for tomorrow, unaware that Rafael Benavides was dead? The man spoke no Spanish, and unless someone had told him, he would have no way of knowing of the death of the man he had vowed to liberate at 2 P.M. tomorrow. Was he even now concealed in some cranny of this sprawling city, waiting for the appointed hour? Was it possible that he would remain where he was until the hour arrived, then, in ignorance, dash forth on the desperate attempt to free the old man? The old one who was beyond all human liberation?

This devastating thought churned at his tired, tortured brain. He struggled for a moment to get up, but the punishment of the past days had numbed his will to fight. In a spiraling dizziness he fell back on his bed and slept.

28

When Mike hauled himself out of bed at 9 A.M. his whole body ached. Examining himself in the mirror he found, with some relief, that the swelling was almost gone from his head. The only remaining evidence of his encounter with Robert Sanders was a yellowish bruise around his eye.

Día de La Libertad would begin with a high mass for the

Armed Forces at ten. The Ambassador and his party were scheduled to leave the Embassy at a quarter to. While Mike drank coffee Nestor busied around, brushing the well-worn dress blues, polishing the brasswork on the Sam Browne belt. Meanwhile Mike kept the phone busy, dialing again all the likely places. There was no trace of Robert Sanders, anywhere. He seemed to have evaporated.

When he arrived at the Embassy, Clapsaddle was already there, looking awkward but very good in his Army dress blues. Alden Clinton was there also, in morning coat and striped trousers. He appeared unhappy and distracted.

When the old man came downstairs at twenty to ten, Mike intercepted him in the hallway.

"General, I can't find the joker anywhere. Do you reckon he don't know about Benavides? You think he might still be planning to spring the old man that's already dead and buried?"

The General made some noises in his throat. "It's possible. As soon as the mass is over, get on your horse." He leveled blue eyes severely. "He's got to be found."

As they approached the Plaza Bolívar they pulled into a slow procession of limousines. The plaza was already jammed with people. The square as well as access streets in all directions were lined with *soldados* in mustard-brown uniforms, their Mausers at parade rest. Old tanks stood at every corner with motors racketing noisily, the pennants on their radio antennas fluttering in the breeze. Half-tracks with machine guns angled skyward were stationed along the way between the blocks. Machia had turned out the entire armed might of Maragua, not just to impress the populace but also to crush any spontaneous uprising, always a possibility when there are people and anger in Latin America.

The big black limousine glided to a stop at the cathedral steps and the General stepped out smartly. Mike followed and they mounted to the stone esplanade before the entrance. All the top dignitaries of the diplomatic corps were there. They gathered in groups, in poses of importance, awaiting the start of the mass, the formal opening of the fiesta.

As the American delegation moved, nodding and saluting, into the assemblage of ambassadors and attachés in their gaudy sashes and sunburst medallions, the military bands of Army, Navy and Air Corps, drawn up on both sides of the esplanade, blasted the air with discordant unsynchronized music. Bright flags on the buildings around the square snapped in the warm wind.

Looking over the plaza Mike saw that the crowd was flecked with the red armbands and white shirts of Machia's bully-boys from the People's Revolutionary Party. They were planted there for a purpose, and would quickly bludgeon any excitable *cholo* who showed signs of starting an anti-junta rally.

It was these toughs who began the coarse, cheering chant when Machia's party of cars snaked down Mercaderes toward the plaza. But the cheering was forced and did not spread. There was an air of tension in the jammed square. It was more an atmosphere of suppressed anger than the pall of grief that Mike had noted yesterday.

Old Marshal Ugarte, then Machia, stepped from the open car. Then they came up the stone stairs leading their retinue of ministers and aides. All three service bands crashed into the Mariscal's March, a good two beats apart, but the sheer din was impressive.

A childish smile played over his wrinkled face as Ugarte led the group into the cathedral. When Machia passed by, he looked straight at Mike. There was an amused glint in his eyes that said he had knowledge of Mike's involvement in the Sanders conspiracy, and that he would remember it.

As the Marshal's party disappeared into the cathedral the diplomats wheeled inward, like two battalions converging on the doors. As he entered the arched entrance into the dim interior Mike saw that the church was already full. The pews were solidly packed with officers of the armed services in dress uniform. They stood stiffly at attention, in rows according to rank. A few ordinary worshipers found standing room in the aisles around the fringes of the church.

In the far distance the altar gleamed through the gloom, a gold-and-jeweled edifice that sparkled richly in the light of its myriad candles. Somewhere in a distant balcony the Maragua Symphony Orchestra tolled out a militant hymn.

The Marshal's party marched impressively to their special seats before the altar. Members of the diplomatic corps filed into reserved pews just behind. As protocol required, Mike dropped off far back in the church and squeezed into a seat by the aisle with the captains of the Army. The General moved stolidly ahead, his sandy cotton head towering above the dark stream of diplomats.

During the next hour Mike sat, knelt, and stood, taking his cue from the disciplined worshipers around him as the ritual unfolded at the distant altar.

At intervals the orchestra played majestically in its loft. Now and then one of the bands could be heard outside striking up a march, providing a weird distraction to the solemn worship. When he knelt, Mike's eyeballs thumped in his head under the choking of his collar. He could not focus his mind to pray, though he felt the need of it.

At last the mass came to an end. The tall doors at the rear

of the church were thrown open, letting in a flood of light. All three bands and the orchestra joined in a wild maelstrom of sound. Double lines of acolytes in crimson gowns filed up the aisle, followed by mitred bishops and priests in gold-brocaded vestments, then two rows of tonsured friars in rough brown robes and sandals, their eyes downcast. Following the clergy came Ugarte and Machia and their ministers, then the high-ranking military and diplomats.

Mike spotted Benito Monclova and caught his eye. The colonel smiled at him gravely and Mike felt sorry for him. Mike was just a visitor, but this was Monclova's country that he deeply loved.

When the General came along, Mike fell in beside him and they walked out into the bright sunlight. The bands were building up to a brassy orgasm. Machia's strong-arm squads were yelling themselves hoarse. From the basilica the procession would journey on foot up Mercaderes, now lined solidly with troops, to the *palacio*. Hundreds of little girls, carefully rehearsed, would throw flowers along the line of march and fill the air with their quavering cheers as the Junta moved along the street to the seat of its power.

The procession would enter the *palacio* for a reception at which champagne would flow in great quantities. The entire officer corps would lift their glasses in a renewed pledge of allegiance to the Junta. Mike had pushed and shoved his way through this same dismal proceedings just a year ago, and he had no stomach for a rerun. After the champagne the officers would retire to their troops for the parade and review. Machia and Ugarte would then lead the upper-echelon dignitaries into the magnificent hall of State for a luncheon banquet.

Afterward they would debouch from the *palacio* and head the parade through the business district, thence out Avenida

Sucre to the municipal stadium, where the Marshal would stand the review of the Armed Forces and, later, Machia would harangue the packed mob on the glories of the revolution, the magnificent future of the new Maragua and the brilliant accomplishments of the Junta to date.

Alongside the General, Mike felt relieved when the old man gave him a nudge and signaled for him to drop out and get about his business of finding Robert Sanders.

Sliding off on a left oblique, Mike pushed his way through the fence of *soldados* and into the packed mob under the arcade. He didn't know where to start. He would begin making the same rounds he had made before, only faster, hoping something would come to him.

He had not gone ten paces when someone pulled at his elbow. Turning, he looked into the pock-scarred face of the secret police agent, the one of the Chevrolet.

"Señor."

"What in the hell do you want?"

"Señor, the young man? Where is he?" Suprisingly the man's voice was not demanding, but friendly, almost fawning.

Mike nearly laughed in the man's face. At least they hadn't found Sanders either.

"What young man?" he said, not stopping.

"You know the one, Señor. The young *americano* with short hair."

"How the hell would I know, *jefe?* I'm not his nursemaid." He strode ahead, pushing through the fringes of the crowd.

The man with the scarred face following along, talking rapidly. "Señor, surely you do not think we would harm him? Nothing like that, Señor. Merely a matter of questioning. For his own good. Possibly we ask him to leave the country."

Mike stopped and grinned at the man. "I don't know where

he is, *jefe*. Why don't you try the *palacio?* Maybe he's having a *copita* with Colonel Machia." He found an empty cab at the corner and jumped in. As the car started up, the detective ran alongside as long as he could follow. The last words Mike heard were, "Señor, he will not be harmed. Señor, I am a family man. Señor, please!"

Mike sat back smiling with grim enjoyment at the thought of the punishment that would be meted out to the man for allowing Robert Sanders to escape.

At home, as he changed from his uniform, Mike kept Nestor busy dialing the telephone, going over the list again—but there was nothing, anywhere.

It seemed hopeless. Mike shifted into last-resort thinking. He told himself that if Robert Sanders had sobered up and was going to try something, he would do whatever it was damned well. If he was in hiding, he would stay well hidden until it was time to come out. Mike could think of but one other thing to do. It was pure hunch, but it took hold of him strongly. He would go down on Avenida Sucre and be in front of the Colombian Embassy when the parade came by at two o'clock.

29

He was there early. Lines of old women and children were already sitting in the hot sun on the curbings, like big and little birds come early to watch the parade. Every building along the street except one was hung with flags. It was imprudent not to show a flag on *El Día de La Libertad*. But there were no flags flying from the Colombian Embassy. A spray of purple funeral flowers tied with a black ribbon hung upon the Embassy door.

As he walked nervously along the sidewalk toward the plaza Mike's gaze swept back and forth over the growing crowd. He didn't see Robert Sanders. That was all right. He didn't expect to see him yet. Sanders wouldn't show himself until he was ready. As he passed through the leafy shade under the seminary wall, under the loggia where he had crouched with Robert Sanders just a few afternoons ago, he wondered if the man was up there now, at this moment, watching, waiting.

Whether he was or not, Mike was convinced that he would come. He felt sure of it. He would come, then everything would be all right.

More people filled the sidewalks now, thickening the lines along the parade route. Men and big boys shouldered their way past the old women and complaining children into the front ranks. It was fiesta and the men had been drinking, but the usual gaiety and laughter of a fiesta day were missing. The old men were grave, and the faces of the young ones were hardened with hidden rage. Some muttered audible insults at the *soldados* who stood at intervals along the street, scowling apprehensively, feet planted apart, backs to the crowd.

It was an explosive day when anger and pisco and patriotism could drive men to attack tanks with bare hands. The tension in the air stirred excitement and apprehension in Mike's chest. He winced at the thought of some drink-inflamed *cholo* setting off a riot. At the slightest show of revolt Machia would splash the gutters with blood.

That is why Mike knew he must be ready. And he was. He touched the slapper he had slipped into his pocket before leaving the house. He would spot Sanders and stay near him, behind him. When the noise of the parade rolled down the street he would apply the leather-covered steel with just the right amount of force, just above the ear. Sanders would drop like an estoqued bull. Mike would catch him under the arms and drag him back across the sidewalk, until the parade was safely past. No one would pay any heed, for the pisco had been flowing and many a man would turn up his toes before the day was over.

Oh, Robert Sanders would definitely come. And it was right and necessary that he should. Because it was the coming that would prove him, the hiding in fear all day and the coming, in spite of the fear. That was the thing. Mike knew he was still trying to justify himself, and he also knew that he had to interdict the tragedy which Sanders had arranged for himself. If he came. . . .

Across the plaza he could hear the racketing noise of tank motors starting up, revving, getting ready to pull out into the marching line. Still no Sanders. He crossed the street and shouldered his way around through the crowd in front of the Embassy. He could not be sure which side of the street Sanders would approach from, though it seemed logical that he would make his move from the side opposite the Embassy, where he would be facing the Embassy entrance and could see Rafael Benavides when he came out—Benavides, who was already sealed in his crypt. Mike recrossed the street, drawing an angry whistle from a nearby policeman.

Pacing back and forth along the walk behind the crowd, craning over the packed ranks of heads, he began to *will* that Robert Sanders would come. It was as close to praying as he could come, a hard straining inside as he said over and over to himself: *Come Robert, come on, boy,* the way a spectator

221

strains and pulls for a tired runner in a distance race, not knowing whether he will make the finish line or not. If Sanders didn't make it, it would be a blinding defeat, not only for him, but for Sadie, and, in a way, for every man alive.

Then the first band marched out of Mercaderes into the plaza, horns blaring and drums bumping, leading out the parade. In minutes the band had squared the plaza and turned into the long march down Avenida Sucre. His belly hard with tension, Mike moved back and forth along the sidewalk, peering over the crowd for a crew-cut head. Then as the brassy din grew louder he retreated across the sidewalk and climbed onto the concrete footing of an iron-barred fence, to have a better view of the street.

Two motorcycle policemen led the procession, rolling slowly along the edges of the avenue, gunning their motors in short bursts, pressing the crowd back ahead of the band. The short-legged bandsmen came even with Mike and marched past with their weird, swinging stomp, blasting deafeningly. Then came a full droning cordon of motorcyclists, followed by the Marshal's car, a long black Mercedes with open top. Ugarte sat on the rear seat saluting and nodding in response to the twittering cheers of the children. Machia sat beside him, a relaxed, malevolently handsome figure in his white *uniforme de gala*. Behind dark glasses his eyes took in the crowd coldly. Two secret police agents walked rapidly alongside, keeping up with the car, their hands resting on the rear fenders, their gazes trained along the borders of the crowd, alert for the slightest sign of trouble. Behind the car a mounted troup of Palace Guards in gold helmets festooned with black horsetails clattered up the pavement under close rein, their scarlet tunics and golden breastplates brilliant in the sun. Stretching behind came a long, twisting column of infantry, bayonets glinting, then tanks, other bands, half-tracks, more troops.

Mike began to curse. He felt like crying. It was too tough and Sanders wasn't coming. He didn't have it. Everybody had lost.

Then the thing started in the crowd straight across the street directly in front of the Embassy gate. At first it was the slightest surging of the crowd, as if someone behind the outer line was shoving to get out where he could see. Then, clearly above the racket of the parade, came a thin quavering yell, *"Viva Rafael Benavides! Viva los Populistas!"*

The effect was electric. The whole crowd seemed to gasp. Directly in the path of the Marshal's car the packed mass of humanity bellied into the street. Shrieks and yells cut the air as people on the edge of the crowd clawed to get back on the curbing.

"Viva Benavides! Viva! Viva!" It was the same piercing voice, strangely familiar to Mike's ear.

Angry shouts echoed up and down the street. The nearest policeman dived into the crowd where the cry came from, truncheons raised. Motorcyclists wheeled around sharply in sudden confusion, dropping their motors on the pavement as they darted in after the miscreant. The Marshal's car was blocked. Machia stood up, enraged, his eyes blazing.

Behind the car, the Place Guard wheeled and turned in confusion, spurring their horses into the crowd on both sides. Screams shivered the tree leaves as the outer lines surged backward. Terrified men and women with children in their arms struggled to get away, only to find themselves trapped in the packed mob.

Once again the cry came, muffled now, as though crushed under the pile of bodies. It was weaker, but still clear and defiant. *"Viva Benavides! Vi-va!"* Mike could see the truncheons rise and fall and hear them thud across the street.

Standing, eyes flashing with fury, Machia shouted an order.

He motioned to the plainclothesmen beside the car, fingering them toward the pile-up. The two men ran around the car, drawing their pistols. They fought their way into the struggling jam of people now completely out of hand in their frenzy to get away from the focal point of danger.

Then Mike saw Robert Sanders. He gripped the iron fence as though he were welded to it, for he couldn't possibly reach the man. Sanders came up from the left, walking casually but swiftly, out in the center of the street. He stepped around a rearing horse, fending off the animal with a hand firmly planted on a glistening rump, but his eyes never wavered from Machia. As he worked his way toward the car, his hand went into his coat pocket. When it came out it held a heavy automatic.

Standing in the car, Machia directed the suppression of the reedy-voiced rebel with sharp commands. Unperturbed, smiling happily, Ugarte nodded and saluted at the bedlam boiling around him. Sanders came up behind them, almost casually. When he reached the rear of the car he placed one foot on the heavy chrome bumper, and stepped upward. Machia's back was toward him. In a swift, sure motion Sanders raised the automatic, raking the cap from Machia's head, exposing dark, oily hair. Then he chopped the heavy automatic down against the man's skull.

The impact made the solid sound of an ax biting into green oak. Machia dropped straight down, like a giant puppet with its strings cut. Vaulting over into the back seat Sanders shoved the inert form aside and seated himself beside Ugarte. Then, to Mike's paralyzed amazement, the man calmly stuck the pistol barrel into the ear of the driver who turned around at that exact instant. With his other hand Sanders pointed straight down the street.

The silent command was clear and deadly. The chauffeur

had a choice: he could drive, or die. It was an easy decision. Squaring around, he jammed the car into gear and roared ahead, tires squealing. Gaining momentum the Mercedes knocked fallen motorcycles aside and plowed into the rear of the band, now lost in its own din, marching obliviously ahead. Startled bleats and honks hit the air as the band was split and scattered by the accelerating car.

Clinging to the fence, Mike let out a yell. The street scene dissolved into chaos. Somebody started shooting. Some of the motorcycle escort attempted to remount and take out after their disappearing chieftains, but the pavement was now clogged with terrorized people, surging in all directions, falling down, covering their heads with their arms, completely immobilizing the parade.

Somehow in the confusion, perhaps by some supersensory attraction, Mike's gaze zeroed in on his *mayor domo*. Out of the hysterical mass he singled out that one face, as Nestor fought his way across the street. The little man didn't yet see him. His shirt had been torn from his back and one leg was ripped out of his trousers. His face was masked in blood which ran in glistening ribbons down his bare chest.

Stepping from the ledge Mike drove his way through the crowd and ran straight into Nestor as he broke into a small clearing near the curb. He grabbed the youth's slender arms and pulled him up, for he was stumbling.

"What dirty bastard did this?" Mike said.

"Capitán!" Nestor cried, rolling his big blood-streaked eyes at him. His voice was high and breathless, and in that instant Mike knew that it was he who had cried out and set off the riot. Nestor was badly hurt. One ear was half torn from his head and there was a terrible white split down the side of his face, but his eyes blazed exultantly.

Half sagging in Mike's arms, he wiped his hand across his

face and showed Mike the blood. Proudly he cried, *"Mire, Capitán! Sangre de Bolívar!"* The same blood as Simón Bolívar, the Liberator!

With an angry yell a secret policeman, hatless and rumpled, burst into the clearing, saw Nestor and started for him. The little man jerked himself out of Mike's arms and darted down the sidewalk. Mike met the onrushing policeman squarely, with a full body block. They hit the curbing together heavily. Jumping up, Mike pulled the man to his feet.

"Perdóneme, jefe!" He apologized loudly, brushing the man's suit with his hands. The policeman cursed him and tried to get by, but Mike stepped in front of him, brushing him vigorously with both hands, holding him back. "Oh, very sorry, *jefe!*" he said. "All my fault. No, please! Let me dust you off! *Very* clumsy of me!"

When he could hold him no longer, he fell aside with a shout of laughter and watched the man charge down the sidewalk. But the little *mayor domo,* proud kinsman of Simón Bolívar, had darted into an open gate and disappeared into the shrubbery at the rear of a garden.

30

Mike got off the *avenida* fast. The parade was piling up like a dammed flood in the street. Infantry officers ran forward with drawn sabers. First one, then several motorcyclists worked free of the crowd and roared off down the street. Mike knew there was nothing more to be done here, and it was not a healthy place for bystanders.

He found himself running down a side street with a stream of hysterical women and children. At the first corner he turned left and headed in the direction of his house. He felt sure that Nestor would go home, if he could get there. Nestor was hurt and needed help.

Mike ran until his chest was nearly bursting. Every cell in his body rang with something greater than excitement. He felt like yelling from sheer exultation. Robert Sanders didn't have a chance of getting away with this. Not a prayer. But he had come.

By the time Mike reached his house his heart was thudding in his eardrums. Hands shaking, he let himself in the front door and started back toward Nestor's room, off the laundry yard. He had got only as far as the kitchen when he saw Nestor, sitting in a chair, leaning against the kitchen table. Big drops of blood fallen from his chin spotted the porcelain table top, but Mike saw that the ugly wound running from cheek bone into scalp was already clotting.

"Damned if you're not a sight," he rasped, falling stiffly back against the doorway.

Nestor was very weak. His chest surged like a small bellows as he turned his big brown eyes gratefully up to Mike. For a moment he did not have strength to speak. Mike stood looking at him, breathing in gasps. In a moment he went to the hall and with trembling fingers dialed the number of his friend Gustavo Melgar at the Clínica Anglo-Americana. Melgar was a young doctor who had interned in the States. Most of the Americans in San Felipe went to him. Mike's call intercepted him just as he was leaving the clinic.

"Tavo—Mike Hodak," he said, trying to control his breathing. "A friend—of mine has been hurt. Bloody as hell. Needs morphine and sewing—maybe plasma. Can't bring him to you—trouble in the streets, and there's gonna be more. Grab your tools and get over here—my house. I'm counting on you, Tavo. *Pronto!*"

He hung up as the doctor began to protest. He knew Tavo would come. He started back to the kitchen, then turned around and ran to the bedroom, to get his pistol. At this moment he had no plan. But he was going to do something, and he was going prepared.

The service automatic was not in its place under his handkerchiefs and socks. It wasn't anywhere in the chest, though he ransacked every drawer, spilling clothes over the floor. As he strode back to the kitchen, suspicion, then anger, then astounded admiration rippled through him, in that order.

"Nestor," he demanded, leveling his eyes on the bloody youth, "was that my *pistola* that Señor Sanders—?"

Nestor rolled his big eyes up at him, then averted them, and Mike knew that it was.

"Nestor," he said, his amazement growing, "did you know where Robert Sanders was, all the time? Was he hiding in your room, *here,* the entire time I was searching this damn town over for him?"

Again Nestor rolled his eyes up and away, as if the shame of having deceived was too great to bear. Almost crying, he said, "But you did not ask me, Señor. If you had ask, I would have told. Almost certainly."

"You nervy little bastard!" Mike went over and picked him up in his arms. He was as light as a thin child. He carried him into the living room and put him down gently on the couch. Nestor's big eyes were on him, like the eyes of a sick pet. As he straightened, Mike heard someone entering. Turning, he stood staring into the white, startled face of Sadie Flippo.

When she saw the wound she gasped and cringed with revulsion. Then with a visible effort she controlled herself and went to the youth. She knelt beside him.

"*Pobrecito!* What happened?"

"Plenty," Mike said.

"Have you called a doctor?"

"Tavo Melgar is on the way."

"Where is Robert Sanders?"

"I don't know. I've got a hunch. I'm going to take your car."

"I'm going with you."

"No, you stay with Nestor."

A wail escaped Sadie. Her face was an agony of indecision. Nestor held up his hand. "I am plenty okay. The surgeon is on the way. The lady must go with you."

Mike hesitated two seconds, then he said, "Yes. I guess you'd better—if you want to see Robert Sanders alive."

31

Mike was not an eyewitness to all that happened the rest of this sun-drenched afternoon. But what he did not see with his own eyes he pieced together afterward from the accounts of an old man who sold flowers from a cart in front of the airport terminal building, from Alvaro Rodriquez, the customs inspector, from a PanAir steward on the afternoon flight, and finally, from the co-pilot on the same flight, a man named Harris.

At exactly 2:20 P.M., more or less, according to the old flower vendor, an open car roared up the airport road, careened around the circular drive and skidded to a halt at the terminal entrance. There were three men sitting on the rear seat, two of them bareheaded. The third—the old flower peddler said he pulled off his hat and stared in amazement—the third man looked for all the world like the Marshal of Maragua, General Francisco Ugarte y Pinilla, whose likeness and fame were known to all patriotic citizens.

The two hatless men got out of the car and went hurriedly into the building. One was very tall and broad and wore a uniform. His face was pale as ashes and he walked unsteadily, as though he were ill, or perhaps he had celebrated too well the fiesta. With one hand the smaller man held the large one tightly by the back of his belt and aided him in walking, supporting him under the armpit with his other hand.

Inspector Alvaro Rodriquez had been sunk in boredom. He was looking over the passenger list for the afternoon flight and reflecting glumly on the hard duty of a public servant which kept him at his post on this *día de fiesta*. When the two men came through the entrance he glanced up in mild surprise. It was too early for passengers to arrive. Then he gave a start. An exclamation escaped his fat lips, for he recognized the Chief of Staff, *Coronel* Lupo Machia.

When the identity of the other man registered in his brain the jaw of Alvaro Rodriquez dropped. Robert Sanders held Machia tightly to his side. The automatic which he shoved up into the big man's armpit was barely visible in his hand. It lifted Machia's shoulder as though it were dislocated. Alvaro Rodriquez opened his mouth to protest, but Sanders silenced him with a look that said *"Make a move and he's dead. Then you are, too."* In any case that is what Alvaro Rodriquez understood the look to say.

Without a word the close-coupled pair marched through the lobby and out the open doors on the far side, to the emplaning gates. Only five other people were in the lobby—a porter, a ticket agent leaning over his counter, a janitor sweeping, and two secret service men who had been assigned to the airport for the sole purpose of preventing an American named Robert Sanders from boarding any outbound plane. The plainclothesmen were slouched on the waiting-room benches. One was dozing, the other reading a newspaper. Alvaro Rodriquez, who thought he knew which side his bread was buttered on, rushed toward them, spitting out the alarm in frantic whispers.

The PanAir steward, a sleek-haired Panamanian boy, had just carried a box of supplies up the steps into the plane and was stowing it away in the galley, making ready for the three-thirty flight. When he heard a noise behind him, he turned and saw two dark figures crowding through the narrow plane hatchway, blocking out the sunlight.

"Por favor, Señores," he protested with annoyance. "You are too early. You cannot board yet." The next instant he was sprawled backward into a passenger seat. The smaller of the two men gave the big one a shove that sent him stumbling into the pilot's compartment. Then he leveled a big automatic pistol at the astounded steward's head.

"You want to die?" the man said softly.

"N-no, Señor. No!" the steward cried.

"Then sit there and don't move till I tell you to get up." Robert Sanders turned into the pilot's compartment after Machia. Then he looked back and said, "Don't try to out-think me, boy. Stay alive."

231

Don Harris, the co-pilot, was in the cockpit checking the gauges, the plane having just been gassed. The chief pilot was in the operations office in the terminal making out a manifest in preparation for the three-thirty take-off. Harris, the co-pilot, first thought a drunk had stumbled into the compartment and fallen into the pilot's seat.

Turning angrily he exclaimed, "What the hell's going on?" and found himself looking into the large bore of a .45 automatic. Glancing upward, he stared into what he later described as the most serious pair of eyes he had ever seen.

The owner of the eyes said, "Start the motors. Pull up the stairs. Let's go flying."

"Now, *look*, Mister—" Harris began a nervous protest. The forty-five exploded in his face. The slug flew past his ear and tore a hole in the plexiglass windscreen.

"I don't want to kill you, Pilot," Sanders said, his voice just above a whisper, "but I will—if I have to."

In shock, the co-pilot squared around and began fumbling with the starter switches. One port engine began to whine and the propellor began to turn.

A khaki-colored weapons carrier with *soldados* hanging all over it screeched to a halt in front of the terminal. The *soldados* jumped to the ground, rifles unslung. Inside the plane Sanders saw them and murmured to the pilot, "Step it up, Pilot. My time's running out and so is yours."

Nobody ever said Lupo Machia was a coward. He wasn't. As the second engine whined and the prop began to spin, the big man grabbed at the window latch next to him. Shoving the window open he leaned toward it and screamed a command to the armed men running out of the building. The barrel of Sanders' automatic came down again across the man's skull. Machia pitched forward heavily onto the instrument panel.

Both port side engines were going when the first bullets hit. They struck motors and wing with a splatting sound. By now *soldados* had fanned out all over the place. Robert Sanders saw the winking of muzzle fire in hedges along the visitors' area as a slug ripped through the cockpit, shattering dials on the panel.

White-faced, the co-pilot turned to Sanders. "You might as well go ahead and shoot me. They've hit the hydraulic system. I've got no controls. Look." He moved the wheel back and forth. It waggled loosely on the control column. With fatal finality he said, "She won't fly, mister. If I tried to take off, we'd roll up in a ball at the end of the runway."

Crouched behind the pilot's seat, Sanders gave a low moan. That was too damned bad. Because he had thought this all out, and decided it was worth a try. Rafael Benavides could no longer be rescued, because he was dead, but Machia could be kidnaped and flown out of the country in a commandeered airliner, creating a chance for Maragua to rise against the leaderless junta. And Robert Sanders could still prove to himself that he wasn't a coward. It really was a good substitute plan. And it had almost worked.

Sanders laughed softly. The co-pilot said he seemed almost to relax.

"Well, as they say in French, that's tough shit."

A puff of black smoke blew against the windscreen. They felt a flash of heat, and smoke was in the cockpit. The co-pilot said, "We're on fire. They've holed the gas tanks."

A sudden sheet of fire arose from the trailing edge of the portside wing, dropping fiery clots of gasoline to the ground.

Quietly, almost thoughtfully, Sanders said, "Pilot, you got kids?"

The co-pilot croaked, "Two."

Sanders hesitated. His eyes cut upward to the shattered instruments, then back into the cabin. Suddenly he jerked the pistol over his shoulder.

"Get the hell out of here."

That was all the co-pilot needed. He spun out of his seat and ducked into the smoke-filled entryway. Sanders said, "Take that steward with you."

It was a modern miracle that the two men were not shot as they tumbled down the steps, because it is said that an Andean *soldado* will shoot anything that moves when he is excited. But this day the reflexes were a split-second slow, and the co-pilot and steward were down the steps and into the building before anyone could sight in on them.

The entire front of the plane was ablaze now and the two engines, still turning, were sizzling and popping. Peering over a window ledge in the building, the breathless co-pilot cursed and waited for the gas tanks to explode.

As Mike spun the Cadillac off the highway and down the road toward the terminal, he heard the firing and saw the smoke. Peering ahead he muttered, "I guessed right, but we're a little late." Sadie sat forward on the edge of the seat gazing through the windshield. At the terminal Mike wheeled the car around the circle to a hard, sliding stop beside the empty weapons carrier, then he jumped out and slammed the door.

He pointed. His voice was an iron command. "This time no argument. Go to the Embassy hangar. Yonder. Fast! The Lodestar is standing by. Tell the pilot to start the engines. Get on board and be ready to take off. I'll bring your boy to you, if I can." When she began to protest he grabbed her and jerked her over under the wheel. "Move!" he shouted. Then he looked at her oddly. *"Adiós,* kid."

He ran around the car and disappeared into the terminal building. In shock, Sadie put the car into gear and drove numbly ahead, toward the hangar at the far end of the field.

Inside the building Mike almost ran over General Ugarte, who was wandering around saluting and bowing like a halfwit. Quickly he crossed to the windows and looked over the crouched heads toward the field. Intuition, luck, and a lifetime's training told him at a glance what he needed to know. Without stopping he turned and ran back out the front of the building.

At that moment he did not know exactly what he was going to do or how. From here on in, it would be played by ear. But he was committed now, beyond turning back—because, except for Mike Hodak, Robert Sanders would not be in that burning plane, and Mike Hodak was going to get him out. Or if he didn't he wouldn't be around to worry about it.

The unguarded weapons carrier stood at the entrance. It was an old World War II model, and was no stranger to him. Sliding behind the wheel Mike kicked the starter. The motor caught and roared to life.

A service road paralleled the landing strip, leading to the private plane hangars at the far end of the field. A chain-link fence separated the road from the runway. The old vehicle responded to Mike's touch and leaped raggedly ahead, gears whining. Fifty yards down the road Mike braked and cut sharply to the right. The truck stopped with a jolt as the heavy bumper-bar butted against a steel post of the fence. Mike jerked the gear shift into low-low and poured on the power. The wheels grabbed and spun, smoking. The steel post bent slightly as the fence tightened and held fast. Then the engine choked down and died. Starting up again, gunning the motor, Mike threw the carrier into reverse, backing jerkily across the road. Then he put the gears in low, sending the vehicle hurtling forward full speed into the fencepost. The impact catapulted him across the wheel, bruising his ribs. The engine died again but the post was bent half over. Again he started the motor, backed up, and again hurtled forward, and again was hurled onto the wheel by the impact, but the post snapped, and the steel mesh of the fence stretched taut, strands popping. Then the whole section of fence collapsed and the truck slid over, rolling out onto the taxiway. Pulling himself back on the seat, grabbing for breath, Mike muttered, "Hooray for General Motors." Then he stomped the accelerator. The carrier leaped forward and roared out onto the taxiway.

With the engine winding up as though it would fly apart, he swung the truck in a tire-singeing arc on the asphalt and headed back toward the terminal. The plane was now burning furiously. Great tongues of oily flame twisted high into the air from the wings.

Then, through the boiling smoke he saw a man appear in the plane doorway and start down the steps.

It was Lupo Machia. He waved his arms and roared unheard commands. It was no good. A dozen guns, triggered by reflex action, cut down on him. Machia fell forward slowly, heavily to the ground and lay in a twitching heap.

Without slowing, Mike aimed the truck straight for the pyre, one thought locked in his mind—if Robert Sanders was alive, he would not stay inside and burn up. He would come out, one way or another.

And he did. Mike saw a head, then shoulders emerge from the emergency escape hatch above the starboard wing, away from the terminal. He gave a shout and veered the truck to the left. Then he eased up on the gas, for two lives, now, depended on timing. On luck, yes, but mainly on timing.

236

Sanders didn't yet see him. Rising half out of his seat Mike gave an open-throated yell and put his foot to the floorboard. Standing now on the burning wing, washed by flames, Robert Sanders stumbled toward the wing tip, arms over his face, intent only upon getting out of the fire. Hard on the plane Mike jammed the brakes and put the carrier into a screeching swerving skid over the dry pavement. It slid to a stop under the end of the wing as Sanders emerged from the fire, clothes smoking, face scorched and blackened.

"Jump!" Mike yelled.

Sanders saw him and left the wing, dropping through the smoky air. He landed heavily on top of Mike, knocking him onto the floorboard. Half stunned, Mike clawed back into the seat. Then he hit the gas and pulled the truck into a hard turn, straight out toward the main runway.

A *soldado* on the left flank of the firing line saw what had happened. Shouting, he jumped up and started out onto the apron, bolting a shell into his rifle as he ran. Then the plane's gas tanks went up with a big gushing sound, enveloping the *soldado*, the plane and all around it in a gigantic twisting ball of fire. Flames leaped a hundred feet in the air and rolled outward, licking the side of the terminal building and driving the men wildly, blindly, out of the searing heat.

Dazed, Sanders righted himself in the back of the carrier. Shaking his head, he recognized the bulky figure behind the wheel as he pulled himself to his feet.

When the weapons carrier reached the main runway Mike careened into a left turn and aimed it straight down the strip like a lumbering dodo trying to take off without wings. He fixed his eyes on the hangar in the distance and tried to push his foot through the floor.

Swaying behind him like a drunken chariot driver, Robert

Sanders crouched forward and yelled in sheer jubilation, "Kick it in the ass, Captain! I don't think you're trying!"

Hunched over the wheel, Mike said, "If you can do any better, get out and run."

The Lodestar stood in the wide opening of the hangar, propellors turning. When the carrier stopped, the two men tumbled out and sprinted for the plane. Sadie jumped from the open plane door and ran toward them. Slowing, Mike let Sanders run ahead to meet her. The two came together, embraced, then kissed, almost savagely. Then to Mike's paralyzed amazement Sadie extricated herself and flung herself into his own astonished arms, sobbing. He pried her away. There was no time for gratitude, and he didn't want any, anyway. Sanders, who had started for the plane, stopped and turned back. The three stood looking at one another.

Mike put out his hand and Sanders took it.

"Pretty fair go, *hombre*. There's nothing wrong with your guts. I can't say about your brains." Mike said. "But that's your problem."

"I understand," Robert Sanders said.

"Get on board. I got something to say to the lady before you go."

Robert Sanders hesitated. He gripped Mike's hand hard, then turned and ran to the plane.

Mike looked at Sadie, "This is where the road forks, kid. You've got a future now. Try to live like it." He stuck out his hand. The trace of a smile crossed his face. "I can't say I'm sorry I met you."

At this moment Sanders disappeared into the plane, the short steps came up and the door slammed shut. Sadie made a signal to the pilot in the cockpit, who hit the throttles. The hangar trembled with a turbulent blast of prop-wash as the plane moved forward.

"Wait a minute!" Mike yelled, running toward the plane, waving wildly. "Wait for her, you dumb bastards!"

"Mike!" Sadie cried, clinging to his arm. "I'm not going! I'm staying!"

"The hell you are!"

"The hell I'm not! I'm staying with you!"

"Jesus Christ, woman!" Mike shouted at her, water of anguish and frustration shooting into his eyes. "This was the point of the whole damned exercise! This is what you wanted!"

"He doesn't need me now. He's got unfinished business back home, and I'm no part of it. It involves a wife and child." She was crying and laughing now, her hair blowing wildly in the propellor blast as she held onto Mike Hodak with both hands.

The plane was now on the taxiway, gathering momentum. It sheered around into the wind, then the engines took hold with a deep roar. The plane moved forward onto the runway and in a moment the tail lifted and seconds later the light-loaded craft leaped into the air, long before it was abeam of the terminal.

Mike could not find any words to say. In that moment he could not even form a coherent thought. The plane was gone, banking and climbing into the mountain-rimmed sky, and instinct alone moved him now, to get away from this place of danger. He grabbed Sadie's wrist and ran for the car.

The bombs began to go off at dusk. They were crude things of black powder, hoarded and rigged by amateurs for the hour of liberation. They did little damage, but they made a great noise. They were important only because they meant defiance. There had been few bombs since the junta took over.

The trouble spread. It could be felt like the closeness in the air before a summer storm, for the revolt was general, the spontaneous upsurge of a whole populace inflamed by anger

239

and the taste of freedom. The shooting started soon after dark. It was hit-and-run sniping, the work of unconnected little bands, desperate leaderless men who drew together in the darkened *barrios,* in the intoxicating cause of liberty. Now and then the crackling of small arms was laced with the long ripple of machine-gun fire when the *soldados* found something to shoot at.

All through the night trucks and motorcycles roared through the streets as squads of soldiers and police were rushed around in the dark, growing confusion to points of resistance. The night sky pulsated with flashes as the bombs continued to explode.

In the blacked-out Embassy the General and his staff tried to follow the chaotic unfolding of the rebellion. A heavy guard at the central exchange kept telephone service in operation most of the night. Mike checked all Embassy personnel that he could reach by phone and passed the word: standard revolution procedure—lock up and stay inside. South American revolutions were not usually dangerous to foreigners who minded their own business and kept out of the way. Embassies were generally respected.

Nestor was ensconced in the Embassy linen room, converted now into an emergency ward. Propped up on a cot, his head swathed in bandages, Nestor looked like a small Eastern potentate.

Radio Central changed hands twice, then went off the air at one-fifteen. Then at first light of dawn, it came raucously to life again, with a proclamation. The Army was in complete control of the city. All citizens were commanded to cease further resistance and obey radio instructions, by order of *Coronel* Benito Monclova, provisional commander of all armed forces in Maragua.

Slowly the situation in the city began to clarify itself. Out of the chaos of the night Benito Monclova had emerged as Maragua's man of destiny. In the crisis he had reluctantly but decisively assumed control of the government.

A little later Monclova himself came on the air. In his sad, resonant voice he spoke to his countrymen. He told them that Maragua had been languishing in a time of sickness. Now it would get well, if they would cooperate with the military authorities, and have faith. At the earliest possible time a constitutional government would be restored and free elections would be held. Of this he gave them his solemn word. Knowing Benito Monclova, Mike had no doubt he would keep his promise, or die trying.

When Monclova finished, the tired group of Americans, huddled around the radio in the Embassy library, broke into spontaneous cheering. The General ordered champagne, and a solemn toast was drunk in the gray dawn to a new and better day in Maragua. Nothing was solved, nothing was settled, but it was a fresh start.

Mike withdrew from the crowd and went out into the early coolness of the garden to try and regroup his thoughts. During the night he had avoided Sadie as much as possible. Thinking about her made his head hurt.

He walked slowly down the path. Under the pergola he paused, watching the light come into the leaves of the eucalyptus trees. Then, as he walked back toward the house she met him beside the fishpool. Her face was fresh-washed and pale and her dark hair was brushed back like a boy's. She walked up to him and held out her hand.

"Friends, *amigo?*" she said.

"Hello, Sadie."

She stood before him and put her hands up on his shoulders. Then she tightened her arms around his neck and kissed him.

"We do have fun together, don't we?" she said. "Let's not ever stop having fun." She looked up at him curiously. "I might even like being married to you."

Bludgeoned by these words and the sensation of her kiss, Mike gripped her arms and stood her away from him. Could this be the moment he had been waiting for all of his life? Or was it just another loaded cigar? The old Marine signals of alarm flashed in his head—do something, even if you do it wrong.

He moved her backward to the edge of the fishpool, and for a long second held her there, looking into her wide, dark eyes.

He said: "I'd just as soon be married to a corkscrew."

Then, firmly, he shoved her and turned her loose. With a wild flurry of arms and legs Sadie hit the water, and presently she came up sitting waist-deep among the goldfish, dripping and crying. Mike turned and strode toward the gate at the side of the house, his brain a raging turmoil. He had let a damn good woman get away. He figured he just had time to hop a plane and intercept Rusty Cobb as her boat passed through the Panama Canal.

At the gate he turned for one last backward glance. Sadie held out her arms and cried to him.

"I mean it, Mike," she wailed. "Marry me and straighten me out!"

Mike Hodak said some dirty words and stormed ahead around the house. By the time he reached the front entrance he had formed a bucolic mental image of himself and Rusty Cobb, riding hand in hand, following an endless herd of goats into the western sunset. As he did he kept on going, right on around the house, instead of turning out to the street toward the new vistas, and a new life.

By the time he reached the garden gate on the far side of the house he had convinced himself that man is put on this earth to solve problems, not to run away from them. Sadie's last words still rang in his ears—marry me and straighten me out!

Having circled the house, he burst through the gate and strode into the garden again and down the walk and over the side of the fishpool into the knee-deep water. He waded furiously down to the small wet figure huddled forlornly in the center of the pool. Flinging himself down beside her, he hooked two fingers into the warm cleft of her decolletage. Then he twisted and jerked her up so that they were staring nose to nose into each other's eyes.

Through his teeth he said, "All right, you little *sonofabitch* —I might just do that!"

The General had come into the solarium with the acey-deucey board under his arm, looking for his aide. When his gaze traveled through the windows to the tender scene in the garden pool, he put down the board.

Molly came into the room just then. With a sweep of his arm the General pointed her eyes out to the pair sitting amid the goldfish. He laid a heavy hand across her shoulder.

"Moll," he said with a deep sigh, "it looks like a whole new ball game."

In the pool Sadie smiled up at the big man beside her, her eyes now shining with a different kind of tears. She plucked a lily pad from the bottom by its stem and draped it, dripping, across Mike Hodak's head, like a garland. Then she kissed him again, tenderly, on his incredulous mouth.

TOM PENDLETON is the pseudonym of a man who finds it convenient to maintain the posture of anonymity. He is fifty years old, has been in succession oil-field roustabout, oil scout, U.S. Marine, lawyer, oil-company executive, negotiator of foreign oil concessions and, most recently, banker. "I haven't yet decided what I'll be when I grow up," he says.

He has a wife whom he describes as "dazzling," and three children who are respectively newspaper columnist, rock musician and juvenile actor, for pay. "All pure ham like father," he reports, "but more talented."

With Tom Pendleton writing is an old love. He has been published in national magazines, and his first novel, *The Iron Orchard,* was co-winner of the Texas Institute of Letters fiction award for 1966.